# The Moment We Fell

## KELLI WARNER

The Moment We Fell
Copyright © 2019 by Kelli Warner
Print Edition

Cover design: Jenny Zemanek at Seedlings Design Studio

Publisher's Cataloging-In-Publication Data

(Prepared by The Donohue Group, Inc.)

Names: Warner, Kelli, author.

Title: The moment we fell / Kelli Warner.

Description: [Springfield, Oregon] : Wave Runner Publishing, [2019] | Interest age level: 013-018. | Summary: "Forced to start over in a new town and at a new school where she's now the principal's daughter, Paige is convinced that her life can't possibly get more complicated--until fate throws her into the path of the only boy her guardian tells her is off-limits ... As Paige tries to adjust to her new life and an uncertain future, a set of unopened journals reveals a dark family secret. When tensions rise to a boiling point, can Paige and Cade make peace with the past before it destroys them?"-- Provided by publisher.

Identifiers: ISBN 9781732717015 (trade paperback) | ISBN 9781732717022 (ebook)

Subjects: LCSH: Teenage girls--Juvenile fiction. | Father and child--Juvenile fiction. | Juvenile delinquents--Juvenile fiction. | Family secrets--Juvenile fiction. | CYAC: Teenage girls--Fiction. | Father and child--Fiction. | Juvenile delinquents--Fiction. | Family secrets--Fiction. | LCGFT: Domestic fiction.

Classification: LCC PS3623.A86332 M66 2019 (print) | LCC PS3623.A86332 (ebook) | DDC 813/.6--dc23

ISBN: 978-1-7327170-1-5

Facebook: fb.me/KelliWarnerAuthor
Twitter: @KelliWarner_
Instagram: kelliwarner_author
KelliWarner.com

# Dedication

To my parents, the best mom and dad on the planet. Thank you both for your encouragement and patience, for teaching me to value what's most important in life, and to find laughter in each day. And Dad—thanks for humoring my obsession with Hallmark Channel movies and watching more than your fair share!

# CHAPTER ONE

## Paige

If someone had asked me a month ago how my life was going, I would have said great. Wonderful. Even excellent. If I were filling out a survey on the subject, I would have ticked the box labeled *extremely satisfied* without hesitation. Because a month ago, it was all that. Then life threw me a craptastic curveball I never saw coming, and now I'm stuck in a plane 30,000 feet in the air and on the verge of puking my guts out.

The flight attendant stares down at me expectantly from behind her beverage cart. *Wait. What was the question again?*

"Are you all right, miss?"

I blink, trying to process what is, on the surface, a harmless inquiry. What this woman doesn't know is that there's a log of dread the size of a Pringles can spinning in my stomach, not to mention I'm carrying more emotional baggage than could possibly fit in my carry-on. Oh, and this plane I'm trapped on is doing some kind of shimmy-sway-bump thing every few seconds. So, no, I'm not all right. I'm a hot mess.

Another unsettling jolt knocks a soft groan from my throat and propels the Pringles can to complete a few more twirls.

"It's just a few bumps, nothing to worry about. Would you like a Sprite or some ginger ale?" The flight attendant's hands poise in midair, ready to pop the tab on a can of soda.

Another thunderbolt rattles me in my seat, and I suck in a breath. *Just a few bumps?* I think this woman is out of her flippin' mind and seriously needs to focus less on pimping me a beverage and take notice of the situation. I can already see our cataclysmic end splashed across the eleven o'clock news. Oh my gosh. *Hot. Mess.*

The flight attendant's thickly lined eyes narrow with sympathy. "There's an air sickness bag in the seat pocket in case you need it."

I manage a shaky smile and wave a dismissive hand as my eyes lock on the blue bag peeking out from among the safety brochures and magazines. Thankfully, without another word, she rolls the metal cart forward to the next row of passengers.

"Not a fan of flying?"

I straighten. I'd forgotten about the woman in the window seat. Since takeoff, she'd been reading a book, nearly as quiet as the twentysomething guy sleeping to my left.

"Is it that obvious?" I ask. Her eyes glance down to my fingers, which I now realize are twisting the leather band of my watch back and forth. I drop my hands into my lap.

"Pretty watch," she says. "I've never seen anything like it."

My hand slides over my wrist, shielding the crystal face from view. My mom gave it to me as a present on my last birthday, and I was disappointed when I unwrapped it. I'd never worn a watch in my life, and because I can check the time on my phone, it seemed impractical. It's funny how things change. Not funny in a laugh-out-loud kind of way, more like ironically tragic. Ironic because the watch I hadn't wanted I now refuse to take off. And tragic because this beautiful watch serves as a constant reminder of the moment my simple existence on this planet was permanently altered.

Twenty-eight days, twelve hours and fourteen minutes ago, my life disintegrated. That was the moment when a man in navy surgical scrubs with sad, tired eyes, placed a gentle hand on my shoulder and told me he'd done everything he could to help my mom and that he was sorry for my loss. In that devastating wake-me-up-from-this-nightmare moment, my world had shattered into a million tiny pieces.

"Turbulence is unnerving, but this isn't bad," the woman says. "Try to relax. Statistically speaking, the probability of a plane crashing is extremely rare."

Hold on. I've never flown before, but I'm pretty sure that talk of crashing is not an acceptable conversation starter. Like—ever.

"The best thing to do is to keep your mind busy." She holds up her book, and several silver bangles around her wrist jingle. The cover is tattered and worn, and I can't make out the title before she returns it to her lap and flips it open again.

Keeping my mind busy isn't my problem. It's practically spinning senseless with all my jumbled thoughts.

"Are you sure you're okay?" the woman asks, leaning slightly forward in her seat, studying me as if there's a complicated mathematics equation etched across my face. She's younger than I first thought, with short, spiky hair the color of a melted Milky Way bar. "Should I call back the flight attendant?"

"I'm fine," I say, refusing to confess that my insides are tied in more knots than the plot of her paperback.

"The first time I flew, I was an absolute wreck," she says. Her words deflect off my distracted thoughts, dissolving into white noise in my ears, and I focus instead on the FASTEN SEAT BELT sign illuminated above me. Will it stay lit the entire flight? More importantly, will this flimsy strap of canvas cinched across my waist actually save me if the plane tumbles out of the sky? Not likely. And how in the world is the guy next to me actually sleeping through this? The air in the plane's confined cabin suddenly feels a little too thick in my lungs.

"Sorry. My husband says I tend to ramble. Am I rambling?"

Yes. Definitely, yes. I shake my head no.

"Once I became more comfortable with flying and accepted the fact that, really, everything happens for a reason,

I stopped worrying."

*Everything happens for a reason.* That might be the most ridiculous thing a human being can say to make someone feel better. I want to inform this woman that I've heard more people say that to me in the last month than I care to count, and that I don't think it's fair to say that everything happens for a reason when no one is able to explain what that reason is. Instead, I purse my lips and nod. Because there's no point in it.

Her thoughtful expression smooths into a smile, and she relaxes back into her seat. Finally.

"Do you live in Oregon, or are you visiting?"

For the love of Pete! What part of my I'm-about-to-hurl body language makes her think I want to have a conversation? And why do they make these seats so small?

"Visiting." I reach for the *Hemispheres* magazine behind the barf bag in front of me.

"Oh, you're in luck! The Pacific Northwest is beautiful this time of year. The colors are incredible. God's artwork, I always say." She sighs as I flip through the magazine's pages, seeing nothing but a blur of color and smears of black ink. "Although, if I had to choose my favorite season—hmmm. I think it would definitely be summer."

If I have my way, I won't be around Oregon long enough to experience fall, summer or anything else for that matter. If I could magically turn this plane around right now, or parachute out the emergency exit, I would do it in a heartbeat. Strap a pack on me and let 'er rip. But because that's not an option, I take my cue from the unconscious guy in the aisle seat and unzip my hoodie, adjust the air nozzle in the panel above me and close my eyes, regretting that I did not snag a cold can of soda when I had the chance.

*Breath, Paige. Just. Breathe.*

A familiar aching claws its way into my chest. I haven't cried since the funeral, and I know that's not normal. It's like something inside me closed up and nothing works right. That's probably why people look at me the way they do, like they expect me to crack at any moment. Even Aunt Faye had gently suggested that I see a therapist. We were sitting in her kitchen a couple of weeks after the funeral when she brought it up. I asked her flat-out if she thought I was going crazy, because sometimes it feels like maybe I am. Aunt Faye was quick to say no but suggested that talking to someone might be helpful. I disagree. Sharing my problems with a stranger won't fix anything. It will only make things worse.

"Ladies and gentlemen, we've begun our descent into Portland." My eyelids flutter open as the pilot's deep voice crackles from the overhead speakers, and it takes me a moment to remember where I am. A quick assessment confirms I'm still strapped into my seat. I swallow, my ears popping against the cabin pressure as I check my watch.

"We should be on the ground in about twenty minutes," the pilot says. "It's currently sixty-eight degrees with a light wind."

I shiver.

"Everything's good. No more turbulence," my seatmate assures me. Her book has disappeared, and instead, she's thumbing through the pages of a *People* magazine. "Landing can be a little bumpy, but it'll be over before you know it."

In no time at all, and much to my horror, there's a ginormous jolt—*ohhhh crap!*—wrapped in a heavy thud as the landing gear wheels meet the hard, concrete runway. My palms splay against the seat in front of me as the powerful momentum that took this plane into the air in San Diego reverses itself, and we go from what feels like a billion miles an hour to a calm Sunday drive. Note to self: No more flying, at least not for the time being.

It doesn't take long for the plane to taxi to the gate. Once the seat belt light dings and turns off, people all around me begin retrieving their belongings from the overhead bins and waiting patiently for the flight crew to open the doors. I stay right where I am while the guy to my left, without a word or a nod in my direction, bolts out of his seat at the first break in the aisle traffic and joins the mass exodus. Twisting, I hike my knees to my chest and rest my feet in the now-empty aisle seat to let my other seatmate squeeze by.

"See? Safe and sound." She smiles and pats my knee. I notice that the silver bangles on her wrist are adorned with small moons. "Take care."

I don't think I can do this after all. I'm not ready. If only there were a way to disappear into the seat cushion. I mean, if it can serve as a flotation device, why not a cloaking mechanism as well? Stalling, I dig out my cell phone from my messenger bag beneath the seat in front of me and hit the Power button. When it comes to life, it alerts me that I have eleven text messages. Three are from Aunt Faye.

*Call me when you can.*

*Have you landed? Call me soon.*

*Are you OK? Please call me. Love you!*

I don't bother listening to the voice messages because I can't handle that right now. Faye had wanted to fly with me, but I'd insisted on doing this solo. The truth is I'm not sure I could have done this at all if she were with me. How could I possibly let her deliver me to this strange place and then watch her walk away? She's already made plans to visit me next month for Thanksgiving. It will be the first family holiday without my mom, and I can't even imagine it. Everything I do now will be the first time I've done it without her. That realization buries itself deep inside me, and loneliness sprouts from every cell in my body.

When the flight attendant asks me if she can help me "deplane," I take that as code for "get a move on," regardless of whether I'm ready or not. Slinging my bag over my shoulder and retrieving my duffel from the now-empty overhead bin, I trudge up the aisle as the rational portion of my brain tries to calmly coax the rest of my cerebral cortex off the emotional ledge it's currently squatting on.

Somehow, my legs manage to carry me across the upper concourse to the escalator, and as it descends, I immediately spot him. The imaginary Pringles can in my stomach does

event of her death. It makes no sense, and Jay, who'd appeared to be lost in the confusion of old memories, couldn't offer any answers to this shocking turn of events.

Now, here he is, standing in the airport wearing the same confused expression. When the crowd shifts around him, the rest of them materialize.

A woman with shoulder-length blond hair stands next to Jay in a red, knee-length coat, clinging to the purse strap slung over her shoulder with both hands, as if she's worried she's about to be mugged. Based on the photos I've seen, this is Jay's wife, Connie. She's a real estate agent, and right now, she is undoubtedly sizing me up like a property listing.

Beside her is a teenage boy, and I instantly know that it's Tanner, who's thirteen. He isn't looking at me; his attention is on the phone he clutches in his fingers.

Rounding out the family is a small girl, her long, dishwater blond curls drawn up into two high ponytails. She holds tight to Jay's hand as she wobbles on her tiptoes, anxiously scanning the people coming toward her. Within moments, I cross through the security gate and come to a stop in front of them, that blasted Pringles can spinning like a carnival ride in my gut.

"Hello, Paige." Jay's greeting is pleasant, but he can't decide if he should attempt to hug me or shake my hand. He settles for a pat on my shoulder. "How was your flight?"

"Good." I shift my duffel bag from one hand to the other.

He practically lurches forward and yanks the bag from

my grasp. "Let me take that for you."

"Hi, Paige, I'm Connie." Her smile is sweet, and she tucks a strand of her hair behind one ear. Without warning, she pulls me in close for a long hug and—what exactly is happening here? I have to be the equivalent of a stone statue in Connie's embrace, but she holds on to me, whispering, "I'm so sorry about your mother." She smells like some kind of flower I can't identify. When she releases me, I attempt to swallow the enormous lump lodged in the back of my throat. "We're so glad to have you here."

I do my best to return her smile, but it feels stiff, like someone glued it on my lips. I planned for diplomacy; I didn't expect affection of any kind, so I'm not quite sure how to process this.

"Tanner, put that phone away and say hello to Paige," Jay instructs. The boy glances up at me with a blank expression and a flat, "Hey," then his eyes drop right back to his phone. Jay leans down and scoops up the little girl. "And this is Lily. Your—sister."

That brings me up short. I mean, I know how it all works, biologically speaking, but that one word said aloud throws me off somehow. I have a sister. And a brother. I'm not an only child as I'd believed. That's a lot to digest.

"I'm five." Lily extends one of her small hands, and I instinctively shake it. "Do you like to play Barbies?"

"Um…I guess?"

"We've got plenty of time to talk dolls," Jay says, setting Lily back on her feet. "Right now, let's get you out of here.

I'll go get the car and pull around up front. Connie, can you and the kids take Paige to baggage claim and get her luggage?"

"Of course," Connie replies, placing a gentle hand on my back.

When we reach baggage claim, crowds of people are gathered around several large carousels, patiently waiting for them to spit out the contents of their flights. We find the correct carousel, and I'm trying to figure out how to insert myself into the perimeter of people hovering around the edges when luggage begins sliding out of the large metal shoot.

Connie's cell phone rings, and she quickly digs it out of her purse. "George! Tell me you have good news." She covers the receiver briefly with one hand and says, "Paige, I have to take this." Then she snaps her fingers harshly at Tanner, who glances up briefly from his phone. "Help Paige get her suitcases. I'll be right over there." She grabs Lily's hand, and despite the little girl's protest, Connie tugs her toward the wall beyond the crowd, already immersed in conversation with George, whoever that is. I glance at Tanner to find that his mother's instructions bounced right off him. His nanosecond of alertness is long gone, and he's engrossed in his phone again. Okay, I guess I'm on my own.

There are a lot of black suitcases, and so many of them look nearly identical to mine. As bodies move in and hands begin grabbing at the contents on the conveyer belt, I can't seem to get near it. Finally, I spot a small opening and slip through. Just as I reach the edge, I catch sight of what looks like one of my suitcases rounding the bend—away from me. Politely, I push my way back through the crowd and quickly work my way around to the other side of the carousel. Just as I extend my hand to claim my suitcase, the bag is swiped right out of my reach. *What the*—? I whirl just in time to see a guy walking away with my suitcase. The dude just stole my suitcase!

"Hey!" I shout, breaking into a jog and hustling after him without any thoughts about my actions. "Stop!" The guy slows and turns just as I reach him. I lunge for the handle, only he doesn't let go. "That's my suitcase," I say, a little breathless from the adrenaline coursing through my veins.

The guy's eyes narrow in confusion. "I don't think so."

"Whether you think so or not, that's my bag," I say, tugging on the handle. The stranger still refuses to let go, and I end up yanking the guy awkwardly closer than intended. "Drop it!"

"Look, I don't know who you are, but this is not your bag," he says firmly, and he has a strange expression on his face, like he's not sure if I'm kidding around or if he thinks I'm legit crazy.

"It is my bag," I insist.

His confused demeanor transforms again, and one corner of his lips lift in amusement. He thinks this is some sort of a game. "Prove it," he says.

"Fine. I will," I retort. Okay, so that wasn't my wittiest

comeback, but this guy has me flustered. He doesn't look like he's much older than me, but he's a good half a foot taller. His intrigue-filled eyes are glued to my face, waiting for me to make the next move.

With my free hand, I reach for the red ribbon that's tied around the hard leather handle of the case. "See this? I put this on here so that I would know without a doubt that this is my suitcase." Actually, Aunt Faye had done that. She'd explained that she uses the ribbon when traveling so that she can spot her bags more easily. And probably prevent thieves like this guy from pilfering her belongings.

I stare up at the guy triumphantly and wait for him to apologize for the mix-up. Only he doesn't. Instead, he chuckles.

"What's so funny?" I demand.

"Take a look behind you. Half the suitcases over there have colored ribbons or tape on the handles. Everyone does that."

"Well—I'm telling you, this is my bag."

With his free hand, he turns over the luggage tag and holds up the suitcase closer to my face so I can read it. "Is this you?"

The tag reads "M. Sinclair." I don't bother reading the address below the name because—well, because I am not M. Sinclair and the blood is rushing to my cheeks so fast, I seriously think my head might explode from sheer embarrassment. *Kill. Me. Now.*

My mouth opens, but it takes a few seconds for any

sound to come out. "I'm—so sorry," I sputter. "I thought—um, it's been a bizarre day and—I'm not trying to make excuses or anything, I honestly thought—"

"Don't worry about it," he says. Then he just stares at me. Why is he staring at me? Because my hand is still wrapped around the handle of his suitcase. Oh my gosh! I immediately release the bag and step back.

"Sorry," I say again. "Can we just agree that this never happened? I'll back away slowly, and you can forget all about the crazy girl who just accosted you in the middle of baggage claim. What do you say?"

"No problem." His smile is friendly, but as I turn and head back to the carousel, I pray I never see it again. I'm pretty sure the epic dose of awkward shame that I'm practically choking on will have a long enough shelf life to keep this memory alive and kicking for years to come.

I nudge my way back into the crowd, in part to retrieve the suitcases that actually belong to me, but also to put a barrier between me and the guy who I will, from now on, associate with "The Great Oregon Luggage Fail." Yup, that's what I'm calling it.

The wall of bodies has thinned, and as I scan the suitcases sliding past me, I'm now acutely aware of how many do, in fact, have ribbons or string or some other paraphernalia attached to their handles. A burst of heat flares once more against my cheeks. I'm not sure I could be a bigger idiot at this moment. At least Connie and her kids didn't see the spectacle I just made of myself.

I spot another black suitcase with a red ribbon and cautiously reach for it. But just as I do, a hand swoops in and yanks it from the conveyer belt. *Seriously, not again!* I clamor after the bag just as the guy I'd nearly assaulted sets it down at my feet, and the air in my lungs swooshes past my lips in a stunned exhale.

"You didn't have to do that," I say.

"I just wanted to make sure there wasn't any more confusion. You know, for the sake of all the other passengers," he says, that familiar smile of amusement still dangling from his full lips.

I blanch. "Funny."

"Are you sure this one is your bag?" he asks.

I want to ignore his comment, but just to be safe, I check the luggage tag. "This is it," I confirm. "Thanks for your help. And again, sorry."

He nods once. "I hope your day gets better."

As he turns and walks away, I dumbly stand there, replaying the last five minutes over and over in my head and cringing a little deeper each time the scenario plays out in all of its humiliating glory.

"Did you get all of your luggage?" Connie asks, stepping into my line of sight.

"What?" I ask.

"Your suitcases. Do you only have one?" She eyes the lone bag at my feet.

It takes a moment for me to forget about the guy who's disappeared through the crowd behind her and focus instead on her words. "Oh! No, I have one more," I say. I turn once again to the carousel, spotting the matching piece of my luggage—double-checking the luggage tag—then return to Connie's side. "Got it."

"All right!" she says with a level of enthusiasm that seems to indicate she was the one who'd single-handedly managed this baggage retrieval. "Let's go find Jay."

Fifteen minutes later, and still reeling from the mortifying encounter at baggage claim, we're in the Chapmans' SUV and on our way. Apparently, the town of Mystic Shores, Oregon—known merely as Mystic to the locals, or so I'm told—isn't big enough to have a commercial airport, and because the family was in Astoria this weekend visiting Connie's parents, they'd arranged for me to fly into Portland. According to Jay, it's about a two-hour drive from here to my new home—120 minutes stuck in a car with my new guardians and their offspring, fumbling over clumsy conversations and occasional moments of stilted silence. What a treat.

Lily talks for a good portion of the time, filling most of the voids that surface. She gives us an earful about her pet frog, Mr. Lily Pad; her best friend, Sophie; and how she loves sour-cream-and-onion potato chips.

"Do you like chips?" Her eyes harbor genuine interest.

"Of course," I assure her. That's all it takes to satisfy her, and she's rambling away again. Jay keeps his eyes on the road, periodically changing the radio station. Occasionally, he glances at me in the rearview mirror and smiles; then his attention goes right back to driving.

Connie eases what silence Lily manages to allow by asking me questions. What do I think of Oregon so far? What subjects do I like most in school? Do I have any hobbies? I answer each one like a baseball player swinging at consecutive pitches. I remind her that, so far, I've only seen the airport, but I heard from the woman next to me on the plane about the rain and the beautiful fall colors. I share that I like science, but I'm not a fan of math. And I'm about to tell her that I'm a dancer and I've had ballet slippers strapped to my feet since I was three, but I abruptly stop myself, biting my lip to barricade the words.

For one thing, they know all about that. Aunt Faye had filled Jay in on most of the details of my life before my arrival here. She'd told him about my mom's ballet studio, her career as a principal dancer before making the switch to teaching and focusing a lot of her time and effort on training me. But aside from that, I don't mention it because—I'm not a dancer anymore. That part of my life abruptly imploded the night my mom died, and that's not something I plan to share with Connie or anyone else for that matter. For the record, omitting information is not technically a lie, or even deceitful for that matter. Sometimes, it's just better to keep things unsaid. So, instead of spilling my guts, I tell her that I enjoy reading and going to the beach, and I hope that's enough for now.

"You've come to the right place!" Connie claps her hands. "We love the beach, isn't that right, kids? Our favorite spot is not far from the house. Maybe we can take you there this weekend." I wait to meet Jay's eyes in the rearview mirror but find myself oddly disappointed when he doesn't glance my way.

Leaning back against the headrest, I stare out the car window and watch the thick jungle of scenery whiz by. There are a lot of trees here. As the road winds, the canopy of foliage thickens, providing a patchy green shield to the midday sun. This place looks nothing like home and—that's all it takes. Within moments, I'm sucked under, missing the house I grew up in and wondering what will happen to it. And the bedroom I've had for as long as I can remember—I'll never sleep there again. One depressing thought spins into the next, and then the next, until I'm swallowed up by a jumbled mess of memories and misery.

I think about the lawyer whose job it was to deliver the stipulations of my mother's will, those dreaded pieces of paper with their big, fancy words that changed my existence in a single day. The lawyer—"*Just call me Howard,*" he'd instructed me—is a short, stocky man who's balding on top but tries to make it look like he isn't by combing a long section of hair across the top of his scalp. Why do men do that? Does he honestly think he's fooling anyone?

I had no idea my mother even had a lawyer. Why would she? She didn't have a regular doctor; she would just pick one at random from a Google search when it was necessary. Unbeknownst to me, she'd found an attorney and paid him money to document her final wishes. I learned about this a week after Mom died. Seven days after my entire world exploded, the next bombshell hit hard.

Aunt Faye contacted the lawyer through the information my mother had left her and headed out on a Thursday morning to meet with him. She told me she expected it to be a short meeting, which is why I nearly paced a hole in the front hallway carpet before she finally pulled into the driveway well after six o'clock that evening. She'd barely managed to stick her key in the lock when I'd flung open the door.

"Where have you been?" I demanded, shaking from a combination of anger and relief that formed a large, barbed knot in my stomach.

Dropping her keys and purse on the small table in the entryway, Faye immediately began apologizing. "I'm sorry, Paige. I never intended to be gone so long."

"You could have called or at least sent me a text. I was worried sick!" I hadn't realized just how upset I was until a well of adrenaline burst somewhere inside me, slathering every panic-stricken word. "After everything that we've been through—after Mom—you just should have called!"

Aunt Faye's arms were around me in a split second, so tight I could hardly breathe. She held me for a long time, and when she finally released me, I took my first good look at her, from her slumped shoulders to her dark eyes and deflated spirit. Faye was always so calm and sure in any situation, but at that moment, she appeared almost catatonic. I was frightened for an entirely new reason. What had happened in the last eight hours to make her look like that?

Taking her by the arm, I'd led her into the living room. "Please tell me what happened," I begged. "You're really scaring me."

Call me naïve, but I honestly thought my life couldn't possibly get worse after Mom died. Turns out, the life-changing tragedy of losing the one person I loved more than anything was just the beginning of my spiraling downfall. With a single sentence uttered from Aunt Faye's trembling lips, my entire being, soul and all, was drop-kicked off its foundation.

"My—*father*?" I sank onto the couch. "That's not possible."

Faye lowered herself onto the edge of the coffee table, lightly touching her hands to my knees, which I hugged tightly to my chest. "I know, honey, I know. It's a shock."

If what she meant by *shock* was an electrical jolt so huge and wielding enough force to obliterate me, then yeah, this was a shock.

"I didn't see this one coming either," she confessed, stroking my cheek. As she pulled me close, my feet dropped to the floor, and our foreheads pressed softly together. I can still hear her heartbreaking sigh. When she pulled back, her eyes glistened.

"What does this mean? I'm gonna live with you," I said. "I'm gonna finish my senior year here and graduate—" Any additional explanation escaped me.

I'm not stupid. Ever since I was little, I'd been aware I had a father out there somewhere. I was the product of a high school romance that went too far and ended abruptly when the guy bolted. He became just a faceless part of a story my mother would occasionally tell me when I was younger to explain why our family was different from my friends' families. They had a dad who was there to play with them and pick them up from school. I didn't. My biological benefactor was long gone, and somehow, Mom convinced me he was not essential to my story. She'd been so convincing, in fact, that I'd never questioned it. My world was simply about Mom and me, and that was enough, and I'd never felt the need to try to find him. As far as I was concerned, my mother filled the role of parent just fine, and I'd accepted long ago that the man whose name I didn't know but was apparently recorded on my birth certificate, was a memory I'd never have. He didn't want us and, therefore, I didn't need him.

Mom told me in no uncertain terms that even though she never planned to have me when she was so young, I was the best thing that ever happened to her. She'd looked me right in the eyes when she told me that, and left no doubt in my mind that she meant every word. The uncertainty that's oozed into every facet of my brain since her death is fueled by all the things she apparently chose not to tell me.

"Paige, Abby made out her will to say that if anything happened to her—she wanted you to live with your biological father and his family." Her voice broke on her final words as tears pooled in her eyes. "His name is Jay Chapman."

As long as I live, I will never forget that moment. It was as if someone had sucked all the air out of the room. All at once, the thoughts swirling in my brain detonated, and I couldn't make heads or tails out of any of them. I wanted to scream at the top of my lungs that I didn't care what his name was. Instead, all that managed to cross my lips was a weak, "No."

"I know, Paige, this is unexpected. I had no idea that Abby was even thinking of doing this. I can't even imagine why—I don't—I don't understand."

"Are you really gonna let her do this?" I demanded, desperation spilling off every syllable. This had to be the part where Faye would laugh and say, "Absolutely not!" This would be the moment when she'd tell me that she'd dismissed the lawyer and the man to whom I was about to be handed over, and that she fully intended to go to court and end this craziness.

Faye brushed a strand of hair from my forehead. "Oh, sweetie."

My heart plummeted into my stomach. "You don't want me?" The words passed my lips, but it took a moment for the full weight of the rejection to drop on top of me.

"Of course I want you!" Faye exclaimed. "More than anything!" Piercing quiet hung between us for a long moment before she said, "When the lawyer broke the news to me, I lost it. I yelled. At him, at your mother. I felt deceived." Faye's watery eyes locked with mine. "You know how much I love you. I've been a part of your life since the day you were born. There isn't anything I wouldn't do for you."

"Then fight for me," I whispered.

Those four small words seemed to break Faye where she sat and her face crumpled. "You don't know how hard it was for me not to tear up your mother's will and pretend it never existed. I would have done it too if—" Faye closed her eyes for longer than a blink. "I loved my sister. I—*love* my sister. And as much as I want to, I can't ignore her last wishes, Paige. What kind of a sister would I be if I did?" She squeezed my hands tighter as a flash of pain washed over her face. "So, as angry as I am with Abby right now—"

*Please don't.*

"I have to believe she had a genuine reason for doing this."

"Are you kidding me?!" Every drop of blood in my veins bubbled to get to the surface. I couldn't catch my breath. If I hadn't been sitting upright on the sofa just then, I would have sworn that someone had pinned me down and put a heavy hand over my mouth.

In an instant, Faye was kneeling at my side, trying desperately to peel my arms from where I'd wrapped them tightly around myself.

"Paige! Paige, sweetie, I know, I know!" she'd whimpered quietly into my ear, her arms encircling me. We swayed back and forth as she kissed the top of my head.

There was wetness on my scalp. Her tears? I wasn't sure of anything at that moment.

No, that wasn't entirely true. I was sure of one thing: someone, somewhere, must be trying to kill me.

"We're coming into town," Jay announces. Startled by the intrusion, I dismiss my thoughts and place a trembling hand on my forehead as I refocus on the world outside the car window. The coastal town of Mystic Shores rolls into view. Population: 8,620. That's what the decorative, wooden welcome sign declares. And it's just what I imagined. Small.

It begins to sprinkle, and Jay turns on the windshield wipers. As he maneuvers the Dodge Durango through town, we're all quiet, except for Lily, who's playing tour guide in the seat next to me.

"That's the McDonald's. And over there's the movie theater. Do you like movies, Paige? I love movies!"

Jay points out a road to the left that leads to the high school. Connie directs my attention to the real estate office where she tells me she's worked for about five years. Tanner's head remains buried in his phone, where it's been since we left baggage claim. Lily points out a few more insignificant landmarks as we drive: the Grab & Go grocery store, the library and the Chinese food restaurant, and then we make a left turn. I catch a glimpse of the street sign as we pass, which reads "Driftwood Drive." On either side of the road sit half a dozen homes with large yards. Jay turns into the driveway of a big two story with a manicured lawn and kills the engine.

"This is it," Connie declares, staring up at the house. "Let's get your things inside."

The family's home is what I would describe as elegant. Not the kind where you worry about touching anything, but the type captured in magazines.

In the living room, thick, burgundy drapes line the windows that stretch from the floor to the ceiling, allowing in a flood of muted afternoon light from the overcast sky. As I step a little farther into the room, my eyes quickly scan over an assortment of family photos that line the fireplace mantel in fancy frames. And perhaps the topper to this *Good Housekeeping* spread is the baby grand piano that sits dust-free and polished to perfection in the corner.

"Your room is upstairs," Jay says. "Would you like to see it?"

Connie takes my suitcase from him and leads the way. Jay doesn't follow.

When we reach the top of the stairs, she stops at the first door on the left. "Here it is," she announces, pushing it open and flipping on the light. I hesitate, then take a deep, you-can-do-this breath and step inside.

It's a decent room as far as bedrooms go. There's a queen-size bed on the far wall and a desk with a laptop in the corner. The walls are painted a pale yellow, and there's a colorful throw rug in the middle of the hardwood floor. I set down my other suitcase and put my duffel on the bed, narrowly missing a gray-and-white cat that's so fluffy and large, I thought it was a pillow.

"Oh, I'm sorry!" Connie says, leaning around me and waving her hand in a shooing motion at the cat. The large animal doesn't budge. Instead, it releases what I think is a cross between a hiss and a growl. Connie sighs and apologizes again. "That's Kitty Poppins." There's a note of disdain in her voice. "We rescued her from the shelter last year. Unfortunately, we've since discovered that she isn't all that fond of people." As if to openly mock Connie and prove her point, Kitty Poppins lazily stretches, rolls over and venomously swipes her paw in Connie's direction.

"If she's so awful, why do you keep her?" I ask.

"She's not awful," Connie backpedals. "More like ornery. But Lily thinks the world of her, so, it is what it is." Her eyebrows shoot skyward in alarm. "You're not allergic to cats, are you? Oh, dear, I didn't even think of that."

"No, I'm not allergic."

"Oh, good." Connie sighs and presses her fingertips to her temples.

Lily appears in the doorway with a pink plastic convertible tucked awkwardly under one arm and dragging a bulging Hello Kitty backpack on the ground behind her. She makes her way into the room like she owns the joint.

"Lily, what are you doing?" Connie demands.

The little girl swings the backpack onto the bed, and a mess of yellow doll hair spills out from the half-open zipper. "I want to play Barbies with Paige. I brought my collection for her to see. Paige, did you know that Barbie has a sister?

Her name is Skipper."

"Oh, honey, not now," Connie says, swiping the pack off the bed before Lily can reach inside to retrieve its contents. She steers the little girl by the shoulders back to the doorway. "Paige just got here. Let's give her some time to get settled."

"But I want to play with her *nooooow*," Lily whines. "You said sisters play together!"

"Later!" Connie whispers harshly, waving Lily down the hallway, much like she attempted to shoo Kitty Poppins. The little girl huffs and stomps off.

Connie closes her eyes and exhales a long breath. The woman is definitely stressed. "Sorry about that. She's just so excited that you're here. You're all she's talked about for the last week."

A small smile blooms across my lips, and it must be what Connie has been waiting for because her shoulders instantly relax.

"I want you to feel like this room is yours, Paige. So, I will talk with Lily *again* about giving you your privacy, but I warn you, she's persistent." Yup, I sort of already picked up on that. "How about next week you and I go shopping, and we'll get you a new bedspread and maybe some framed art for the walls?"

"Sure." I don't know if I will ever have anything meaningful to say to this woman, but I'm trying. Right now, I just want to be left alone, behind closed doors, where I don't have worried eyes sizing me up and trying to assess how damaged I really am. "I think I'll unpack, if that's okay?"

"Great, sure, absolutely. I'll start dinner, and I'll call you when it's ready. We're having chicken." She pauses, then looks momentarily concerned once again. "Do you like chicken? Or are you vegetarian? I could make something else."

I have to give her points for effort. "Chicken is fine. Really."

"Great! Chicken it is!" Her attempt at a lighthearted laugh comes out more like an odd, strangled sound as she backs toward the door.

I muster another quick smile, and thankfully, she disappears, closing the door behind her. As the clacking of her heels grows distant, I take a full, cleansing breath and slowly release it. Now that it's just me and Kitty Poppins, the room is quiet, and it's the best sound I've heard all day.

I unzip my suitcase. Tucked protectively between my clothes are two silver-framed pictures. The first is of Mom and me at Disneyland last summer, in front of Sleeping Beauty's castle. I run my finger across the glass before placing it gently on the nightstand. The other photo is of Aunt Faye and my cousin Tyler. He's Faye's only child, and he's two years older than me. Ty just started his sophomore year at the University of Oregon, so at least he isn't too far away. That's the most comforting thought I've had since I left San Diego this morning.

Encased in those two frames is my entire world. I glance

around my new room. I suppose that's no longer true. Thanks to what has to be my mother's worst decision ever, and with help from the law firm of Johnson, McCrory and Taylor, I now have a father. How in the world am I supposed to handle this? I reach out a hand and stroke Kitty Poppins's fur. She cracks open one eye and gives me a once-over that borders on uninterested. Then, as if I've met her feline expectations, the cat's eyes close once again. No hissing, no growling.

I pull out my cell phone and shoot Aunt Faye a text, explaining that I've arrived and that I'll call her tomorrow. I can't talk to her right now. She'll keep me on the phone forever and expect me to tell her everything that's happened since I boarded the plane. Call me a crappy niece, but I just don't have it in me to put on a happy voice and tell her everything is fine. Because it's not. And I'm not sure if it ever will be again.

I sit on the bed, looking around the room that doesn't really belong to me. I think about the people downstairs who don't know me. And those aren't even the greatest of my worries right now. Monday will be my first day at a new school where I have no friends and will basically have to start all over again. And to top it all off, I am the principal's kid.

There's no way I can fly under the radar on that one.

# CHAPTER THREE
## Cade

*Two hundred and sixteen days until graduation.* That mental countdown is what gets me out of bed every morning and convinces me to go to school. Today, though, I should have just stayed in bed. I know that the instant I pull my motorcycle into the student lot and spot her.

She's standing in the shadow of a large tree, her back against the worn brick wall that leads to the school's entrance. She kicks distractedly at the asphalt with the toe of her boot, trying to dissolve into her surroundings like a chameleon desperate to hide from predators. What she can't hide from me is the despair that's nearly tattooed across her face.

"Hey, Hannah."

I barely get those two simple words past my lips when she blurts out, "I need help."

That's what I was afraid of. I scan the space around us, trying to identify who's within earshot before I say, "What's going on?"

Hannah pushes off the wall. Her heeled boots add some stature to her small frame, but she barely brushes my shoulder. "I'm out. I'm leaving town." Her attempt at bravery can't mask the quiver in her voice.

"Why? I thought you were going back home. You told me you worked everything out with your parents."

"Yeah, well, I lied." She brushes a strand of hair away from her face. Her usual sparkle, so mesmerizing that I've seen her take down a guy with a simple wink, is nowhere to be found. Instead, light purple bruises bloom in the hollows beneath her eyes, a track record of many sleepless nights. "I've gotta get out of here, Cade."

"Wait a second." I release a slow lungful of air, giving my mind a moment to catch up. "You promised me you weren't gonna do this. You said you would—"

"I don't have a choice!" A couple of students walking by look over, and Hannah lowers her head. She doesn't like to draw attention to herself. "I don't have a choice," she softly repeats.

When Hannah and I first met, we were just kids, and the worst things either of us worried about were getting grounded for not doing our chores or not getting what we wanted for Christmas. But things changed, and life got more complicated than either of us knew how to handle.

I was thirteen when it started. One minute I was living a pretty good life and the next—I'd lost everything that held me together. First, my mom. I can thank cancer for that one. Then my dad. But I refuse to take any of the blame there. He knew what he was doing, and he knew it would destroy us, so it really shouldn't have come as a surprise when it did. The final casualty was me. I'd splintered beneath the weight of devastating loss and insurmountable betrayal, and I let it engulf me until I couldn't see straight. I did things I'm not proud of, and I got caught up in a life that no longer resembled anything good. I hurt a lot of people. I know that, and no matter what I do, I will always carry the weight of the guilt on my shoulders. But despite all of it, I'd been lucky, because I'd had people in my life who'd helped pull me back up. My sister, for one. She'd refused to give up on me, and she was right beside me through it all, until I finally figured out how to crawl my way back to the surface.

Like me, Hannah got mixed up with the wrong crowd a couple of years ago. And because her parents were more concerned about their reputation and social standing, they found it easier to disown her than to forgive her. She's been bumming on the streets and crashing on friends' couches ever since. I've tried to help her when I can, but things don't seem to be getting any better. When our senior year began two months ago, Hannah promised me she would try to get her life back on track, and she'd start by making amends with her parents. Instead, she was ditching class by the end of the first week.

"What about your brother?" I ask, my jaw tightening against the sick realization that her loser sibling might be the only person in her family who could stop her from making this enormous mistake. "I thought you said you could talk to him."

"I'm an embarrassment to him, too. Just like I am to my parents. I was an idiot to think he was any different from the rest of them."

"Running away isn't going to fix this," I say, but the words sour on my tongue. I'm the last person who should be lecturing her. I shake my head, trying to suppress the bitter memories and the guilt I now feel. "Where are you gonna go?"

Before she can answer, she spots something over my shoulder and curses as she drops her head, trying to hide behind the veil of her hair.

"What's going on here, Miss Sloane?"

I roll my eyes just before Principal Chapman enters my peripheral vision, suspicion plastered in stern lines across his brow.

"Nothing, Mr. Chapman," Hannah says, so sweetly I almost believe her. "We're just talking, sir."

I'm quick to notice the girl standing two steps behind him. Our gazes meet, and I barely have time to focus on her face before she averts her eyes, brushing her long hair over one shoulder as if she's trying to go unnoticed, and glances at her wristwatch. At first, I think maybe she's a new student, but she looks familiar. Wait—*the airport*. I shake my head, convinced that I must be hallucinating, and this girl is some strange mirage that's morphed from my subconscious. I study her face. Oh, yeah, it's her. The girl who was convinced I was stealing her suitcase. The spitfire who'd nearly tackled me over a piece of luggage is now standing in front of me. What in the world is she doing here?

"The bell's about to ring," Principal Chapman says. He eyes me with disapproval so thick, I could slice it with a knife and serve it on crackers. He's not my biggest fan. Never has been. "And you, Miss Sloane, can't afford any more unexcused absences. I suggest you get to class or we'll be seeing you in detention again." He glances at Hannah and then back at me, the stern lines deepening across his forehead.

"We're heading in," Hannah says, offering another sweet smile.

The girl beside Principal Chapman glances up at me, but this time when her eyes meet mine, she holds my gaze for a long moment, a perplexed expression on her face.

"Get moving. You don't want to be late," he warns.

Yeah, because being tardy would be the end of the world. I bite back the retort as my eyes drift once more to the dark-haired stranger, who looks as curious as she does uncomfortable.

Principal Chapman motions toward the building. "Come on, Paige, let's go."

The girl offers me a half smile, and I watch as she follows him into the school, then I return my attention to Hannah, who's avoiding my eyes.

"You aren't going inside, are you?"

Dipping her head, she shrugs her rail-thin shoulders. "I bought a bus ticket to Portland. I have a friend there. I can probably stay with her for a while."

"Probably? Hannah—"

"I'll make it work. I always do." She nods as if she's made her final decision and skims a hand through her hair. "I need a fresh start, ya know?"

Yeah, I do know. I know all about trying to run from your problems and finally realizing that no matter how fast you move and how far you go, your demons will always be faster than you.

Hannah should never have been on the streets in the first place. Her family is loaded, and they gave her everything she could ever want, except for the two things that matter: unconditional love and forgiveness. I can't be a part of that world anymore, the world where Hannah and I were friends who bonded over bad luck and crappy circumstances. It served me well when that was all I had, but I'm not that guy anymore. Even if no one else bothers to notice.

"I just don't feel right letting you go. Not like this," I say.

"Then come with me," she says. Before I can process her words, she raises up on her tiptoes and wraps a hand around my neck, tugging me toward her. I grab her wrists.

"What are you doing?"

She exhales deeply. "Taking a chance. Cade, we've been through so much together. You've been so good to me, even when I haven't returned the favor. Come with me to

Portland. We can start over."

"I can't."

"Why not?" She reaches for me again, and I step back.

"Because we're just friends," I remind her. "And because I've finally gotten my life back together. I have responsibilities now. I can't just leave."

To my surprise, she smiles. "Yeah, that's what I thought. But it was worth a shot."

I reach out a hand. Hannah's cheek lifts and I pull her in for a hug. She's so small and fragile. I should say something, stop her from making what I'm pretty sure will be another bad decision in her extensive collection. Her hands press into my back as she draws me closer with unsettling desperation. I think she knows she's making a mistake.

"Is there any way I can get you to stay?" Hannah shakes her head against my chest. "Come on. Don't do this. Let me help you."

Tilting back her head, she gazes up at me, her brows drawn together. "You have helped me, Cade. You were always my friend. And that means a lot to me." She gives me one more squeeze, then drops her hands and steps away. As she reaches down to sling the strap of her backpack over her shoulder, she adds, "I don't think I would have made it this far without you."

It's because of me that she's in this mess in the first place. The guilt burns.

"Is there anything I can do?"

Hannah's eyes trail a path from my forehead to my chin, like she's trying to memorize my face. She straightens and clears her throat. "Well, if I can't get you to come with me, I could use some cash."

Without hesitation, I pull my wallet from my back pocket and fish out my last twenty-dollar bill. "Keep in touch, okay? I want to know that you're all right."

She takes the bill and slips it into her boot. "I'll be fine."

"Promise."

The color drains slowly from her face with the last of her smile, and she stretches up once more, pressing a kiss to my cheek. "Bye, Cade."

Hannah pushes past a couple of guys making their way into school, the last of the morning migration. Her shoulders slump against the weight of her backpack, which as heavy as it appears, might as well be carrying all the rejection and loneliness that shrouds her. She can't seem to escape it. And dammit, it's not fair.

I continue to stare after her, long after she disappears around a dumpster in the parking lot. Long after the bell rings and quiet settles over the school. Long enough for a slow, simmering anger to build in my chest.

*Just 216 days until graduation.*

# CHAPTER FOUR
## *Paige*

Mystic Shores High School is nothing like I'd imagined. For one thing, it's much smaller than my old school. *Way smaller.* When Jay pulled into the parking lot, I'd nearly bolted from the front seat. I didn't want to be seen walking in with him, but there was one simple flaw in my plan: I had no idea where I was going.

The second he shifted the Durango into Park, Jay transformed into principal mode. It was like Clark Kent racing into a telephone booth, only much less cool. With just a few stern words and a look so heavy with authority it was blinding, almost like looking directly into the sun, he could spot trouble at fifty paces—which he made abundantly clear when he'd practically interrogated a couple outside the school's entrance. But if that wasn't awkward all on its own, I'm pretty sure Jay's target was the guy I'd nearly accosted at the airport. What are the odds that I would end up at the same school with the dude I bitterly humiliated myself in front of not even forty-eight hours ago? Pretty darn good by the looks of it.

"I think you'll like it here," Jay says, holding open the door to the main office. "If you have any questions at all, I should be in my office most of the day. If not, Karen knows where to find me." He gestures to the woman with a well-coiffed updo who stands behind the long counter assisting a lanky boy with an unfortunate case of acne.

"Be right with you, hon," Karen says with a smile.

Once I have my schedule in hand, I convince Jay that I do not need an escort through the hallways. He looks unsure but lets me go without assistance. "Well, then, have a good day, Paige. I'll meet you back here after school."

American history is my first class. It's one of my favorite subjects and the teacher, Mr. Jennings, looks just like a history teacher should, at least the way I picture them: a sweater, a tie and a pair of horn-rimmed glasses that droop low on his nose. He clears his throat a lot as he summarizes the plot points of the Great Depression. I try to ignore the stares from the students around me, but it's not easy.

Fifty minutes later, I make my way to health class. The teacher, Mrs. Barlow, welcomes me warmly, and she leads me to a seat in the back, much to my relief. Again, all the heads in the class follow me.

It's not until English literature that someone actually tries to speak to me.

"You must be Paige Bryant," a petite redhead says shortly after I slide into the seat across from her. I nod as pleasantly as my discomfort allows. So far, no one has seemed to know my name.

"I'm Quinn Talbot," she whispers, pulling a hair tie from around her wrist and sweeping her thick, fiery mane into a messy knot at the back of her head. "My mom teaches chemistry here, so I know what it's like to have a parent on staff." She shrugs and smiles, a warmness in her blue eyes. "It stinks like cheese, but you'll deal with it."

I stifle a surprised laugh and return her smile before letting my eyes fall to the reading list in front of me. Maybe this class won't be so bad. I like Quinn, and because it's been less than a minute since she introduced herself, I'm not entirely sure why.

I don't get another opportunity to talk to her until the bell rings. We walk to our lockers together, which are in the same section of the hallway, and she insists that I sit with her at lunch and meet her friends. I don't hesitate to accept her invitation because my alternatives are to eat alone or hide out in the girls' restroom, which would really take a hit on my self-esteem.

When Quinn and I squeeze in at a large table with our lunch trays, she kicks off the introductions. "Everyone, this is Paige."

"Are you really Principal Chapman's kid?" The question comes from a dark-haired boy sitting across from us. By the way, he's sizing me up, I can tell I'm not what he pictured, but I nod.

When he turns to speak with the boy next to him, Quinn whispers, "That's Gio."

"Gio?" I mouth.

"Short for Giovanni. Cute, don't you think?" Again, I nod, my bobblehead persona resurfacing.

"Where're you from?" This next question comes from a girl with short, curly blond hair who sits diagonally across the table from me.

"San Diego."

"Oh, your ocean is warm," she says. "Ours is freezing. Just a warning." The group laughs in agreement. Quinn tells me her name is Samantha, but to call her Sam. I feel like I should be taking notes.

"So, Paige," the guy sitting next to Gio says. He has the most amazing eyes that crinkle at the corners when he flashes me a mischievous grin. "Do you surf?"

"Yeah, a little bit," I say, picking at the French fries on my tray. I sense an odd stillness, and when I glance up, all the guys at the table have their eyes locked on me. What just happened?

"Hey, Dane, you have a little bit of drool right there at the corner of your mouth," Quinn says, balling up her napkin and tossing it at him, then flashing me an apologetic look. "Sorry, they're surfing freaks, but trust me, it's miserable. *So* cold," she says, agreeing with—what was her name? Sam?

"Don't listen to them," Dane says, and he and Gio proceed to tell me all about Otter Rock and Agate Beach, their two favorite spots for surfing by the sound of it.

"You've gotta come with us. It's a rush," Dane says.

"What do you say? I'm a pretty good tour guide." What I think is that his smile could melt sugar.

Before I can respond, Quinn grabs my forearm with both of her hands. "Hey! How long have you been a dancer? Do you do hip hop? Or is it just classical?"

The hand holding my can of soda freezes halfway to my lips. *What the what?*

"Are you really as good as they say?" Quinn presses, but I'm still working on her first question.

"How do you know about that?" The words slip from my lips, but I already know the answer. The only way anyone in this dinky town could know about my dancing is through Jay. I have no doubt that in one of his many conversations with Aunt Faye, she'd told him that I'd been preparing for an audition at a prestigious dance academy before—well, before everything happened. But my dancing is none of his business and certainly not something he has the right to share with his staff, who must blab to their children—

"I Googled you," Quinn says, drawing her phone from her back pocket. "There are pictures and everything."

Oh. Well, sure, there's that.

Apparently, Quinn misses my moment of shock and awe because she just keeps talking. "Here's the sitch—we desperately need another body on the dance team. We're going to state this year."

"You know it!" two other girls at the table chime in, apparently confident in the dance team's abilities.

The discomfort that spiked inside me just a moment ago was mild compared to the tidal wave that's rolling through me now. "I don't dance."

Quinn's eyebrows pinch together in confusion and her questioning eyes drop to her phone. "Well, according to the internet—"

I gently push down her phone. "What I mean is, I'm just trying to get settled with my classes. And at some point, I'm gonna need to look for a job. So, I really don't have any time for that right now." And I desperately need to change the subject.

"There are a couple of openings at the movie theater," a girl named Zoey informs me. She has sharp, angular features and long, glossy black hair that she constantly twirls around her finger. "It's a pretty easy paycheck."

I don't actually need a job. It's more of an attempt to find something to do with myself, to get me out of the house and out from under the watchful eyes of Jay and Connie. And if I can earn some money to pay for the airplane ticket home the second I turn eighteen, even better. I've never worked a day in my life outside our ballet studio in San Diego, and I spent nearly every free moment training, rehearsing with Mom and performing, so I'm not sure that I'm qualified to do anything *but* dance. But at least this conversation has rerouted itself.

Quinn stills beside me. "Uh-oh," she says, her voice low. "Angry hot guy at twelve o'clock." I follow her gaze across the cafeteria and see a dark-headed guy—the guy from the airport—heading in the direction of our table. And she's right; he looks angry.

"Ohhh, this is not good," Sam whispers.

"What's happening?" I ask.

The guy stops at our table, right behind Dane, his hands fisted at his sides. "What the hell did you say to her?" he demands.

Dane is out of his chair so fast, I blink back surprise.

"That's none of your business." He steps forward so that he's nearly nose-to-nose with the other guy. A thick tension coats the air and every head at the table, including mine, is glued to what appears to be a fight about to go down.

Hot Angry Guy's dark eyes narrow and a muscle thrums along his jaw. "I'm gonna ask you one more time, and I strongly suggest you pick a better answer. What did you say to Hannah?"

"Get lost," Dane says. "This doesn't concern you."

"She's gone," he spits. "Did you know that? She's gone because of you."

"That's bullshit! She brought this on herself. She's got no one to blame but herself. And you," Dane accuses. I don't know who Hannah is, but clearly, there's no love lost between her and Dane.

"You're a coward. And you know it."

Dane begins to turn back to the table, then without warning, spins and punches the guy in the jaw. He just hit the guy! Hot Angry Guy stumbles back, and before he can recover, Dane lunges at him, and the two are embroiled in an all-out fight on the cafeteria floor. A full-on fight with fists swinging and—everyone is just watching it happen and cheering like it's some pay-per-view match on TV.

"Knock it off! Right now!" The second those words touch my ears, Jay appears in the middle of the brawl, alongside another man. They scramble to pull Dane and Hot Angry Guy off each other, and they have their hands full. Both boys are still swinging at each other as they're hauled apart. Dane's nose is bleeding, and a small trickle of blood appears at the corner of Hot Angry Guy's mouth.

"You! Both of you!" bellows Jay, his hands outstretched as if that's enough to bar the two from going at each other again. "In my office, now!"

"Coward!" Hot Angry Guy manages to spit once more at Dane before Jay gives him a shove toward the cafeteria doors. Chest heaving, Dane wipes the blood from his nose as the other man takes hold of him by the upper arm.

"Okay, okay, I'm going!" Dane snaps, yanking his arm free. He runs a hand through his hair and slowly heads for the doors.

When they're gone, it's like they took all the words left at our table with them. Gio is the first to break the silence with a heavy sigh. "Well, I'm pretty sure this means Dane won't be making it to lacrosse practice this afternoon." He huffs, picks up his tray and heads for the garbage cans. The stunned silence that momentarily consumed the cafeteria quickly breaks apart, and conversations resume at the tables around us.

47

"What was that about?" I ask. No one answers me, so I try again. "Who is that guy?"

Quinn and Zoey exchange a look, then in unison say, "That's Cade Matthews."

"And who's Cade Matthews?" I press.

"He's a senior," Quinn says.

"He's stupid hot, but kind of a loner," Zoey adds. "Oh, and his dad is in prison."

"Prison? Really? For what?"

Quinn shrugs. "I think he killed a guy." She turns her attention to her granola bar as if she just rattled off the weather forecast. Is she joking? My wide eyes trail back to the cafeteria doors. Maybe I'm not the only one who has problems.

Lunch passes quickly and talk of the lunchroom brawl ebbs and flows throughout the afternoon as I make my way through my classes. Art is enjoyable. Calculus is uneventful. Spanish seems manageable. And overall, I am pretty satisfied with my day when I emerge from the door of my forensic science class.

After collecting my bag from my locker, I make my way to the office where Karen, the secretary who gave me my schedule earlier, tells me Jay has someone in his office and I should take a seat and wait for him.

She gestures to a row of chairs outside the door marked "Principal," but I hesitate. Slumped in one of the chairs is Cade Matthews. I glance around and realize that there are no other chairs in the office. Swallowing, I take a seat, leaving the last open chair between us.

I risk a glance at my neighbor and immediately wish I hadn't. Lazy, contemplative eyes framed by long lashes are fixed on me. I check my watch. Then, I pull out my cell phone from my bag and check for new texts. There aren't any.

He's still watching me. I can feel it.

Shifting in my seat, I avert my eyes to the other side of the room, to where Karen is typing at her computer. I recheck my phone. Another glance at my watch. And then my patience runs dry.

"What?" I ask, turning to face him. Even with the split lip and the angry red and purple bruise that spiderwebs its way across his jaw, he's definitely easy on the eyes. I suppose I'd been too flustered at the airport to take inventory of his appearance. I mean, I thought the guy was trying to swipe my luggage, so seeing anything beyond his criminal activity wasn't exactly on my radar.

"Nothing," he answers, his expression blank. He leans forward, propping his elbows on his knees and sighs heavily.

Then I sigh.

He swivels his head in my direction and—he's staring at me again.

"Can I help you?"

He huffs out a laugh. "What is your deal?"

"You're staring at me," I say.

"No, I'm not."

"Yes, you were." I notice he has a thin, white scar

slashed across his right eyebrow.

"You're right, I was," he says and—I have no idea how to respond. "You're new here."

"Yup." Look, everyone, Captain Obvious is in the building.

"The principal's daughter? Seriously?"

Geez, did they send out a flipping memo or something? Unease ratchets up my spine as his eyes linger on me, and I feel entirely exposed. "Does everyone and their dog know who I am?" He chokes back another small laugh, and my irritation flares. "Is that funny?"

"No," he replies. "It's a small school. People talk. And right now, you're the one they're talking about." Deep copper eyes clouded with cool curiosity travel the length of me, then he raises one sardonic eyebrow. "The luggage stealer."

I frown. "I'm pretty sure everyone is still talking about the fight in the cafeteria. Nice show, by the way."

Cade's eyes narrow for a moment, then he relaxes back into his chair.

"Do you do that often? I mean, are lunchtime brawls your thing or something?" I'm not sure where exactly my words come from. I'm not usually the chat-with-strangers type. But after seeing this guy throw down in the cafeteria, I have to admit I'm intrigued.

"Not usually."

"So, how come today was the exception?" I prompt, feeling bolder than what's typically my nature.

"Why don't you ask your buddy, Dane."

Before I can respond or ask any more questions, the office door opens, and Jay steps out, followed by a dark-headed man in a uniform. I glance at the badges on his shirt. The embroidered patch on his upper sleeve that reads "Mystic Shores Fire Department."

"Thanks for coming in. I wish it could have been under different circumstances," Jay says, shaking the man's hand. "We don't tolerate violence at this school, and when it occurs, there are consequences." He glances at Cade, then back at the man. "Hopefully, this suspension will help Cade understand that he can't just start a fight anytime he wants."

Cade rolls his eyes as he begrudgingly stands, shoving his hands into the pockets of his jeans like this whole thing is just an annoying inconvenience in his day.

"Again, my apologies for the disruption," the man says. "You can be sure that Cade and I will talk about this when we get home."

I'm not sure exactly how it happens or why, but I'm suddenly on my feet. "Cade didn't start the fight," I blurt out.

All three heads turn in my direction. "What did you say?" the man asks.

"Paige, why don't you head into my office. I'll be there in a minute." Jay gestures to his open door.

"Wait." The man holds up his index finger in Jay's direction, but his eyes are still on me. "What did you just say?"

"I said—Cade didn't start the fight. Dane did. I was there in the cafeteria; I saw it."

"Is this true?" the man asks Cade in an odd tone, bewilderment wrapped in frustration, as if he's relieved to hear the news and yet not entirely surprised that it came from someone else. "Then why didn't you tell Mr. Chapman that?"

Cade lifts one shoulder.

"Paige, are you sure?" Jay asks. "That's not what the other students I talked with reported."

I have no idea what the other students thought they saw. If they're Dane's friends, maybe they were just sticking up for him. "Positive. I saw it with my own eyes." Cade looks away, his jaw tense. "Cade approached Dane, but he was just talking. It was Dane who threw the first punch." Slowly, I sink back into my chair.

Jay mulls over my words, dipping his head and rubbing the back of his neck. "Cade, I'm at a loss here. We just spent the afternoon discussing this at length. I gave you ample opportunity to give me your side of the story. Why didn't you tell me this yourself?"

"Does this mean he's not suspended?" the man asks, placing a hand on Cade's shoulder.

Jay hesitates, his gaze bouncing from me to Cade and back again. "I suppose—in light of this new information— no. We'll forgo the suspension for now, until I can sort this out. But you will serve two days in after-school detention for not being honest. School policy doesn't tolerate violence or dishonesty, Cade, and neither do I. You and I are going to talk about this tomorrow. Come see me before your first class."

The man extends his hand to Jay. "I'll make sure he comes to see you."

Cade reaches down for the backpack sitting on the floor between us. As he retrieves it, he leans close and, surprised, I freeze.

"Don't believe everything you hear," he says in a voice so soft that only I can hear him. "Or you're no better than the rest of them." And with that, he slings his pack over one shoulder and heads for the door.

*What in the world?* Before I can begin to dissect Cade's ominous message, Jay exhales deeply. "Come on in, Paige."

Dutifully, I follow Jay into his office and close the door behind me while he slips off his suit jacket and hangs it on a hook on the wall.

"So, how did it go? Did you have a good day? How are your classes?" He ruffles through some papers on his desk and glances up at me when I don't answer. "Did you have any problems?"

"No, it was fine." I glance over my shoulder at the closed door. "Who's Hannah?"

Jay's head lifts. "Who?"

"Hannah? That's who Dane and Cade were talking about before the fight in the cafeteria," I say. "I was just wondering who she is."

Jay works his jaw in thought before dismissing my question with, "No need to concern yourself with that. It's best if you steer clear of Cade Matthews."

The roar of an engine pulls my attention to the window. Just as I spot a helmeted rider on the back of a large, silver motorcycle, it peels out of the parking lot and shoots up the street, out of view.

I turn my attention back to Jay. "And why's that?"

He contemplates his response before saying firmly, "Because I told you to."

Okay, then. Clearly, this is not a topic he wants to discuss, which is unfortunate because I have a lot of questions. Instead of pressing it further, I make a mental note to ask Quinn my questions tomorrow and drum my fingers on the desktop next to a framed photo of Jay and his family. It's one of those pictures taken in an actual photography studio, in which everyone is positioned just right and told to smile on cue. I've never seen Jay smile like that. I squeeze my eyes tight. I'm so angry at my mom, and it drives me crazy that I will never know what she could possibly have been thinking when she decided to give me to a stranger.

"I hear you met Mrs. Talbot's daughter, Quinn." Boy, news travels fast around this school.

"Yeah, she introduced me to a bunch of people at lunch."

"Great," Jay says, his attention buried in the paperwork in front of him. "She hangs with a good group of kids." Um, okay—including a kid who just punched another guy in the middle of the cafeteria. I keep that thought to myself.

I stand and cross the room to look at another set of framed pictures on the bookshelf. In one of them, a much younger Jay is wearing a blue-and-white football uniform. I lean in to take a closer look.

"I played quarterback in high school," he proudly says.

"Is that when you were dating my mom?" Silence. I turn and wait for an answer.

"Abby and I dated for about a year and a half."

"And then—you just broke up?" I press.

Jay stands and moves a few items around on his desk. "It was complicated."

"Complicated because she got pregnant with me." It isn't a question, and Jay's face pales. He loosens the knot on his tie.

"I didn't know about you, Paige. I told you that."

"How is that possible?" I ask.

"Look—"

"Then why did you break up? Can you answer that?"

"What did Abby tell you?" he counters.

"She just said you went off to college."

Slowly, Jay comes around his desk and leans against the edge, thick lines of thought creasing his forehead. "Her father didn't particularly like me."

I wasn't expecting that. "I never met my grandfather," I tell him. Now it's Jay's turn to look surprised.

"What do you mean, you never met him? Abby was so close to her family."

"We've lived in California since I was born. We never

went to visit my grandparents in Florida, and my grand-mother was the only one who came to visit us in San Diego." I try to explain the best I can, but I don't really have an answer to what Jay is asking me.

"Well, anyway, her father made it very clear that it would be better if Abby and I didn't see each other anymore," he continues.

"So, that's it? You just left the girl you supposedly loved because her dad didn't like you? That's weak."

He shakes his head. "It wasn't that simple, Paige. Martin Bryant was—a difficult man." He's still for a moment, his brow furrowing at unpleasant memories. Before I can say anymore, Jay stands, moves back around his desk and begins shoving papers into his satchel.

I'm aware that something happened many years ago that blasted that branch of my family tree into splinters. A disagreement with her father, that's what Mom had called it, but even I know that a disagreement, no matter how big, can be mended. What can't be repaired by my mother's standards is a betrayal. Whatever happened between her and my grandfather was enough to make her pack her bags and abandon her pedigree.

Mom rarely talked about her father. I only saw his name on Christmas and birthday cards each year, and I know his signature had been scrawled in my grandmother's perfect penmanship. Mom kept in touch with her, and while she occasionally visited us, she always came alone; her only traveling companion was the excuse that Martin couldn't get away from his work.

My grandfather passed away four years ago after suffering a massive stroke. I wasn't sad that he died because it's hard to mourn what you never knew. What bothered me the most was the sadness that took up permanent residence in Mom's eyes. While I don't know if she would have done anything differently if she'd had the chance, I know she wished their long, silent separation had never happened.

I like to think, or at least hope, that there were times when my grandfather wanted to reconcile with my mother. Maybe he even went so far as to dial her phone number, but it was the years of detachment and the chasm of miles between them that sadly convinced him it couldn't be done. That thought is so much better than allowing myself to accept the alternative—that a man could just let his daughter walk out of his life for whatever reason and never wish to have her back. With only Martin Bryant and Jay Chapman's sudden appearance in my life as my reference points, I hold little faith in that universal order known as fatherhood, or the men who are, for better or worse, card-carrying members.

Is Jay the reason my mom never again spoke to her own father?

Jay removes his jacket from the hook and slips it on, a gesture that clearly states this conversation is over and we're going home. Reluctantly, storing my questions for another day, I pick up my backpack and follow him out the door.

# CHAPTER FIVE
## Cade

I try to put some distance between Shawn and me as we leave the school, hoping to give him some time to cool off before his impending lecture. What I really want to do is take my bike up the highway and ride as fast and as far as I can until I forget this day ever happened. But I was never really good at running from my problems without creating more of them, so, instead, I head for home, and right on par with the rest of my crappy day, I hit what has to be every red light on the way.

This wasn't how today was supposed to go. Hannah wasn't supposed to leave. Dane wasn't supposed to take the first swing, but I guess I didn't really think that through when I cornered him, given everything that's gone down between us. And I don't even want to think about what's going to happen when my sister comes home. I was relieved to see Shawn at the school instead of Macy. While he was clearly disappointed, facing her would have been so much worse.

I drop my backpack and helmet on a chair at the kitchen table, shrug off my jacket and open the fridge. I was a little preoccupied at lunch, so I'm starving. The backdoor screen wrenches open and then, as if a prelude to what's about to go down, it bangs shut.

"Look, I know what you're gonna say, but it wasn't entirely my fault," I begin. Keys clatter on the counter behind me.

"You got another letter today."

Audible silence drowns the space between us as that unexpected plot twist sinks in. Recovering, I pull a can of soda from the fridge and turn to face Shawn, who's leaning against the counter with a white envelope in his hands.

"Not interested."

He sighs, lips drawn tight. "Cade, sit down."

"I have homework."

"It can wait."

"If you're planning to start in again on my misguided feelings for my father, can I at least make a sandwich first?" Right on cue, my stomach growls. Nice.

"Sit. Down." At the thin tone of warning in his voice, I drop into a chair at the table. "Contrary to what you may think, I don't particularly like having these conversations with you." Shawn slides the envelope across the table. I glare at the return address. "I don't want this letter lying around when Macy comes home. It upsets her too much."

"Fine." I swipe up the envelope and flick it into the garbage can two feet away. "Problem solved."

"Problem *not* solved, Cade!" Shawn paces in front of the table, one hand on his waist, the other in his hair, his head tipped back like he's searching for something lost among the ceiling tiles. His patience maybe? His last nerve? I seem to get on top of that one a lot. "What is going on with you? What really happened in the cafeteria today?"

"I told you. The guy was a jerk and he had it coming."

"That's not what the girl in the office said," Shawn reminds me. "Who is she? And why in the world did she stick up for you when you didn't bother to stick up for yourself?"

That's the question I haven't been able to get out of my head since I tore out of the school parking lot. Why did she stick up for me? She knows nothing about me, and all I know about her is that her name is Paige, she has a habit of stealing suitcases, and she comes from an unfortunate lineage.

"Why didn't you say something when Principal Chapman accused you of starting the fight?" Shawn takes a seat across from me and waits for my answer. I try to remember that he means well. When he married my sister two years ago, I wasn't exactly in a good place. Neither was she. But when he signed on for better or for worse, the guy really meant it. I just wish I could find a way to stop disappointing him.

"Well?" Shawn prompts.

"Because it doesn't matter."

"What do you mean it—"

"It doesn't matter, okay? It doesn't matter because whatever I could have possibly said in that office wouldn't have a made a difference. I broke the rules. I screwed up. Again." Shawn opens his mouth in rebuttal, but I cut him off. "And don't give me that crap about second chances. Sometimes, there are no second chances. No matter what I do, no matter what I say, I'm the screwup. Let them think what they want." I slump back in my chair.

"You're not a screwup. You screwed up. There's a big difference, and that was over a year ago." Shawn stands and crosses to the garbage can, where he fishes out the letter and places it in front of me on the table. "And there is such a thing as second chances. You just have to be willing to forgive."

"I'm not doing this," I murmur.

"Cade, he didn't choose to leave you. And you know that."

I stand abruptly, nearly knocking over my chair. "What I know is that I don't want to talk about this again—for the millionth time!"

"He's in prison," Shawn continues, ignoring my comment. "And I don't think it's too hard to imagine what it's like to be locked away from your family while you're serving time for making poor choices."

Nice dig. If I weren't getting more annoyed by the moment, I'd have to give Shawn credit for knowing just what to say to get under my skin.

"I thought you were on my side."

"There are no sides here," he says. "I'm the neutral third party, remember? I'm the only one in this house who doesn't have an agenda on this. So, please, can we just have a reasonable conversation?"

I swallow against the stillness filling the space between us. Even when Shawn's off the clock, he's still trying to help people. When he finally raises his eyes to meet mine, they're clouded, strangled by a mix of emotions I can't fully identify. I hate it when he looks at me like that.

"Why are you doing this to her?" he asks.

My chest constricts as each of those seven words sucker punches me right in the heart. I was two seconds away from leaving the kitchen, but the weight of Shawn's words on my shoulders drops me back into my chair.

He folds his hands on the table between us. "Every time one of those letters arrives, your sister gets hopeful, even though there must be twenty more in that drawer over there. And each time you don't open one, it kills her, Cade."

I stare at the rip across the knee of my jeans and nod.

"Then why do you do it?"

I attempt to count the lines in the grain of the tabletop, but my vision blurs.

"Why do you insist on hurting her?"

"That's not fair."

"No?" Shawn sucks in his bottom lip and turns his eyes skyward once more. "Then why don't you tell me what it is."

"Look, what happened in the cafeteria today and whatever you think is going on with those letters are two very different things. Why don't you get that?"

"Because there's a lot of anger inside you, Cade, and it's not doing you any favors. You've finally put some of the pieces of your life back together, and I don't want to see you throw that away because you're holding on to things you need to let go." Shawn stands. "Please, do me a favor and think about that."

He heads for the living room, leaving me alone with my thoughts, which is, ironically, a form of punishment in itself. I stare at the envelope, wanting so badly to chuck it back into the trash can, but I'm not a jerk. I respect Shawn too much to do something so spiteful. Instead, I snatch it up and cross to my mom's antique hutch, which still displays her china, like it did when she was alive. Some days, I'm glad Macy kept it, and other days it's just one big reminder of all we've lost.

That one memory is like a match, igniting white-hot resentment inside me. I yank open the top drawer, scooping up a bundle of identical, unopened envelopes bound together by a thick rubber band. If I had my way, they'd all be in the trash, long gone without an ounce of remorse or regret. I don't care what's inside them. I have no plans to read them. But because my sister hopes I'll change my mind, she insists on keeping them.

I slide the new envelope beneath the band, then shove the thick stack back into the drawer. It takes a few moments and a couple of deep breaths, but slowly, my anger simmers to cool disgust. I stare at the pile of letters, trying not to think about the suffocating hatred I feel toward the man who wrote them. I couldn't care less what he has to say. He lost the opportunity to tell me a long time ago. I slam the drawer and head for my room.

A small part of me wishes I could let go of the toxic feelings I have for my father, to finally be free of the loathing that coats my insides when I think about him. It consumes me, but I'm just not ready to release it. Not now and maybe not ever.

# CHAPTER SIX

## *Paige*

"Is there anything you'd like to talk about?"

I stare blankly across the desk at Marilyn Hopkins, Ph.D., her name etched into the gold, rectangular placard facing me from the edge of her desk. The slender blonde's laser-sharp gaze walks a fine line between interest and concern.

"No, I don't think so."

"How are your classes going?" She breaks eye contact long enough to inspect the contents of the file spread open on the desktop in front of her. "I see you're taking several honors classes. Very nice. Quite a workload for a new student."

"It's probably quite a workload for any student." I twist my watchband in a circle and glance at the wall clock above the door.

Mrs. Hopkins shoots me a close-lipped smile. "According to your transcripts, you're a solid student."

I lean slightly forward, trying to see what else those

papers say about me.

"Jay mentioned that you dance. Have you had an opportunity to connect with the dance team here at Mystic High?" Her curious eyes probe mine.

I shake my head.

"Why not?"

Because I don't plan on staying. Because dancing makes me happy and I can't be happy right now. Because—

"You know, Paige, connecting with student groups can be very beneficial."

"I'm sorry. I don't mean to be rude, but why exactly am I here?"

She smiles, but this time I get the full grin, perfectly aligned pearly whites displayed behind glossy pink lips. "I like to get to know all our new students. Find out what your interests are and help you make your time here at Mystic a positive and successful experience." I wonder if she memorized that from the school brochure.

"That's what the guidance counselor said to me yesterday. When he called me into *his* office," I say.

During our brief meeting, Mr. King, who seemed too young to have received much guidance himself, and who'd likely only been dispensing it to students for a year or two at the most, had plied me with a smorgasbord of questions about my interests and plans for the future. He'd wanted to know if I'd given much thought to my career path and which colleges I might be considering attending. I'd almost felt bad for him. He'd tried so desperately to stir some small spark of hope in me, but the truth is, I can't conceive of a future without dancing, or a future without my mom there to guide and support me. So, suffice it to say, despite his best efforts, disappointment was all I'd left him with. And now it's Mrs. Hopkins's turn.

"Are you sure I'm not here because my father is your boss, and he wants you to find out if there's something wrong with his kid?" Yup, there it is, a little bit of uncomfortable surprise warming her cheeks.

Mrs. Hopkins blinks several times. "Paige—"

"Oh, I get it." I stand. "Trust me, I get it. I'm sure Jay has told you all about me and our...*situation*. He has, right?"

Closing the folder and lacing her fingers together on the desk, she nods.

"So, just ask me what you want to know. I don't mean for that to sound obnoxious, honest. But please, get to the point, because I'm tired of people treating me like I might break." My boldness feels good.

Mrs. Hopkins opens her mouth to speak, but a knock at the door interrupts her. Without waiting for an invitation, Karen pops her head in.

"So sorry to interrupt, but could I steal you for a minute?"

"Can this wait?" Mrs. Hopkins asks.

"I'm afraid not," Karen says.

"My apologies, Paige." Mrs. Hopkins stands and smooths out her pencil skirt. "Make yourself comfortable.

I'd like to continue our conversation when I return. I won't be long."

Take your time. I'm in no hurry to talk.

While she's gone, I move to the window, which over-looks the cafeteria courtyard. Kids are beginning to gather for lunch. I'm not sure which irritates me more: that I'm here in Mrs. Hopkins's office and not with my friends, or that Jay has his staff doing his dirty work for him.

In my first three days at this school, I've managed to find myself in every administrator's office. Although I will say, as the school's assistant principal, Mrs. Hopkins has the nicest office of all. Instead of institutional gray, her walls are painted a robin's-egg blue, and there's a small sofa with decorative throw pillows. But she's still the assistant principal, so—how messed up does Jay think I am? Maybe he'd have some idea if he bothered to take the time to ask me himself. But Jay's been distant since picking me up at the airport. Nice and all, but distant, like he's not exactly sure what to say to me, or worried I might unleash more questions on him that he doesn't want to answer. Not like Connie; she's gone a full 180 in the opposite direction, nearly smothering me with her time and attention. I honestly don't know which is worse.

And I can't seem to make the nightmares stop. I had another one this morning. This time, I was young, maybe six, and I was performing in a ballet recital. I'd practiced for weeks, and I was confident and excited, but as I took my first steps onto the stage, my legs became as heavy as mud. I glanced down and discovered that they were no longer my legs, just thick blocks of cement. I couldn't move. Everyone was staring at me, and all I could hear above the murmurs of the audience was my instructor, some faceless presence calling out to me to begin, and then her growing agitation when I couldn't respond to her commands. She just kept yelling at me, but no matter what I did, I still couldn't react. The audience began to snicker and then laugh. When the laughter reached a fever pitch, it morphed into something wicked. The screeching of tires and the explosion of metal against metal assaulted me. The laughing turned to bloodcurdling screams that pierced me to my core, and all I saw was broken glass—and my mother. She needed me, and I was helpless, unable to move, unable to reach her. Unable to save her.

I'd woken, just as I had from all the other nightmares, dizzy and disoriented and covered in sweat. I suppose that's the kind of thing I should share with Mrs. Hopkins, but there's no way I'm going to do that.

I drum my fingernails on the windowsill and spot Quinn, Sam and Zoey at a table near the cafeteria doors. They're laughing about something, and I wish I were there with them. How many more questions will I have to answer before Mrs. Hopkins lets me go, satisfied that she's somehow managed to help the principal's emotionally wounded daughter? Ugh.

Mrs. Hopkins sweeps through the door and repositions herself at her desk. "Sorry for that. Where were we?"

"You were wondering just how messed up I am," I innocently remind her, taking a seat across from her once again.

That close-lipped smile returns. "No, I wasn't," she says gently. "But I do know what you've been through and—"

"And Jay's wondering if I'm okay," I finish.

"Paige, I will always be honest with you. So, yes, he's a little concerned. And I don't blame him. You've been through a lot. First, losing your mother the way you did—" My hand slides over my watch as a familiar heaviness liquifies in my chest. "And then moving to Mystic. You've been asked to handle some pretty heavy issues that would be hard for an adult to comprehend, let alone a seventeen-year-old girl. It's okay if you're struggling." Mrs. Hopkins pauses and gazes at me with sympathetic eyes. "But it's not okay to struggle alone."

The pressure of unshed tears pulses behind my eyes. I wish they would just finally spill out. Maybe if I could cry, I could feel normal—and finally forgive myself. And maybe, if I unloaded my tears, Mrs. Hopkins and every other adult in this building would stop looking at me like some project that needs fixing. But I can't cry, so I stand abruptly.

"I appreciate your concern, but I'm doing okay. Yes, this whole place is a transition, but I'll figure it out. So, if you don't have any more questions, could I head to lunch? My friends are waiting for me."

"Of course," Mrs. Hopkins concedes. I lunge for the door at lightning speed, but not quite fast enough. My hand is on the doorknob when she says, "Let's check in with each other next week."

"Really?" I ask.

"I'll see you on Wednesday. Bring your lunch and meet me here."

I sigh, then nod and walk out of her office, not even bothering to acknowledge Karen as she gives me a little wave.

After picking up my lunch bag from my locker, I locate the girls at a table in the center of the courtyard.

"How bad was it?" Quinn asks as I take a seat next to her. She's purging the lettuce from her sandwich.

"It was fine," I mutter. "What did I miss?"

"We were talking about dance team practice after school and how you just have to come with us today," Quinn says. "Seriously, Paige, do not make me beg again."

"'Cause she totally will." Sam winks.

"I can't. I have to take my car to the mechanic. Jay's orders."

"I can't believe your dad gave you a car!" Zoey squeals. "I've been saving for a car for like a billion years, and you get one handed to you."

Zoey referring to Jay as my dad is like being forced to wear a sweater that's two sizes too small, but I let it go. The car thing was a complete surprise. Jay explained that when they bought Connie's Prius last spring, they intended to save her old Camry for Tanner. Instead, after what felt like an interrogation about my driving record—which is shiny and clean, thank you very much—and a lecture about the responsibility of operating a motor vehicle, he handed me the keys, then insisted I take it to his mechanic for a tune-up.

"Have you dropped off any job applications yet?" Sam asks.

"I'm working on it," I say.

"I would sooner die than work in fast food." Quinn makes a face. "The uniforms are awful!"

"That's not true," Sam corrects. "My uniform at the Burger Shack is really comfy. T-shirt and jeans. What's wrong with that?"

"Well," Quinn says, tearing the crust from her sandwich. "Just stay away from the Arcade. Mr. Gordon is kind of weird."

"Oh, and the dry cleaner is run by old lady Miller. Some people think she's a witch," Zoey informs me. She works at the wad of gum in her mouth until a perfectly symmetrical pink bubble swells from her puckered lips.

"Let me guess, the movie theater is owned by a vampire, and the Grab & Go is run by Robin Hood and his Merry Men," I quip, stripping the peel from my orange.

Quinn shoots me a sour face. "Ha ha. Laugh all you want, we're just trying to help."

I appreciate it. They can't possibly know how much their friendship means to me. Being the new kid hasn't been as awful as I'd expected, even though plenty of eyes still turn in my direction when I walk down the halls or stare at me during classes. I have the feeling that the stigma that comes with being the principal's daughter is forever etched somewhere on my skin for all to see. But I can handle it now because Quinn and her friends make me feel so included. Even though I don't plan to be here long, I am grateful to feel I belong somewhere.

"The fast-food applications are just to cover the bases. I'm actually hoping to find something that inspires me, you know?" I open my milk carton. "Maybe something that betters the world in some way."

Quinn chokes on a laugh. "Good luck with that one." She puts down her sandwich as a serious expression consumes her fair-skinned, lightly freckled face. "What inspires me is that Miranda Campbell's sister is having a party next week and we're invited!"

Zoey and Sam squeal as I ask, "Who's Miranda Campbell?"

She's in our lit class," Quinn replies. "Some of the girls in her sister's sorority rented a beach house for Halloween weekend."

"So, we're crashing a sorority party?" I ask.

"Nooooo," she drawls, rolling her eyes. "Miranda invited us. And where there are sorority girls, there are always frat guys!"

"Miranda and her sister are really close. Her sister graduated three years ago, and she's famous for her parties. If you get the chance to go to one of them, you don't miss it unless you're in the hospital or dead," Zoey says as matter-of-factly as a Wikipedia page.

"I hate to be the buzzkill here, but there's no way Jay is going to let me go to a sorority party on Halloween. Your parents are seriously okay with you doing that?" I ask.

"Of course not," Quinn replies as Zoey and Sam shake their heads. "That's why we're not going to tell them. You're going to tell your dad that you're staying at my house on Friday night. Just say it's a slumber party."

"And what about your mom? She works in the school, remember? They're bound to talk," I point out.

Quinn's eyes lose some of their excitement. "It'll be fine. My mom won't even know we're gone." Before I can begin to decode that, Quinn sits up tall and with renewed excitement says, "Frat guys will be a nice change from immature high school guys."

I'm surprised Quinn doesn't have a boyfriend. She's pretty and flirty, and I've seen the way guys look at her. "So, none of you are dating anyone?" I ask.

Sam shakes her head as Zoey says, "Quinn doesn't do relationships." I glance at Quinn, who's suddenly very interested in the nutritional label on the back of her Vitamin Water.

"Why is that?" My eyes ping-pong between the three of them and finally rest on Quinn.

"Because they don't last," Quinn says, in a tone that implies everyone should know that, and if they don't, they're stupid. I want to ask her more, but she's already moving our conversation in a different direction. "Paige, you're new here, so you should know what you're dealing with. We don't want you to make any mistakes."

Sam nods resolutely. "At that table over there are kids from the Chess Club." She wrinkles her nose.

Quinn jerks her chin toward the table across from us and lowers her voice. "Those are the band kids. They're nice, but—you know what I mean. Now, over there you have the jocks, obviously. They're fun, but proceed with caution."

I scan the crowd where she indicates. Several of the guys, including Gio, wear letterman jackets and the others look like they could be wrestlers, football players or bench press their own weight—or at least the weight of a couple of the band kids.

"Isn't that a little stereotypical?" I ask.

"I'm trying to help you."

"But I'm not looking for a boyfriend right now," I say.

Quinn grabs my shoulder, and I nearly jump out of my seat. "Exactly! And it's when you're not looking for one that you are most likely to find one. And we're here to make sure you don't find the wrong one."

As she continues to point out the various kids at different tables, my eyes scan the courtyard and abruptly stop when I spot Cade Matthews talking to someone through the chain-link fence. I can't get a good look at the guy on the other side, but they appear to be in a serious conversation.

"Hey, Quinn. Look over there."

She stops her monologue in midsentence and shifts her

focus to where I'm pointing.

Cade glances around, then reaches into his pocket and passes something small through the fence to the guy on the other side. The guy shoves whatever he's received into the front pocket of his jeans.

"Who is Cade talking to?" I ask. Just as the last word crosses my lips, Cade catches my gaze. My eyes drop to my lunch. When I glance up a few seconds later, he's walking away from the fence toward the school. The guy on the other side is several yards away, getting into a junky old car parked at the curb.

"I don't know who that is," Quinn says. "Cade hangs out with an older crowd. They don't go to school here."

"What kind of crowd?" I ask.

"Let's put it this way: your dad would crap bricks if you went anywhere near them."

Again with the dad reference? I dismiss it and continue to probe her with questions. She seems to be pretty up-to-date with most people's business at this school. "So, what's this Cade guy's deal?" I'd heard bits and pieces of the gossip shortly after the fight in the cafeteria, but some of it seemed a little too dramatic to be true.

Quinn rests her elbows on the table and steeples her fingers beneath her chin. "Why so interested?"

I shrug. "I'm not. Just curious. I mean, Cade and Dane did throw down in the middle of the cafeteria three days ago. Guys like that have to have a backstory."

"Well," Quinn pensively says, "I told you his dad's in

jail, right?" I nod casually. "I'm not exactly sure what happened, but his mom died when we were in middle school."

I swallow hard as my half-eaten lunch roils in my stomach. My fingers drop my sandwich on the table and instinctively drift to my wrist, to the feel of smooth glass. "What happened to her?" I whisper.

Realization dawns on Quinn's face, and she straightens, looking like she wants to take back the words, but can't seem to figure out how to do it. "I'm not sure," she says.

Oblivious to the unspoken conversation about the loss of my own mother wedged between Quinn and me, Zoey blurts out, "When we were freshmen, Cade stopped coming to school. Just disappeared. Rumor was, he got messed up with a gang or some bad crowd like that. Just fell off the radar. Then boom! Last year, he was suddenly back in school."

"Where had he been?" I ask.

"Some say juvenile detention, others say drug rehab. I'm not sure. It's kind of sad either way," Sam finishes.

That is sad, and I'm not sure what to say. I have so many questions, but they aren't ones that Quinn, Sam or Zoey can answer. Only Cade has the information to quell my curiosity. And who knows? Maybe someday, I'll get up the nerve to ask him.

# CHAPTER SEVEN

## Cade

"Dude, you're so late," Jared says, glancing at the wall clock as I enter the break room.

"Where's Mac?" I ask, shelving my motorcycle helmet on top of my locker and shaking out of my jacket. I quickly button up the work shirt I'm wearing over my T-shirt and smooth the front. "Did he ask where I was?"

Jared flips a page in the magazine he's reading and takes a big bite of his sandwich before he answers, "He's old, but he's not blind." A few crumbs fly out of his mouth as he responds, and he wipes them off the magazine with his forearm.

"Where is he?"

"He's been under a Chevy out there for over an hour." Jared shrugs. "Maybe, if you're lucky, he forgot about you."

You know that feeling of being wound too tight and things just seem to keep piling on? That's where I'm at. I head out the door and into the hallway, quickening my steps as I reach the auto bay. I scan the ample space, and when I don't see Mac, I exhale the breath I'm holding and snag one of the work orders off the wall.

"Nice to see you could squeeze us into your schedule today, Cade."

I cringe, hang the clipboard back on its hook and turn. Mac Williams stands behind me in his faded gray coveralls, wiping his grease-stained hands on a rag.

"Yeah, sorry."

Mac's in his midsixties and is built like a workhorse, which is pretty impressive. But all those decades of what I suspect involved some hard living—although he's never talked about it in any confirmable detail—have definitely left their mark, visible in the rooted lines etched across his forehead and around his eyes and mouth. He looks worn, like a piece of leather that's been left in the sun too long.

"Walk with me," Mac says, clapping a hand on my shoulder and steering me toward the side door of the shop. Once outside, Mac sits down on a wooden bench that rests alongside the building and faces out toward the massive dunes. He takes his smoke breaks out here every day, even on days he has to huddle under the awning to shield himself from the rain. Today, though, there's some blue sky peeking through the gray clouds and a stiff breeze. Right on cue, Mac slides a pack of cigarettes out of his pocket and taps it against his palm.

"How come you're late?" he asks, raising a cigarette to his lips. He gives his silver lighter a flick and shields the flame from the wind. Just before he touches it to the tip of the cigarette, he glances up at me and mumbles sternly between pinched lips, "Don't you ever think about smoking or I'll kick your butt."

He says that every time he lights up around me, but he does it anyway. Issuing that warning must make him feel a little less guilty about his addiction.

Mac's a good guy. And considering he took a risk eleven months ago and offered me a job when I wasn't the most ideal employee, I owe him a lot. That's putting it lightly. The truth is, Mac and I met when he was volunteering with the county's youth corrections diversion program. It didn't take long to discover that the guy with the grizzly, hard-nosed exterior was a softy at his core. And from time to time, when he made the right connection, he offered internships at his garage to kids who he felt were serious about getting their lives back on track. Why Mac took a liking to me, I'm not really sure. But he did, and it was part of what saved me from the hole I'd dug for myself after my dad went to prison. For one, I met Jared, Mac's grandson, and we've become good friends. And as a mechanic in this town for over thirty-five years, Mac's taught me a lot. He's even helped me soup up my motorcycle and discounted the parts. So, as payback, I've come to accept that these weekly one-on-one chats are part of the deal. Usually, it's just a lot of "How're ya doing?" followed by "Not too bad" with an "Anything new?" and a "Nope, everything's good" to wrap it all up. But today, Mac's in for a treat.

"I planned to call, but they confiscated my phone in

detention," I finally admit.

Mac's quiet for a few seconds as he takes a long drag from his cigarette. "Detention, huh?"

"It's no big deal. I got into a fight earlier this week. It wasn't serious, and it wasn't my fault."

"I never took you for a fighter," Mac said. He scrubs a hand across the back of his neck. "But I suppose every man can be one, given the right circumstances." His warm brown eyes settle on mine. "Find yourself in some circumstances, did ya?"

"No," I say. "Just a disagreement."

"Wouldn't be over a young lady, would it?"

"A friend," I clarify. Mac nods, as if he's somehow gathered some great knowledge from those two words. "It won't happen again."

"The being late part or the detention?"

"Both," I quickly answer.

Mac gestures to the empty space beside him on the bench. "Take a load off, Cade. This is the only break you're going to get today."

"Fair enough." I take a seat.

"What gives, kid?" Mac asks.

"I just told you."

"That's not what I'm talking about. I had a chat with Shawn yesterday."

"Of course you did," I mutter, shaking my head.

"He brought one of the command rigs in for servicing, and we got to talking." I can feel his eyes on me as I kick at a patch of dune grass. The silence between us grows thick until I realize he's waiting for me to make the next move.

At first, I refuse, squinting up at the sky and avoiding him with everything I can possibly muster. But then I break and say, "Do I have to open those stupid letters just because they want me to?"

"Nope," Mac says, exhaling curls of smoke. "That's your business."

"Maybe you could tell Shawn and my sister that. Because apparently, when I say it, they can't hear me."

"Look, Cade, I'm not one to even attempt to tell you that life is easy. Sometimes, son, it just stinks, and you have to deal with it the best way you can."

I wait for a few beats, but the only thing that passes between us is a gust of cold wind that ruffles my shirt collar. "That's it? That's all you've got?"

Mac raises a thick eyebrow. "Were you expecting something else?"

"Well, yeah," I say. "Maybe some morsel of enlightenment? A tiny nugget of wisdom, if nothing else. What am I supposed to do with 'Life stinks sometimes'?"

He scratches his stubbled chin. "If you're looking for wisdom, Cade, you picked the wrong guy. My enlightenment tank is a little low this afternoon." He takes another drag from his cigarette, then flicks the butt into the patch of sand at his feet and squashes it with the toe of his heavy work boot. "The fact is, life does stink from time to time, and it can be that way for a while. I think you and I both know that."

"Well, that's helpful," I say, and I don't even bother hiding the sarcasm in my voice.

"But I will say this. And if you pay no attention to anything I say from here on out, hear me loud and clear on this one. Life is not something you want to handle alone, Cade." Mac stands and places a firm hand on my shoulder, and a serious expression crosses his face. "Disagree with the people you love all you want. But don't shut them out. You know good and well what happens when you try to teach them a lesson."

Classic Mac. He manages to come off like some run-of-the-mill guy with no real agenda, and then he proceeds to nail me with a zinger that hits dead center.

"Now, get back in there. I need you to clean the front office today."

I nod, and with his words still lingering, I head back inside, but I stop short at the sight of the customer waiting at the front desk. She's nibbling on her thumbnail, her head cocked so that she can get a look through the open doorway to the automotive bay.

"Can I help you?" I ask, stepping up to the desk.

Principal Chapman's daughter whips around, her eyes wide when she meets mine. "Oh! Um, hi."

"Hey."

"I didn't know you worked here."

I tap in my password on the computer, and the screen comes to life. "What can I do for you?" I repeat.

"Oh, um, I brought my car." She gestures behind her, and I see a maroon Camry parked in one of the front stalls. "It needs a tune-up. I think Jay, um—I have an appointment. For a tune-up. I think." Something has her flustered. I locate the appointment in the schedule and grab a clipboard from under the desk.

"Can I have your key?"

She stares at me blankly, as if my words are on a two-second delay, then snaps to attention. "My key? Yes, here. Here it is." She slides the key across the counter.

"I'm gonna grab an odometer reading. I'll be right back." She nods, and I head out the front door, chuckling a little to myself. When I return, she's got her nose buried in her phone. She glances up, and even with a look of unease returning to her face, she's stunning. I thought that the minute she nearly tackled me at the airport in defense of her luggage. Shifting quickly, I refocus on the computer screen before she catches me checking her out and thinks I'm some kind of perv.

"Hey, you aren't by any chance looking for an office clerk or know of someone else who's hiring, do you?" Paige asks, leaning a little closer to the counter with anticipation.

"Not unless you've got experience as a diesel mechanic," I say dryly, adding the odometer information into the computer. My attempt at humor falls flat when she frowns.

"Nope," she sighs. "Not in my skill set."

As she scrolls once more through her phone, I have an undeniable urge to help this girl, and I have no idea why.

"You should check out the waterfront," I offer. "There are a few businesses down there that are looking for holiday help."

Her eyes instantly lift and a small smile, although fleeting, flashes across her lips. "Really?"

"Yeah, there's a bookstore on Marina Drive that has a 'Help Wanted' sign in the window. At least they did yesterday."

"Thanks." She leans to her left to get a better glimpse of something behind me. When surprise registers on her face, I turn to see Jared pass by the doorway.

"Was that guy carrying a guitar?" Paige asks.

"Yeah," I say. "The owner lets our band rehearse here a few times a week after closing." That's another thing about Mac that makes him a cool guy. He even rearranged the staff room to give us a place to store our instruments and equipment in between gigs. All he asks in return is that we not invite people into the garage after hours and make sure everything is locked up tight when we leave. It's a rule we've never broken.

"You're in a band?" Curiosity lightens her eyes. "Where do you play?"

"Kind of all over the place. Mostly parties. We're playing at a college house party near the north jetty next week."

"I think I'm going to that one," she says. "Miranda Campbell, right?"

Is she serious? "You know Miranda?"

"Not really," she admits. "But my friends do. Why are

you looking at me like that?"

I straighten. "Sorry," I offer. "I never pegged you for that kind of party."

Her eyebrows arch. "A sorority party?"

I scratch the back of my head and hit <shift> <P> on the computer. The gears of the printer under the counter come to life. "It's not a school-sanctioned event, that's all," I clarify. "Your *pops* might not approve." I can't keep the mockery out of my voice.

"Well—I'll be there," she says airily, but I can see her brain is working overtime to decipher my words, and a hint of concern inches its way across her brow.

A horn honks. Over Paige's shoulder, I see a Prius out front.

"That's my ride," she volunteers. "When do you think the car will be done?"

I pull the work order off the printer and slide it across the top of the counter toward her, along with a pen. "Sign here. You should be able to pick it up tomorrow after school unless there are additional repairs that need to be made. We'll let you know."

She slides the paper and the pen back to me. "Okay, thanks." My eyes follow her to the door.

"Hey," I call after her, then mentally kick myself when the question that's been gnawing at me for days makes its way past my good sense and onto my lips. I should just shut up and let her go, but instead, I ask, "Why did you stick up for me? After the cafeteria thing. Why'd you do it?"

Paige's eyes sweep the floor. "Because it was the right thing to do."

"And do you always do the right thing?" I ask.

She bites her lower lip, and when she lifts her eyes to meet mine, there's an unmistakable sadness in them. Shaking her head, she answers, "No, I don't. But I'm trying to change that." And with that simple response, she leaves, closing the door behind her.

# CHAPTER EIGHT

## *Paige*

I return to the mechanic's the following day to pick up my car, and I'm thankful that Cade isn't behind the front counter. From the minute we crossed paths, I've been nothing but a bumbling idiot around that guy, and I'm half embarrassed and half annoyed that I can't seem to pull myself together.

When I get back to the house, I quickly change my clothes and scoop up a few more résumés to drop off downtown. I need to focus on more important things than Cade Matthews. I'm heading out the door when Connie stops me in the kitchen.

"Paige! I'm glad I caught you. I need a favor."

"What is it?"

"Could you take Lily to ballet this afternoon? I wouldn't ask, but it's an emergency. I've got to show a house at four thirty and Jay's tied up in a staff meeting."

Lily tugs on my forearm. "I'm a ballerina," she proudly announces. I blink hard and stare down at her as she twirls at my side in her pink leotard.

"Paige? Are you all right?" Connie asks.

My head snaps up. "What? Yeah, ballet class. Got it. No problem."

Relief floods her face. "Her class is at the Gold Coast Dance Academy on Front Street. Here's the address." She scribbles the information on a scratch pad on the counter and hastily hands it to me. "Lily can show you how to get there. I'll put her booster seat in your car." She slides a small stack of papers into her bag. "You know," she adds lightly, "they have a full schedule of classes. It's quite a prestigious program, actually. You might want to check in to it."

"No," I say, too quickly and too loudly. Connie's mouth forms a small "o" of surprise as she realizes she's over-stepped, which is odd because we haven't figured out yet where exactly the boundaries between us are.

"I'm not interested," I manage, fingering a strand of hair and avoiding her eyes. "I'm still trying to settle into school." My attempt to sound nonchalant misses its target miserably, but I can't have this conversation with her. When Connie smiles apologetically beneath concerned eyes, I turn my attention to the cute little blonde holding my hand. "Okay, Lil, let's get you to ballet!" She claps and jumps up and down.

Connie scoops Lily's dance bag off the center island and hands it to me. "I'll pick her up at five thirty. Oh, and this evening, we've got Tanner's soccer game, so we won't be back until about eight. There are leftovers in the fridge when you get hungry." She kisses Lily on the forehead, then, to my surprise, leans in and kisses my cheek. She grabs her car keys and disappears through the door, calling out, "Thanks so much, Paige!"

"Anytime," I answer.

The Gold Coast Dance Academy is housed in what looks like an old warehouse, right next to a mixed martial arts gym. When we step inside, there's a large lobby and a crowd of girls in leotards and ballet slippers bustling about. An equal-size crowd of mothers occupy the bank of chairs scattered along the perimeter; some are on their phones, while others are engaged in conversation as their children scamper about. Lily nudges me forward, and I come to a dead stop in the doorway of a spacious room that's lined with mirrors on three sides.

"This is my class, Paige!"

Something strange happens at that moment. Weightlessness envelops me, but my feet are somehow anchored to the floor, refusing to allow me to take another step, as if they're mired in mud. Thoughts of my recent nightmare come rushing back. I wipe clammy palms on the hips of my slacks, and there's a dull ache in my stomach that matches the sensation pulsing behind my temples.

"Come watch me!" Lily says, her little hand tugging at my own, urging me farther into the room. I resist, my breathing growing shallow and stunted. I manage to swallow, a frantic attempt to open my airway for a cleansing breath, but it doesn't work. My head is swimming like I'm encased in glass and everything around me has morphed into slow motion.

A large group of girls, all several years older than Lily by the looks of it, are lined up at the barre along the far wall. Their attention is scattered, but one by one, at the teacher's repeated command, they fall into sync and begin their warmup. It's a routine I could do with my eyes closed.

*First position. Demi-plié. Tendu front. Back to first.* My throat tightens and sweat beads along my upper lip.

*Tendu side. Back to first.* My short, quick attempts to gather air into my lungs are audible.

*Tendu back. Back to first. Demi-plié.*

My hands twitch at my sides as the throbbing of my heart grows thunderous against my rib cage, panic welling into a tight ball lodged at the base of my throat. I can't for the life of me understand what is happening, why my body is reacting the way it is, only that I have to lean against the wall to steady myself. Frantically, I search the room for something that can draw my focus until this light-headedness passes.

A peal of laughter immediately draws my eyes to the instructor across the room. The woman is tall and statuesque and—*familiar*. I'm so stunned at the sight of her, an invisible force takes hold of my heart and squeezes the life out of it. The woman's long, dark hair is pulled back into a tight chignon, and she releases another laugh across the space that pierces my consciousness like an arrow dead center against its target, sharp and quick, unleashing a memory so vivid, I gasp. Her infectious laughter swirls amid girlish squeals and fills the studio from wall to wall, stabbing right to the nucleus of my existence.

*Mom?*

The spinning that's taken my brain hostage intensifies as my mother—*my mother!*—executes a flawless pirouette for Lily and her young classmates, who've managed to form a mismatched line near the doorway. She's right here in front of me, and she's vibrant and mesmerizing—*and alive!*

No. No, no, no! Pressing my hands to my eyes, I silently order them to refocus, to regain some measure of control over this madness.

*It can't be her. It can't be her. It cannot. Be. Her.* I chant the words silently over and over to myself, willing, no, begging my mind to believe them.

But I want it to be her. So badly, I would trade my soul for it. I scrunch my eyes tight, warning my conscience that it's a twisted deception, an unhinged illusion. Swaying under the weight of it all, rationality spars with desperation. Music bleeds from speakers somewhere in the room, but it's disjointed to my ears. The sounds of childhood echo off the walls, the walls that are now closing in around me and sucking what feels like the last of the air from my lungs.

"Stop!" The word explodes past my lips, shattering the suffocating memories into a million shards and thrusting me back into my cold, empty reality.

I'm gasping for air when my eyes reopen. Then, I'm frozen by a new horror. The wide eyes of two dozen young dancers and their teacher—the apparition of my mother replaced by a woman I've never seen before in my life—stare back at me in surprise and confusion. I'm mortified.

"Sorry!" I cry out in a high-pitched voice that I don't recognize as my own. My cheeks burn and the pressure to escape is so urgent that I begin to back away, bumping into the doorjamb in my scattered state.

"Paige, stay and watch my class!" Lily calls. I shake my head, trying in vain to swallow the large lump that remains wedged in my throat.

"I can't," I manage. "But have fun. Your mom will pick you up."

As I rush for the exit, two women ask me if I'm okay. I brush them off with a nod and a curt smile and shove open the front doors. I can't get outside fast enough. The instant the cool breeze touches my cheeks, I cling to the railing and drop onto the cement steps to catch my breath.

What the hell was that? I have never experienced such a debilitating panic, not since that horrific night at the hospital. *That horrible, horrible night.* There had been no warning that merely walking into a ballet studio would set it off. I shudder as a chill rolls down my spine, prickling the skin on my arms and neck.

What did I expect would happen? That my mother would actually appear? That the last two months could simple dissolve away and everything would go back to the way it had been? Even though that's what I want, so badly it hurts, it never occurred to me for a second that my mind could create *that*—whatever that was. Tendrils of icy sadness consume me, seeping into my bones with the undeniable realization that ballet, something I've sacrificed time, friends and opportunities to pursue, endured physical pain beyond measure to immerse myself in, and my most sacred connection to my mother now riddles me with unforgiving anguish and despair. My insides feel like a washcloth that's been run under scalding hot water, then rung out again and again until it no longer resembles its original shape.

I brush my forehead with the back of my hand, wiping sweat from my brow. Pathetic. That's me. Crumpled on the cold concrete, heartbroken and helpless, assaulted by my own memories—pathetic.

The heavy metal doors of the gym behind me open and a group of guys spills out onto the steps, talking and laughing as they head for the street. I shift so that my back is against the railing and drop my head, allowing my hair to fall forward over my face. Tilting slightly, I watch their feet bound down the steps behind me. When I'm confident that the pitiful girl huddled on the steps has gone unnoticed, my shoulders relax and I exhale. The last thing I need is—

"Hey!"

My heart stutters, and I'm staring at a pair of athletic shoes.

"Paige? Is that you?"

At this point, I'm not sure if this day could get any worse. Tapping my forehead with the heel of my palm, I lift my head, a beyond-fake smile perfectly in place. "Hey there."

Dane Sloane takes a seat on the steps on the other side of the railing. "What are you doing here?" He's wearing black athletic shorts and a hoodie that's pulled up over his head. He rolls his keys around in his hand.

"You know, just, uh—"

"You do martial arts?" he asks in disbelief, gesturing over his shoulder.

"No, my sister takes ballet over there. I just dropped her off."

"So, you're waiting for her?"

"No, I—" I have nothing. No response. No excuses. Just the truth, as embarrassing as it is. I turn my head and meet Dane's curious eyes with a shrug. "I'm kind of having a bad day. Just taking a break."

He nods, like he totally gets it. "That's cool."

"Dane!" a guy from the street calls. "You comin'?"

"You should go," I encourage him.

To my disappointment, he ignores my words and shouts back, "Go on without me; I'll catch up!"

"No, really, you should go with your friends," I say, nearly begging him. "I have things to do anyway."

"It's fine. You look like you could use a friend."

That's sweet, but I'm not sure he qualifies for that role, seeing as we barely know each other. Then again, I'm not really in a position to argue.

"Do you want to take a walk?" Dane asks. "The water-

KELLI WARNER

front is just a couple of blocks that way. There's a great coffee house down there."

"No, really, I have things I have to do," I repeat, standing and brushing a hand across the back of my pants. "Honestly, I don't think I'd be good company right now. But thanks anyway."

"We can grab a cup to go," he offers. I try to think of another way to decline his invitation, but I can't come up with anything before he adds, "Come on. A little caffeine will perk you right up."

I sigh and concede with a smile. "Sure, why not?"

We walk the first half block in silence. Dane's tall; I guess I never paid much attention to that before. But then again, why would I?

"So, you do martial arts?" I ask, trying to kickstart the conversation.

"Kickboxing," he corrects. "It's not a bad way to spend my time since I got suspended."

Oh, yeah, *that*.

"I'm not allowed to work out with the lacrosse team until next week, so this is the next best thing to stay in shape," Dane says.

"I don't want to pry," I say, which is precisely what one says before the prying commences. "But what was that fight about anyway? If you don't mind me asking."

A muscle in Dane's jaw ticks like I hit a nerve. "Matthews was just stirring up trouble," he says, like it's no big deal and could have happened to anyone. "I'm not sure why

96

I'm the one who got suspended. Coach benched me for the next two games." His words sting with bitterness.

"Sorry about that," I offer.

"It wasn't your fault."

Well—that's not technically true. The words *I ratted you out to Jay* are on my tongue, but I swallow them down. There's no appropriate place for them in this conversation. "Yeah, I know, but I'm related to the executioner, so I feel like I should say that."

"No worries. Coach wasn't happy about it, but it's school policy or some crap like that. Anyway, because I can't practice with the team until next week—" He gestures over his shoulder toward the building in the distance behind us. "That's what I'm doing to stay in shape."

We reach the waterfront, which is lined with historic-looking shops that somehow possess a modern-day beach-front charm. When cool raindrops pelt my jacket, Dane and I duck inside Java Joe's Coffeehouse, and he orders for us while I grab a table by the window and frantically run my fingers through my hair, trying to put my windblown strands back in order.

Dane returns with two coffees in to-go cups, just like he promised, and a brown paper bag. I peer inside to find a chocolate chip muffin that's twice the size of my fist.

"Help yourself," he says.

I break off a hunk of muffin and place it on a napkin in front of me as Dane pulls the lid off his coffee and starts adding several sugar packets. I do the same.

We make small talk for the next fifteen minutes until the rain subsides and the overcast skies part just enough to let the remaining fragments of the day's earlier sunshine bleed through. Dane downs the rest of the muffin, and we take our coffees and walk another half block while talking about nothing of great importance. He tells me he's going snowboarding with his family in central Oregon over Thanksgiving break. I try to reroute the conversation when he asks personal questions, but he's persistent.

"No one even knew Mr. Chapman had a daughter in high school," he says.

*Not even Mr. Chapman*, I want to say. But I don't. Instead, I direct Dane's attention to the candy display in the window of the Old Town Ice Cream Parlor and fight the urge to go inside and buy an obscene amount of chocolate to ease the lousy afternoon I've had. My eyes drift across the street to a brick shop on the corner. The sign over the door reads "Moonlight Books." There's a "Help Wanted" sign in the window, just as Cade had said. Hope blooms in my chest.

"Do you mind if we go in there?" I ask. I step off the curb, but a hand grabs hold of my wrist and tugs me to a stop. Dane's frowning.

"Let's keep walking. There are more shops a block over. And there's beach access that way." He motions down the street.

"But I really want to go in there. I won't be long. Come on, it'll be fun." I jerk my chin toward the bookstore, but

Dane takes a small step backward.

"Nah, not my kind of place."

Not his kind of place? A bookstore? Who says something like that? Before I can ask, Dane says, "Look, I should meet up with my friends. But it was nice spending time with you, Paige. Do you think we could hang out again? Maybe go to a movie?" His charming smile is back, but not quite strong enough to penetrate my puzzled expression.

"I'll only be a couple of minutes," I say.

He shakes his head, his smile still in place. "No, take your time. I really gotta get going. But I'm serious about seeing you again. Can I text you?" He fishes his phone out of his pocket, taps a few buttons and offers it to me. "Put in your number."

Slowly, I take it and do as he instructs, still confused over why he wants my number when he's trying so hard to get away from me.

"Cool," he says, retrieving the phone and sliding it into his pocket. "I'll see you at school on Monday."

"Sure. Thanks for the coffee. And the muffin." I give a small wave and look up and down the street before crossing. I expect Dane to take off, but when I reach the opposite curb, I turn to find he's still standing there, watching me. He holds up his hand, then turns and heads up the street.

Shaking my head in confusion, I turn the door handle and step inside. A bell tinkles overhead.

The shop is quaint and cozy. Two overstuffed sofas sit in the center of the room with a big, wooden coffee table between them. Several comfortable-looking club chairs are strewn about with big, red throw pillows. A combination of aromas catches my attention: new books with crisp pages and a hint of something sweet.

I'm the only one here, so I slip out of my jacket and begin to browse the shelves, running my index finger along the glossy spines and occasionally pulling one out to read the back cover.

"Hey there! May I help you?" A young woman appears from a door in the back, a stack of books in her hands.

"Just looking," I say.

She steps behind an old wooden desk that serves as the store's front counter. "Anything in particular?"

I give the shelf in front of me another glance. "No, not really. Actually, I'm looking for a job. I noticed you have a sign in the window."

The woman lifts her head. "Yes, I do. Do you have any experience working in a bookstore?"

"No," I admit, making my way to the counter. "But I love books, and I'm very responsible." She extends her hand, and that's when I see them. Several silver bangles adorned with small moons jingle about her wrist. I study her face. "You're the woman from the plane." Short, spiky hair the color of a melted Milky Way bar. Kind face. Sweet voice. Yup, that's her.

Recognition fills the woman's eyes, and they twinkle with amusement. "What a small world!" I realize her hand is still extended, so I quickly shake it. "It's good to see you again. I'm Macy. Welcome to my shop."

"I'm Paige. Paige Bryant. I just moved here from California. That's why I was on the plane that day."

"Mmm, I wondered why you seemed so nervous," she says. "So, how do you like it here in Mystic?"

"It's—nice." I refrain from giving her any additional commentary. "So, you're hiring?"

"I am. But you should know it's just part-time. Only about sixteen hours a week at minimum wage." She looks apologetic.

My heart flutters. "That sounds perfect, actually."

A brightness returns to her eyes. "Well, then, what do you say we take a seat and get to know each other a little better?" Macy comes around the counter and gestures to one of the sofas.

"How much do you know about Mystic Shores?" she asks, straightening the throw pillows before she takes a seat, curling a leg beneath her. I sit straight-backed on the sofa across from her.

"Not a lot," I answer.

"Well, for starters, we're a tourist town," Macy explains. "Because of that, business has been a little slow since the summer ended. We're in the off-season now, which consists of business from locals, as well as storm watchers."

"What are storm watchers?" I ask.

"People who like to watch the waves during winter storms. Our piece of the Pacific is quite a draw. They come from all over. The waves get pretty crazy, up to a hundred twenty feet high at times."

"Really?"

Macy nods. "There are some lookout shelters that provide cover for storm viewing, but lots of people choose to rent hotel rooms with a view," she says. "Those visitors help restaurants and shops pad their bottom lines until the next summer season gears up."

I glance down at my side to pull a résumé out of my bag, only there's no bag. Shoot! I left it in my car at the dance studio.

"I had a part-time employee, but she's a college student, so she's not available during the school year. I tried to run the place myself, but my husband says I'm never home so—voilà! The 'Help Wanted' sign in the window." Macy's smile is confident and warm.

"What would you need me to do?"

"Stock shelves, help customers find what they're looking for and ring up orders." She holds up a copy of what looks to be a murder mystery resting in her lap. "We offer a lot of books by local authors, as well as unique and hard-to-find volumes. Although it isn't easy competing with those big online retailers, so I'm always looking for ways to make the shop unique. I was actually coming back from a book buyers' conference in San Diego the day we met on the plane."

I nod. "What are the hours for the position?"

"After school until seven on Tuesdays and Thursdays, and you'd be responsible for closing up the shop on those nights. We'd work together on Saturdays."

The schedule is perfect, but because I don't have the job

yet, I push down my excitement and pleasantly say, "That sounds great."

"Tell me a little about yourself, Paige. What do you like to do in your spare time? Any hobbies?"

I quickly bypass the truth and anything that might lead to additional questions I'm trying to avoid. "I like to read."

Macy smiles. "Good answer. Are you involved in any activities that might conflict with your work hours?"

"No," I say.

"What grade are you in?"

"I'm a senior."

"So's my brother," she says.

"Who's your brother?"

"Cade Matthews."

I blink hard. Okay, now I'm convinced Karma is just playing with me. "Cade's your brother?"

"Do you know him?"

"Um, not really," I say. "I mean, I've seen him around."

She sits up in her seat. "Cade's actually here today, help-ing me with inventory. I'll get him."

"That's okay, you really don't have to—"

It's too late; Macy's off the sofa and calling toward the back room. "Cade! Can you come out here for a minute?"

Adrenaline spikes in my veins and I have a sudden urge to swan dive under the table, as if someone just set the hem of my pants ablaze—which is ridiculous on so many levels, I don't even know where to start. I shift in my seat and smooth down my hair as the door to the back room opens.

# CHAPTER NINE

## Cade

The second Paige lays eyes on me, she looks like she's swallowed something sour. She and Macy are sitting across from each other, my sister with a book in her lap like always, and Paige—well, the only way she could possibly be more uncomfortable is if someone slapped a blindfold on her and forced her to walk a tightrope over the Grand Canyon. I waver between acting surprised to see her or appearing reserved, like it's no big deal. The truth is, I saw Paige long before she ever saw me.

I was stocking books on a shelf by the front window, a favor to my sister because she currently doesn't have any employees, when I'd spotted Paige standing on the street corner with Dane Sloane.

I wish I could say that it hadn't bothered me, that it was no big deal when the jerk made her laugh, and that I was utterly uninterested when he handed her his cell phone and it looked like she gave him her number. I'd like to say that I'd ignored it all and just focused on my work, but I hadn't.

I'd stood there watching them as a weird tightness grew in my chest.

It's not that Paige was with a guy. She has every right to hang out with whoever she chooses. It's that she's with *that* guy. That jerk doesn't deserve to be within two feet of her, and someone should warn her. When she'd crossed the street toward the bookstore, I'd headed for the back room. But now—here we are.

"Cade, this is Paige Bryant."

Paige glances my way but quickly looks down at her hands, fiddling with her watch.

"Yeah, I know. We go way back," I say, a hint of amusement in my tone. "This is the girl who tried to steal your suitcase at the airport."

Paige's face pales and then floods crimson as my words hit her like a blow from a hammer. She clutches a hand to her chest. "Oh my gosh. You're—M. Sinclair? Macy *Sinclair?*" Paige asks, abashedly dipping her chin at the realization. "This can't be happening," she murmurs.

Macy's eyes grow wide, and she collapses into laughter. "That was you?"

"Uh, yeah. Not my finest moment." Paige looks like she wants to wring my neck and dissolve into the floorboards at the same time.

"I honestly thought Cade was joking when he told me that story. That's so funny!" Macy's giggles finally subside, but Paige's unease doesn't waver. "I retract my earlier statement about this being a small world," my sister says, registering Paige's discomfort and trying hard to compose herself. "This was obviously meant to be. I don't usually make impulsive decisions, but I have a good feeling about you, Paige. If you want the job, it's yours."

"Really? Yes, definitely yes!" Paige's embarrassment dissipates, replaced by a beautiful, white-toothed grin that illuminates her face, and I find myself smiling back at her. "Thank you so much! I can't tell you what this means to me."

Macy pats her shoulder, choking back another giggle. "Let me just grab some forms for you to fill out and we'll make this official."

My sister disappears into the stockroom, leaving us alone. Paige presses her palms to her cheeks and sighs, her larger-than-life smile still in place. "Wow," she says in joyful disbelief.

"She's a big believer in fate," I say.

"What?" she asks, as if she forgot I was in the room.

"Macy." I gesture to the door. "I'm pretty sure she thinks you two met on the plane that day because the universe somehow knew she needed you to work here. That's how her mind works."

Paige's smile weakens, barely lifting the corners of her mouth. "That's not the reason."

"What is it, then?" Maybe I'm overstepping, but this girl is a mystery. I've listened to the talk around school, hoping to pick up some bits and pieces of her story, but as far as I can tell, no one seems to know for sure how Principal

Chapman's daughter suddenly materialized out of thin air.

She shrugs off my question with, "Just a happy coincidence, I guess."

"Macy doesn't believe in coincidences."

"Well, whether she believes in them or not, that's all this is," Paige says firmly, avoiding my eyes. She fingers a stack of books on the counter, inadvertently knocking the paperback on the top to the ground. In her haste to pick it up, she fumbles and drops the book one more time before returning it to the stack, bumping her hand into a display of bookmarks beside it on the counter. She grabs for the display, ensuring it doesn't tumble as well, and exhales a sharp lungful of air, closing her eyes for a moment before issuing a curt, "Sorry."

"Do I make you nervous?"

She snorts. "What? *No.*" Still refusing to look at me, Paige's eyes dart around the shop and then land on the stockroom door with such intensity that I wonder if she's somehow trying to send Macy a telepathic plea to come back and rescue her.

Right on cue, the stockroom door opens and Macy reappears with several sheets of paper in her hand.

"All right, here we go." She hands Paige the paperwork from across the counter. "Welcome to Moonlight Books. Here's to many new adventures to come."

# CHAPTER TEN

## Paige

I drive home that evening with a ridiculous smile on my face, singing along with the radio like I just won the Grammy for Best New Artist. Macy's job offer salvaged what had started out as a pretty sucky day.

I'm scheduled for my first shift at the bookstore next Saturday. The hours are perfect, so Jay can't object, and I really like Macy. She's down to earth, and I feel comfortable around her. I definitely regret not being a better seatmate on the plane now. But even more surprising than crossing paths with Macy was the revelation that Cade is her brother. I did not see that one coming.

I pull into the Chapmans' driveway beside Jay's Durango. I thought Connie said they were going to Tanner's soccer game? The house is dark except for the kitchen light. I unlock the back door and, once inside, drop my jacket on one of the stools at the island counter and slowly make my way toward the living room.

"Is anyone here?" As I round the corner, I spot a small,

orange glow in the fireplace silhouetting Jay's form. I switch on the lamp on the end table and find him with his back to me, his hands firmly planted on the mantel.

"I'm home." Taking a couple of steps into the room, I glance about, trying to identify what it is I just interrupted. On the coffee table lay two open photo albums. I step closer and see that the pictures in those albums are of me. A photo taken in the hospital after I was born. Another holding a basket of colored Easter eggs—I couldn't have been more than two years old in that one. A photograph of me in a pink leotard at my first ballet recital.

I lower myself onto the sofa, pulling one of the albums onto my lap and fingering the plastic page protector over a photograph of me with my mother at the park. "Where did you get these?"

When Jay finally speaks, his words are bitterly hard. "I'm so angry at Abby."

"What did you say?"

His back rises and falls in slow, controlled breaths. "I said, I'm angry." I'm still processing his words when he finally turns to face me. His expression is dazed, wavering between frustration and—anguish?

I swallow, preparing myself for the conversation I knew would happen sooner or later. Of course Jay's angry. Who wouldn't be after having a teenager suddenly plunked down in the middle of what I'm guessing has been a pretty perfect life for this man? My mind swims with all the reasons Jay could possibly have to be pissed off at my mother. The list is pretty long by my estimation. I don't blame him for resenting her, but before I can tell him so—that I, too, have as many reasons to be furious with her—he speaks again. And this time I'm completely derailed by his words.

"When I look at you, all I see is nearly eighteen years of things I missed." Jay runs his fingers through his dark hair as the muscles in his cheek pulse. He clears his throat and tilts his face toward the ceiling. "Damn it, Paige, I missed your first steps."

What is happening here?

I try again. "Where did you get these pictures? Did Aunt Faye send them to you?" It's as if he can't hear me, like he's looking right through me, lost in memories I know he doesn't have.

"When did you get your ears pierced?"

My lips part, but no words form.

Jay chuckles, and it's both bitter and brief before the heavy shadow over his eyes returns. I nibble on my lower lip when his gaze touches mine for a fraction of a second, then shifts to other points of contact in the room, like he's not sure what to focus on. "I could have been the one to teach you to surf. I would have liked that."

I flip through the album. School pictures, middle school Science Night, birthday parties. And just as I suspect, there it is. The photograph staring up at me was taken at a youth surfing invitational three years ago. In my hands is an honorable mention ribbon from the first and only surfing competition I'd ever entered. My surfboard is planted firmly in the sand beside me. My fingers fidget with my watchband as something turns over in my stomach.

"Ten," I murmur.

His eyes lock with mine. "What did you say?"

"I was ten when I got my ears pierced."

Jay nods as sorrow fills his face. I must look as confused as I feel because he asks, "What is it?"

I struggle to get the words out. "Well—you have all these memories, or you will, with Tanner and Lily," I say. "I guess I don't understand why this matters so much."

Jay shakes his head in disbelief. "You're my daughter. You're just as important to me as Tanner and Lil." He dips his chin and sighs with frustration. "But I don't know how to do this."

"Do what?" Goose bumps prickle along my arms, like they do when I'm expecting bad news. His green eyes catch mine in his apologetic gaze.

"I don't know how to be a father to a child I didn't raise."

And there it is. Even though I'd expected it, Jay's words sting and my heart stutters at the rejection. Closing the photo album, I place it on the coffee table. Finally hearing the gravity of his own words, Jay's eyes widen, and in a flash, he's sitting beside me on the sofa.

"No, Paige! That's not what I meant." I think he wants to comfort me because he's acting all awkward and hesitant, but I don't think he has a clue how to do it. A consoling touch on the arm would be a nice gesture, but I don't get one. Instead, he leans forward, his elbows on his knees and his hands fisted against his mouth as we sit in silence for several long moments.

I almost feel bad for the guy. I mean, I'm not the only one who had my world turned upside down. He'd received the same legal order from the will of a woman who'd lied to him all these years. Jay hadn't wanted this—hadn't wanted me—and that's why he's been distant and detached since the moment I got here. Because biological or not, I am an undeniable disruption to his life.

Jay sits up and faces me. "Let me try this again."

"You don't have to," I say. "You don't owe me an explanation."

"Yes, I do," Jay says. "Look, I have no idea how Abby raised you—her values, her beliefs. I want to do what's best for you, what she would have wanted for you, only I'm not exactly sure what that is. What if I get this wrong?"

"You know more than I do," I offer, but my optimism falls flat. "Don't worry, I'll be okay."

"You deserve better than okay," Jay says.

Another awkward moment of silence slips between us, and suddenly the ticking of the wall clock and the crackle of the fire are deafening.

"Can I be honest?" I ask when I can't take it any longer.

"Please," Jay says.

"This is weird. This entire situation. You get that, right?" I have to say it. It's the enormous pink elephant in the room, the one that seems to have been in every room with Jay and me since the moment I got here. The elephant isn't just pink; it's wearing disco pants and twerking on the coffee table. At some point, someone has to acknowledge the absurdity of it all. Calling our new living arrangement awkward just doesn't quite do this whole situation justice.

Jay flips the page of one of the photo albums in front of him. "Yeah, it's weird." He sighs. "But hopefully soon it won't be and—" I can feel the weight of his eyes boring into me as I stare down at my watch. "We'll figure this out, Paige. This is your home now. At some point, I hope you'll feel comfortable here, and then we can figure out how to fit into this relationship that started seventeen years later than it should have. If that's what you want," he says.

What I want is my mother. I want a second chance to save her, to erase the pain and the misery that sprouts from roots so deep inside me, I can't wrangle my way free. I'm not sure how much more I can take. First, it was Connie trying way too hard to fill my mother's shoes. Now, Jay is doing whatever *this* is and trying to bond with me as my father. And despite his words tonight, I'm not entirely convinced it's a role he's fully committed to playing.

# CHAPTER ELEVEN
## *Paige*

I am officially a liar, liar, pants on fire. And I feel kind of bad about that as I ring Quinn's doorbell on Friday evening.

When she flings open the door, she takes one look at my face, rolls her eyes and pulls me into the house. "Will you relax? We're not going to get caught. You're making this a way bigger deal than it really is."

Am I? Let's break this down. First, I lied to Jay and Connie about exactly what I would be doing tonight, completely bypassing any mention of the party at some strange house with a bunch of people I don't know. And if that wasn't bad enough, I took my storytelling to an entirely new level by adding an intricately woven yet fabricated backstory.

"We have a big math test coming up on Monday and Quinn's really struggling," I'd told Jay that morning before I'd left for school. "She needs my help studying, and I thought it would be a good idea if we jumped on it now, so she'll have the rest of the weekend to practice and prepare for next week's test."

"I think it's great that you've made friends so quickly," Jay had said, and Connie had stood beside him nodding approvingly and looking like she wanted to bake me a cake as a reward for my gallant gesture of friendship. "It's admirable that you're willing to help Quinn with her schoolwork, Paige. We're proud of you."

I think that's what did me in. Hearing Jay and Connie say, "We're proud of you," when I was not only planning to sneak around behind their backs but lying to them about it too. In my defense, this is not something I typically do. I never lied to my mom to sneak out to a party. She either trusted me enough to let me go, or I'd had enough common sense not to sneak out in the first place. I hope Quinn's party invitation is worth it, because I'm pretty sure I'm getting a one-way ticket to hell for this one.

"I'm not sure this is a good idea anymore," I tell Quinn.

With a dramatic sigh and another roll of her eyes, she drags me by the wrist through the large living room, calling out to no one in particular, "Paige is here; we'll be in my room studying!"

I glance around, expecting Quinn's parents to appear, but they don't.

Quinn's room is at the end of the upstairs hallway. Once we're behind her closed door, I release the breath I'm holding. "What if your parents ask where we're going, or wait up for us to come home?"

"For the third time, calm down!" Quinn roots around in one of her dresser drawers. "My mom has her own stuff going on. We won't see her until tomorrow morning. Trust me, it's totally fine. My track record for this kind of thing is nearly flawless."

I narrow my eyes. "What do you mean, *nearly* flawless?"

Through her sheepish grin, she says, "You don't want to know."

*No. No, I do not.*

Stray articles of clothing are strewn across Quinn's bed, along with the scattered contents of her school bag. I notice a couple of sheets of paper peeking out from her math book. One of them has an unmistakable "58%" written in red ink at the top.

"You really are flunking math?" I'm starting to understand why this part of our plan is so believable.

"No biggie." She waves her hand dismissively. "I don't plan to use it later in life."

"Not even to get into college? I hear it comes in handy for that."

Quinn smirks and flips on the stereo next to the bed. Her walls are covered with photographs, some in frames, others simply tacked up on the wall or collaged on a bulletin board above her desk. I peruse the room, taking them all in, and I'm about to ask her where her collection came from when I notice two cameras on her desk.

"Did you take all these?" I ask, inspecting a photograph of a sunset with the most spectacular pinks and oranges I've ever seen.

"Most of them. I collected a few for inspiration."

"How long have you been in to photography?" I pick up a black-and-white photograph from the desk and study it. It's a photo of Mrs. Talbot, apparently taken without her knowledge. She's gazing off into the distance, and she looks nothing like the woman I see in the halls every day at school. This woman radiates sadness and pain and—Quinn snatches the photo from my fingers, and I jump.

"So, what's your story, Paige Bryant?" she asks, placing the photograph facedown on the desk and leaning against the edge. She studies me like my autobiography is written somewhere on my skin.

"What do you mean?"

"If we're going to be best friends—and I'm certain we're well on our way—I need to know your deepest, darkest secrets," she says. "So, spill."

Her words catch me off guard, and I can't seem to come up with a response. "I don't have any secrets."

"Everyone has secrets," Quinn says. "Some people are just better at keeping them tucked away. And you, my mysterious friend, strike me as a master in that department."

I stare wide-eyed, wondering what she might already know about me that's prompting this bizarre and uncomfortable conversation. "I don't know what you're talking about."

"Okay. Playing it aloof. I respect that technique."

I sit on the bed. "Quinn, seriously, I have no idea what

you're getting at."

Her eyebrows lift. "Google, remember?" Hopping onto the bed beside me, she tucks her legs beneath her. "What gives? You're apparently this amazing dancer, but you're avoiding the dance team like we smell or something. Aside from the fact that you had to come live with your dad, I hardly know anything about you. So again, I have to ask, what is your deal?"

"You know why I'm here," I say. The entire staff at school knows about my mom and how I ended up in Mystic. That's no big secret. But I didn't have control over the sharing of that information, so I'm not exactly ready to volunteer additional details.

"Okay, fine. You're not ready to share yet, I can see that," Quinn says, surprisingly jovial and nonchalant. "But when you are, know that your best friend is here to listen."

"I'll keep that in mind," I answer, still dumbfounded by this odd exchange.

"Check this out." Quinn pulls me by my forearms to her closet and flings open the doors to reveal a large walk-in, filled with clothes from floor to ceiling.

My mouth drops. "Whoa! Did we just teleport to the mall?"

"I know, right? I'm obsessed with clothes."

"Clearly." I run my hand across a stream of colorful fabrics on hangers. There are enough skirts, dresses, shirts and sweaters to clothe a third world country. One wall of the closet is dedicated entirely to a collection of jeans; light wash, dark wash and what appears to be everything in between. "You can't possibly wear all these."

"Oh, I will," Quinn says. "Or die trying!"

For the next hour, we try on half her wardrobe. Fortunately for me, we're the same size. By the time we're ready to leave for the beach, I've thrown my own outfit back into my bag and borrowed a cute, lacy top from Quinn's collection, along with a soft, button-up sweater and a to-die-for pair of jeans that I silently hope I won't ever have to return.

"You look perfect!" Quinn says from her vanity, which is cluttered with an obscene collection of cosmetic tubes, bottles and compacts. She's placing the last few curls in her silky hair with her hot iron.

"Is it wrong that we're going to a Halloween party but we're not wearing costumes?" I ask.

"Don't worry, I've got you covered," she says, hopping up and heading back into her closet. When she returns, she's holding two headbands with black cats' ears on top. "What do you think?"

"I think that looks like we're phoning it in," I reply. A flimsy headband does not constitute a Halloween costume, not in my world.

"Do you want to freeze your butt off? A beach house party in late October is no joke. So it's this or risk hypothermia. Your choice." Since I'm not used to the change in weather here yet, I take one of the headbands from her.

"Will I know anyone else at the party tonight besides

Miranda?" I ask, sliding the headband into place and checking my reflection in the vanity mirror.

"Mmm, I think she invited Dane and a couple of his buddies. Miranda's had a thing for Dane since sophomore year. She's not exactly subtle about it."

"How come they've never gotten together?" I ask.

Quinn shrugs. "I don't know. But I'm pretty sure he has a thing for you right now."

"Why do you say that?"

"He practically fell all over you the first time he laid eyes on you. And Dane's not really the fall-all-over-girls type of guy. Girls fall for him. All he has to do is catch the ones he wants."

I'm surprised and flattered, but a little confused, thinking back to that day outside the bookstore when he couldn't seem to get away from me fast enough. I think Quinn might be a little off on her assessment.

She stands and fluffs her hair, her own cat ears perfectly in place. "How do I look?"

"You're the cat's meow," I say, and we laugh at my stupid punch line.

After Quinn gives herself one final approving look in the mirror, we head for the stairs. She pauses beside a closed door. "Oh, shoot, I forgot something."

"What is it?" I ask.

"Nothing big. Just go downstairs and grab my coat, will you? It's the blue one in the closet by the door. I'll be right down."

"Is everything okay?"

"Yeah, of course. Go. I'll be there in a minute."

I nod and descend the staircase, but just before I reach the landing, I hear a door open at the top of the stairs and Quinn's muffled voice.

I hesitate, but curiosity propels me back up the stairs. I move carefully, making my way to the door. It's not my intention to eavesdrop, but the door is ajar, and I hear Quinn softly speaking to someone inside.

"Mom, Paige is here."

A woman moans. "I can't see her, sweetie, not now." It must be Mrs. Talbot, and there's a note of panic in her muffled words.

"It's okay," Quinn says, her tone low and soothing. "You don't have to. Just rest. We'll be fine. We're going to watch movies and order pizza."

There's a soft whimper, and I hear the woman's tormented and broken voice ask, "Did he call?"

The bedsprings creak. Quinn either sat down, or her mother rolled over. "No, he didn't. I'm sorry."

A small, emotionally saturated cry escapes past the door, and I take a quick, surprised step backward as Quinn urgently tries to calm her weeping mother. "Shhh, take it easy. Here, drink some water."

"You'll tell me when he calls, won't you?"

"Yeah, of course I will."

"Promise me," Mrs. Talbot begs. "I need to talk to him. I need to tell him—"

"I promise. Now, lay back and get some sleep, okay?" Quinn gently says. "Things will be better in the morning. They always are."

After another small whimper and a sniff, her mother mumbles something unintelligible.

I'm trying to process what is happening, what it is that's wrong with Mrs. Talbot, when Quinn backs out of the room, softly closing the door. I freeze because there's nowhere for me to go. Biting my lip, I flash Quinn an apologetic look. We stare at each other for a long beat, then Quinn sighs and hurries past me for the stairs.

"I told you to wait for me in the living room."

"I know, I'm sorry," I say, trailing after her down the staircase. "Is your mom all right?"

"Yeah, she's fine. I think she might have the flu." She rummages in the foyer closet for her jacket.

"She seemed fine at school today."

"It came on pretty suddenly."

"Do you want to stay home and make sure she's okay? I'm all right with staying," I say.

"What? No, she'll be fine. She'll be asleep soon, if she isn't already." Quinn grabs her wallet and keys off the entry table. "Which means we're in the clear, so let's go."

"Quinn—" I glance back up the stairs and then return my eyes to my friend, who looks like she can't get out of this house fast enough. "What's going on?"

"I told you." She opens the door, and a gust of crisp evening air wafts in.

"You know you can talk to me if you want. Besties and all that?" I remind her.

Quinn pales. "You're being ridiculous. Can we please go now?"

"I don't feel right leaving your mom like this," I say. From what I just heard, Mrs. Talbot isn't in any condition to be left alone. She might need a doctor.

Quinn closes her eyes. When she opens them, she peers down at her hand wrapped tightly around the doorknob. After a few seconds of deliberation, she closes the door and steps back. "Fine. You want to know the truth? My mom isn't sick. She's a mess." Disgust laces her words. "She does this every weekend."

"Does what?"

"Falls apart." A nanosecond after her blunt words leave her lips, Quinn's eyes fill with anguish, and she sits down right in the middle of the entryway. Her wallet and keys slip onto the hardwood floor as her head falls into her hands.

I kneel beside her. "What are you talking about?"

"Swear to me that you won't repeat this," she says firmly. "I mean it, Paige. *No one* can know."

"Know what?"

She tilts her head and stares me down. She's not messing around.

"Okay, I swear," I say.

Quinn rubs her forehead with the heel of her palm. "I told you, everyone has secrets. Mine is that my dad walked out on us a few months ago."

"Oh, Quinn, I'm so sorry."

"Don't be." She chuckles harshly. "He's a jerk who's been cheating on my mom for months. He didn't even have the decency to try to hide it."

My lips part, but I don't know what to say. All I can muster is, "That's awful."

"He's a professor at the university. The distance made it pretty easy for him. At first, he told my mom that the drive back and forth was getting too difficult, so he got an apartment near campus and only came home on weekends. Convenient, huh?"

I try to think of something useful to say, but I find myself at a complete loss for words that could temporarily medicate her pain. I wonder if this is how people feel when I talk about losing my mom.

"When she found out about the affairs—because there was more than one," Quinn sneers, "she confronted him. He wasn't even sorry." She throws up her hands, as if releasing an armful of disbelief into the space around us. "Can you believe that? Instead, he told her he wanted a divorce. Then he packed his bags, and we never saw him again."

"Never?"

She shakes her head. "He's always sending me money to try to make up for the fact that he's an ass, but no, I haven't seen him in months. At first, I thought about sending back his checks, but then I realized that would be too easy. So, now I just blow it all on clothes."

"Wow," I breathe, trying to process her words. I'm not quite able to make all the pieces fit, but at least I understand where all the clothes in her closet came from. Each item is her father's attempt at buying her forgiveness, and I now feel uncomfortable in my borrowed outfit. "I don't know what to say," I admit.

"Because there isn't anything to say. I mean, what can you possibly say about a man who threw away his family?" A tear forms at the corner of Quinn's right eye, and she hastily brushes it away. "And you know, I'm fine with that. Whatever. But my mom—she didn't deserve that. She didn't deserve to give twenty years of her life to a creep who just discarded her when something better came his way!" Her eyes drift to the top of the stairs. "She's completely ruined. And the thing is, I don't know how to make her better. Somehow, she manages to hold it together at school, but on the weekends she gets depressed, and then she breaks down and completely checks out. It's like she unravels—and I'm the one who has to take care of her. I hate him so much for that."

"Is there anything I can do?"

Quinn clears her throat and brushes a stray tear away from her cheek. "Well, it would be all kinds of awesome if you could forget about this uncool meltdown that I'm having in front of you on the floor right now." She readjusts her cat ears and searches my face with pleading eyes.

"Don't worry about it. But if there's anything I can do, please tell me. I'll help any way I can."

"Thanks." Quinn clambers to her feet, picking up her wallet and keys, and I follow her. "But honestly, the best thing you can do is get me out of here and get me to that party."

"Really? I mean, I want to go to this party, too, but what if your mom needs you?"

Quinn shakes her head, dabbing at her eyes to remove any remnants of smudged mascara. "Once the wine kicks in, she's out for the night. I spend most of my weekends alone."

I make another attempt at mustering the words that will make this better in some way, but again, I come up short. "Have you thought about talking to someone?"

Quinn rolls her cornflower blues skyward. "Like who? Mrs. Hopkins? How did that work out for you this week?"

Message received. I'd met with Mrs. Hopkins for our second lunchtime meeting on Wednesday, and it had been exhausting. She'd asked more questions about my mom and my living arrangements with Jay, and I could see she was a little disheartened when I offered her nothing of any value. The consequences of not spilling my guts is that I have yet another meeting scheduled with her for next week. I'm pretty sure she thinks the third attempt at trying to get inside my head will finally be successful. I hate to tell her, but the only thing that will be on next week's agenda will be another heaping dose of disappointment. I don't plan on sharing my secrets with anyone, especially not someone trying to analyze them.

"Look, I'm sorry I laid all this on you. And if it's all the same, I'd really appreciate you keeping it to yourself. Not even Zoey and Sam know," Quinn says. "My mom will freak if anyone at school finds out."

"I swear," I say again. "But you shouldn't have to deal with this by yourself. I'm here for you."

"Thanks. You're good people, Paige. And don't forget, that offer goes both ways, if and when you decide you want to talk." We hug, the kind of hug that's quick but tight enough that we have another separate conversation within our brief embrace. I smile, and she bends down, swiping her coat off the floor at her feet. It feels good to be there for someone else.

"All right, now that that mess is over, let's go get our party on," she says.

"Okay, but not too late. I'd feel better if we didn't leave your mom alone for more than a couple of hours. You know, just in case she wakes up and needs you."

Quinn nods. "I can work with that."

# CHAPTER TWELVE
## Cade

I spot Paige the second she steps out onto the patio of the beach house. I try to convince myself that I haven't been watching the door for the last twenty minutes, waiting for her to arrive, and that instead, I've been preoccupied with the drunk sorority chick and her friend who've been trying to chat up any member of the band who will give them an ounce of attention.

"Is that her?" Jared asks from beside me, ignoring the blonde who's dressed like a slutty nurse and nearly draped all over him, and instead training his eyes on Paige and her friends. I give him what I think is an inconspicuous nod, but Ash looks up from his drums just in time to catch it, and he's suddenly a little too interested in our conversation.

"Which one? The hottie in the blue coat?" he asks, pushing his Batman mask up onto his head to get a better look.

"The other one," I correct, my attempt at playing it cool quickly disintegrating now that we've also caught Zeke's attention. He glances up from where he's kneeling in front of one of the amps and zeroes his gaze on Paige and her group of friends. They're exchanging a round of hugs with Miranda, who's dressed as Jasmine from Disney's *Aladdin*.

"The hottie in the sweater," he croons, a little too loud, and I chuck my guitar pick at him like it's a Chinese throwing star.

With quick reflexes, probably from all the other times people have thrown things at him, Zeke deflects the pick with his forearm and laughs. "Looks like I hit a nerve." He scoops up the pick and pitches it back at me. "Seriously, man, she's cute. What's her deal?"

I shrug, because I need them to take it down a couple of notches and quit acting like grade-schoolers. And because I have no idea what Paige's deal is, and I've given it way too much thought since our encounter at the bookstore.

"All right, let's do this," Jared announces, snapping me out of my thoughts. "We're not being paid to analyze Cade's schoolgirl crush." I kick out a foot, but he jumps out of the way with a devilish smile. These guys can be jerks sometimes, and they get way too much pleasure out of reminding me that I'm the youngest one in the group. But they are as close to brothers as I'm ever going to get, and at the end of the day, they always have my back.

With a grin still plastered across his face, Jared launches into a riff on his guitar to get the crowd's attention. It works, and heads turn in our direction amid a few whoops and whistles. I lock eyes with Paige for a brief second, and she smiles, giving me a small wave.

As we dive into our first song, I try to concentrate on the music as Jared croons the lyrics I wrote, his cool, Keith Urban-like persona—shaggy blond hair and all—drawing the attention of most of the female population that's now gravitating toward us. The guy can work a crowd, I have to give him that. I glance up occasionally and locate Paige beyond the dozens of bodies now pressed in close in front of us. She's settled on a bench on the far side of the stone firepit, sandwiched between Quinn and—Dane Sloane. I grimace. The douchebag is dressed in a long white coat with a toy stethoscope dangling from his neck. Despite Miranda's attempts to command his attention, he's entirely focused on Paige. I exhale against the tension that's coiled beneath my shoulder blades.

Paige's hands are outstretched to the flames, absorbing the heat. Occasionally, she laughs in response to the conversation unfolding around her, and that perfectly pitched sound wafts through the space between us. Then— her gaze lifts and our eyes meet. It's kinetic, and my first instinct is to look away, to focus on the crowd and pretend that I'm too in to what I'm doing to notice her. But damn, she's all I see, so I hold her gaze. When her attention shifts to the clearly intoxicated girls dancing in front of us, she frowns and turns away to talk to Quinn.

And that's all I get. Paige doesn't so much as throw me another look during the next three songs. At one point, she disappears into the house with Quinn, and when she returns, she gravitates to the far corner of the patio, where she's leaning against the railing. Sloane is practically glued to her side, leaning in too close, and that damn tension is back, biting into my spine like it has claws.

"Dude, you've got total stalker eyes," Jared says after the song comes to an end.

"Shut up," I growl.

"I get it," he says. "But unless you're willing to go over there and talk to her, you need to holster the daggers you're throwing at that guy."

I ignore him.

"All right, have it your way," Jared says with a disappointed shake of his head. "I'm sure those two will be very happy together." With a jerk of his chin, he signals Ash, who nods, then knocks his drumsticks together four times, cueing our next song. This one's a ballad, and couples quickly begin to form, entwining together and falling into rhythmic swaying. As pathetic as it is, my eyes stray back to the corner of the patio in search of Paige. She's not there.

When the song finishes, Jared announces that we're taking a break. I turn to place my guitar in its stand as I hear a voice behind me.

"Hey." Paige offers a single wave, then shoves her hands into the back pockets of her jeans. The three groupies to my left take her in, their expressions souring when their eyes shift to me.

"Nice costume," I say, glancing at the cat ears perched on top of her head. The smile that begins to form on her lips immediately derails when the girl in the nurse getup slides between us and leans in to me, nearly throwing me off balance with the force of her weight. She snakes her arm around mine, stroking my forearm with her fingers.

"Hey, cutie," she slurs. "Let's go get a drink."

"No, thanks," I answer, extracting my arm from her grasp. As I step back, she stumbles at the absence of my body. She immediately turns predatory eyes on Paige in a nasty glare that I swear just lowered the temperature of the night air by ten degrees. But thankfully, without another word, she ambles off toward the house with her two friends in tow.

With arched eyebrows, Paige watches them go. When she shifts her attention back to me, the smile I missed out on the first time lazily returns to her mouth. "Your band sounds great."

"Thanks. Jared was a little off on that last song," I say, raising my voice just enough that he is sure to hear me. He flashes me the middle finger, and I laugh. "You look nice," I say.

"Thanks." Paige's shoulders relax, but she nibbles on her lip. "So, what are you supposed to be?"

"What?"

"Your costume?" She waves a hand over the length of my torso. "No offense, but this is a Halloween party."

I lift the bottom of my sweatshirt up above my chest to reveal my Captain America T-shirt. "Superheroes are always undercover."

She laughs. "All right, I'll give you that one. So, how long have you all been playing together?"

"One year, two months and nineteen days," Ash says, slipping a hand between us and extending it to Paige. Surprise fills her eyes, but she shakes his hand as he says, "But who's counting, right? Cade's awful at introductions, so let me help him out. I'm Ash. That's Jared, and over there is Zeke." Jared nods and Zeke throws her a two-fingered salute from behind his drum kit.

"Nice to meet you," Paige says.

A loud whistle shoots through the crowd, and a girl calls out, "Can I have everyone's attention?"

I pull my eyes from Paige to see that Trina, Miranda's sister, has climbed up on a chair. With two hands cupped around her mouth, she yells, "Helloooo? Everyone, listen up!" It takes a few seconds, but conversations begin to settle around us as the brunette, who looks a little shaky from her perch, waves her hands at the crowd. "In just a few minutes, we're going to head down to the beach for a game of capture the tag."

"You mean capture the flag!" yells a guy.

"Noooo, Ethan," she drawls. "I mean just what I said. Capture the *tag*. I need everyone to pick a partner, then each team gets a flashlight and a colored flag." Trina reaches into her back pocket and pulls out what looks like a red handkerchief. She waves it in the air. "You must protect your flag while you avoid being tagged."

"How do you win?" the same guy shouts.

"*You* don't!" another dude shouts back, and his response is met by laughter from the crowd.

"The last team standing has to single-handedly steal the flag from the team that's it, without getting tagged. If you can do that, you win!" Trina declares.

"Who's it?" a girl shouts from the doorway of the house.

A tall guy with dark hair swoops Trina off the chair and into his arms as he announces, "Trina and I will be it. And the rest of you—prepare to go down!" He spins her around as another barrage of whoops and cheers bursts from the amped-up crowd.

"Now, pick your partner and come get your flag!" Trina instructs. The guy sets her back on her feet as people rush in around them.

From my peripheral vision, I see movement and immediately zero in on Sloane, who's making a beeline for Paige. *Oh, hell no.*

"How about it?" I ask. "Want to be partners?" My words are just loud enough that Dane slows his approach when he hears them.

"Are you sure?" Paige asks. "I don't know if I'll be any good at it."

Dane's eyes meet mine for the briefest of seconds, and I'll admit, it feels pretty damn good when the realization that I just shut him down registers in angry lines across his face. Jaw tight, he turns and heads back toward Quinn and her friends.

Without hesitation, I reach back and tug the neck of my sweatshirt, pulling it over my head. I offer it to Paige.

"Here. Put this on. It's nice and warm."

She wraps her sweater tighter around herself. "No, thanks, I'm fine."

"You won't be in about ten minutes. The wind on the beach is harsh." I shake the sweatshirt at her.

"But then you'll be cold," she protests, glancing at my long-sleeved T-shirt.

"Just put it on. I've got a jacket over there." She glances over my shoulder, then does as I instruct, slipping the sweatshirt carefully over her head and readjusting her cat ears. She releases a relieved breath the instant the warmth surrounds her. The sweatshirt is at least two sizes too big, and she's practically swimming in it, but she looks cute as hell. I retrieve my jacket and slip it on. "All right. Let's do this."

"Wait." Paige grabs my forearm and glances around at the couples gathering up their coats and flashlights and whispering to one another, no doubt strategizing, as they head for the stairs that lead down to the beach. She lowers her voice. "Shouldn't we have a game plan?"

"Trust me, you're in good hands. I'm undefeated at beach tag and capture the flag," I say proudly.

She narrows her eyes. "What's your secret?"

"Don't get caught."

She shoots me a bland look. "Obviously, Einstein, but how do we avoid that?"

I take her hand in mine. She stares at our entwined fingers, then her questioning gaze lifts. I wink. "Stick with me, and I'll show you."

# CHAPTER THIRTEEN

## *Paige*

"Where exactly are we going?" I whisper, stumbling over a ridge in the sand but managing to regain my balance. With a white-knuckled grip on the hem of Cade's jacket, I can barely see anything in the surrounding darkness. Cade has a flashlight, but he refuses to use it because he says it will give away our position, or some boyish nonsense like that. At this rate, I'm going to break my ankle or possibly my neck. "I think we're going the wrong way. Shouldn't we be going toward the beach?"

"Trust me," he whispers over his shoulder.

Because I don't really have a choice, I tighten my hold on him, and after another near fall, Cade finally slows his steps. When we reach the top of a small bluff, he tugs me down so that we're perched behind a low ridge, giving us a hiding place as well as a bird's-eye view of the beach below. Beneath the pale silvery moon, half-shrouded by clouds, I can just make out the scattering of dark forms darting about on the sand. High-pitched squeals and laughter from the girls invade the peaceful night, along with occasional swear words shouted by their partners. The gameplay echoes against the crashing waves as the couple who's "it" picks off the competition, one by one.

"Okay, so now what?" I ask, gulping in the cold, salty air as I try to catch my breath from our blind hike up the sand dune.

"We wait," Cade says.

"For how long?"

"Until there's only one team left. Then we take them down, steal their flag and claim our victory."

"Isn't this technically cheating?" I ask.

"You really suck at this," he says, which might have ticked me off if it wasn't for his amused tone. "Tag and capture the flag are both games of calculation. The best way to win is to let everyone do the work for you, and then you swoop in and seal the deal."

I roll my eyes, even though I know he can't see me, but I consider his words. Cade's strategy for winning is a foreign concept to me because I've always played by the rules. Whether it was a silly game of tag or checkers or whatever, I was raised to respect the process and put in the effort to achieve my goals. But then, where did that get me? It couldn't save my mom when everything went wrong. In the end, all those years I'd spent diligently training to be the best dancer I could be, soldiering through the blisters, the pain and the fatigue, all in the slim hope of achieving a future I'd dreamed about since I was six years old, hadn't matter one bit. So, maybe Cade is on to something. Maybe following the rules is pointless when you can still lose everything.

Cries of surprise and more peals of laughter swirl up from the beach as rogue flashlight beams arc and swirl like fireflies below us. I pull my borrowed sweatshirt tighter around myself. "So, Captain, what exactly do we do until it's time to 'swoop in and seal the deal'?"

"We could make out."

If my surprised horror had a sound, it would be in the octave range of a lighthouse's foghorn. What I actually hear is Cade's soft laughter.

"Classy," I mutter, shifting my legs beneath me and sending thanks skyward that it's too dim for him to see me blush.

"I'm kidding, Bryant. Let's just talk," he says.

I'm not entirely sure why, but talking with this guy makes me more nervous than the thought of a make-out session in the dark. "What do you want to talk about?"

"Well, for starters—" Even in the obscured light, I can feel his eyes on me. "Where in the world did you come from?"

"California." A shower of something hits my side. Did he just throw sand at me? "Hey!" I protest. "Not cool."

"Why do you take everything so literally?" Cade asks.

"How was I supposed to take that? That's where I came from. And by the way, you're a jerk for throwing sand," I say, brushing at my side.

"What I meant was—how does Principal Chapman's daughter suddenly appear out of nowhere?"

I knew what he meant. It's the million-dollar question. "I guess you could say he won the genetic lottery. Only he didn't know he was playing."

"What does that mean?"

I cough, trying to get rid of the lump in my throat. "Why did you tell me not to believe everything I hear?"

"What?" Cade asks.

"That day outside Jay's office, after the fight," I remind him. "You told me not to believe everything I hear."

"You didn't answer my question," Cade counters.

"Ohhh, sorry, times up. It's my turn now," I announce.

"Says who?"

"Says me."

Cade's silhouette shifts, and I can see that he's shaking his head. "You're unbelievable."

"That's not an answer," I say. "Anytime you're ready, lay it on me."

Just when I think he's not going to answer, he says, "If you haven't already figured it out, I'm not exactly part of the popular crowd."

"So?"

"So, how many people have already warned you to stay away from me?" Several beats of silence pass between us. "*That's* what I'm talking about. But just so you know, those people know nothing about me."

"Well, for your information, I don't listen to gossip. If I

judge people, I do it based on my own information," I say. "Not the opinions of people I barely know."

"You're judging me?" Disappointment colors Cade's words.

"Haven't you already judged me on some level? It's human nature."

Cade's quiet for a few moments. "So, what have you decided?"

I cock my head and study his profile. "I think you're a gentleman." Cade snorts. "I'm sorry, do you have some commentary you'd like to share?"

He shakes his head. "I can't figure you out."

"I'm not that complicated."

"Since we met, I've managed to get into a fight and land in detention, and you have to know by now that I'm not on Principal Chapman's list of favorite students. What could possibly make you think I'm a *gentleman*?" He says it like it's a dirty word.

I turn my face up to the night sky, feeling the bite of the cold wind on my cheeks. "Because you helped me with my suitcase at the airport, even after I nearly tackled you because I thought you were trying to steal it." I cringe at the humiliating memory. "You must have thought I was a complete whack job. But despite that, you came back to help me."

"I just wanted to make sure you found your bag. I mean, I didn't want you to end up assaulting some other unsuspecting passenger."

I smile. "That's what I'm talking about. It's the things you do when you think no one is paying attention that matter the most. So, whether you like it or not, buddy—" I nudge his shoulder with mine. "You're a gentleman."

"You're crazy," he murmurs, but I can hear the smile in his voice. I tug down the sleeves of Cade's sweatshirt until my hands are safely tucked inside and shiver. "Are you warm enough?" Cade asks, inching closer to me. I could use another sweatshirt, but because that's not an option, I nod. "There aren't a lot of beach parties on Halloween. The weather isn't usually this mild."

"This is mild?" I ask. "You mean for the North Pole?"

He laughs softly. "Are you gonna tell me anything about yourself?"

"On top of being uncomplicated, I'm also not that interesting."

"Oh, I don't know about that. The whole school is practically chomping at the bit to know more about you. The principal's mystery daughter," he says in a low, ominous voice. "There are a lot of people trying to figure you out."

"You're one to talk."

"What does that mean?"

"Is that a serious question?" I ask. "You're a total mystery to most of the kids at school. And you're either oblivious to that fact or you just don't care. Which is it?"

"I don't care."

"I think maybe you do. Otherwise, you wouldn't have

warned me not to listen to the rumors." Cade doesn't respond. "If you want to set the record straight, do it."

"What are you talking about?" He sounds annoyed.

"I'm right here. Tell me the truth." I can feel his eyes on me.

"Fine. What have you heard?"

Okay, I guess we're really doing this. Honestly, I didn't think Cade would be so willing to take me up on my offer. "Well—" I draw a deep breath. "Did your dad really kill someone?"

Cade exhales a bitter laugh. "No."

"But he's in jail?"

"Yup."

"What did he do? I'm sorry, is it okay to ask that?"

"Ask me anything you want." The context of his words seems genuine, but his tone is guarded, like he's not entirely ready for all the questions I might ask. Interrogating him was never my intention. I turn my focus once more toward the gameplay unfolding below us.

"My dad was convicted of embezzlement," Cade finally says. "He took a lot of money from a lot of people. They wanted it back." More shrieks and laughter rise up from the beach. "Next question?"

I stare at his profile in the darkness. "Okay. Do you sell drugs? Or hang out with people who do?"

"No." His answer is immediate and firm, and I feel as if I've put him on trial. He interprets my silence as doubt. "Do you not believe me?"

"No, it's not that."

"Come on, Bryant, spill it. You're holding out on me."

"It's just—a couple of weeks ago, at lunch, I saw you by the fence in the courtyard."

"Yeah? So?"

"You passed something to a guy on the other side. It looked, well, suspicious, I guess."

"That was Ash. I passed him a flash drive with some new songs I'd written on it. We played two of them earlier tonight."

A combination of relief and embarrassment washes over me. Why did I jump to conclusions? And why did I listen to Quinn? Cade's right; believing the rumors makes me just as bad as the people spreading them. "So, you didn't spend time in juvenile detention?" I ask, preparing to apologize for being so ridiculous.

"Uh, yeah. That one's true."

"Oh." The relief I'd felt moments ago oozes away from my body at warp speed. His sigh is audible, heavy with annoyance, and I don't know whether to blabber an apology or keep talking.

"Ask me why."

"You don't have to tell me," I say, convinced that if there were an award for being a complete idiot, I would be a mighty strong contender.

Cade's breathing deepens. He reaches down and scoops up a handful of sand, letting it slide through his fingers. "I went through a tough time after my dad went to prison. I guess you could say I didn't handle it very well."

Despite the pile of questions that pulse on the tip of my tongue, I press my lips tightly together, waiting for him to volunteer more information.

"I got mixed up with the wrong crowd. We did some stupid stuff."

"Like what?"

"Well, let's see." Cade tips back his head, looking skyward, as if the list is so long it has to be gathered from the clouds above.

"Please tell me you didn't kill anyone," I whisper.

"Is that what you heard?" he asks incredulously, then mutters, "Bastards!"

"No, no one said that." I'm at a loss for my next words when he takes my hand in his, single-handedly bringing my swirling thoughts to an abrupt halt. Did I just stop breathing? The warm tingling radiating across my chest most definitely confirms that my lungs are in perfect working order.

"I stole a car. Spray-painted a few things I shouldn't have. Nothing as serious as murder, I swear."

"Sorry," I blurt out.

"It's okay. I knew it was wrong, but I didn't care."

"Why not?"

"Because I was angry. And—because I was lost," Cade confesses. "Acting out was easier than accepting what had happened."

Bravely, I scoot closer to him. Without hesitation, he

puts his arm around me and pulls me into the shelter of his body. I rest my head in the crook of his neck. A soft whisper of musk tantalizes my senses and—oh my gosh, it feels like I just downed an energy drink.

"What finally changed?" I manage.

"I realized that wasn't who I was. I was trying so hard to rebel, and where did it get me? I wanted to hurt my dad. The last thing in this world I want is to be like him. I figured out that being reckless and stupid wasn't the answer. And I didn't want to hurt Macy anymore. I saw what it did to her when I started messing up."

"And the bad feelings you had toward your dad—did they just go away?"

He dips his head. "No. I hated him for what he did."

"How did you get over it?" I have to know how some-one that angry can move on; how such deep emotions can just vanish, or at least soften. Feelings like that, the kind that take root in your center, don't just go away. In my experience, they not only take hold, but they also grow, intertwining with the very depths of your soul until you're consumed.

"I haven't," he says. "Not yet."

"When was the last time you saw him?" At some point, I know he will stop me and say *enough with the questions,* but until he does, I press on.

Cade shakes his head. "Not since he was arrested. He's been writing me letters for the last three years."

"What does he say?" I ask.

"I don't know. I stopped opening them after the first one." He shifts uncomfortably at the memory, and I draw back. I can't help myself; I have to know.

"What was in the first letter?"

"It doesn't matter."

But it does matter. I can see that in the sudden change in Cade's demeanor. Whether he knows it or not, his body language tells a different story.

He clears his throat. "My turn."

Instinctively, I pull away and begin to get to my feet. "Come on; we need to focus on the game. Let's go claim our victory."

"Whoa," Cade says, securing his hold on my hand and gently tugging me back down to his side. "I don't think you understand how this works, Bryant. You can't play twenty questions with me and not give me anything in return."

I sigh heavily as any remnants of the euphoria I was basking in just moments ago dissolve. Unease builds slowly inside me at the thought of giving Cade control of the questions. But he's right; this one-sided quiz show isn't fair. Swallowing hard, I say, "Fine. What do you want to know?"

# CHAPTER FOURTEEN
## *Cade*

"Where's your mom?" I ask.

Paige's back straightens, as if someone just dropped a steel rod down her spine, and I'm convinced that if I weren't holding her hand, she would have bolted at my question. Instead, she stares out at the inky black horizon.

"She was killed by a drunk driver about a month and a half ago."

Surprise punches the air out of my lungs. "Shit. I'm sorry."

"Yeah, I get that a lot," she says, wrapping her free arm around herself. "She was a dancer. She was on her way home from our ballet studio when it happened." Paige pulls away from me, and her face falls into her hands. "Sorry," she whispers.

"You have nothing to be sorry for," I say, guilt washing over me in waves. It wasn't my intention to open such a gaping wound, but I didn't know it was there. Now I understand why Paige looks like she carries the weight of the world on her narrow shoulders.

"I just made you extremely uncomfortable, didn't I? Sorry for that," she says.

"If I'd known, I swear I wouldn't have asked."

"Don't worry about it."

"Are you okay?" That has to be the stupidest question. I mean, she clearly isn't okay, but the words tumble out before anything more reasonable can derail them.

Paige lifts one shoulder. "Sometimes."

"And how about the other times?"

"You want the truth?"

"Always."

She sighs. "Other times—it's like I'm drowning and I can't find my way to the surface." She gives another shrug. "I don't belong here, but this is my home until graduation. There's nothing I can do about it."

"Do you not get along with your dad?" I ask. With only my personal interactions with Principal Chapman as a reference, I can't imagine him as a father. Not a good one anyway. But for Paige's sake, I hope I'm wrong.

"I don't really know him," she answers. "I didn't even know he was my father before this happened." Paige shakes her head and attempts to stand again, but I grab her hand, preventing her escape. If I let her go, this moment will disappear. I can't let that happen.

Pointedly, I ask, "Do you wish you'd been with your mom that night?"

Even in the dim light, there is astonishment in her wide

eyes. "Why would you ask me that?"

I just asked her if she wishes she'd died beside her mother. And maybe on the surface that makes me an insensitive jerk, but I need to know the answer. I understand that level of pain. I know what it's like to lose the most vital person in your life, to wish for just one minute that you could make it all go away. I cock my head, attempting to see more through the darkness than what my eyes will allow.

Her silence is lost in the wind, but finally, she answers. "At first I did."

"And now?" I press, studying her face for a response.

"No. Not anymore."

"What changed?" Turning our hands over, I gently trace the soft lines of her palm with my index finger. Sensitive to my touch, her hand tenses and she shifts beside me.

"Oh my gosh, you ask more questions than Mrs. Hopkins," she breathes. "Maybe *you* should be the assistant principal."

I huff. "So, she's focusing on you now, is she? It's nice to see she's branching out."

"You too?" she asks, surprised and relieved.

"Are you kidding? I was her project for most of last year."

"She's intense," Paige says.

"That's because she was a psychologist at a high school in New York. She moved back here a couple years ago to take care of her parents."

"Why do you know so much about her?" she asks.

"That's weird."

"Yes, it is," I say. "But I think she was hoping that sharing about her life would get me to open up about myself. Psychologists are tricky like that." Paige nods and leans in, and I steal the opportunity to pull her close once more. "Turkey on wheat," I whisper against her temple.

She stares up at me, an odd smile parting her lips. "Turkey on wheat? What's that?"

"That's Mrs. Hopkins's favorite sandwich," I say. "Bring that to your lunch meetings and offer her half and she'll be putty in your hands."

"Seriously?"

"Well, you may have to throw in a few insights into your soul, but if you do that, I can practically guarantee those meetings with her will be more like a book club than the third degree." She laughs, and the sweet sound is like a bolt of warmth against the wind. I want to hear her laugh again.

"That's all it takes, huh?"

"I told you—not my first rodeo with that woman." I'm just about to pull Paige tighter against my side when she abruptly stands, and whatever this is that's between us washes away with the night air.

"I think the game is almost over," she says. "Time to swoop in."

I don't move. Instead, I gaze up at Paige. She shoves her hands into the pockets of my sweatshirt, looking around uncomfortably like we didn't just spill out our guts to each other.

"That's all I get? I think you owe me one more question."

"I think your math calculations are a little off," she says.

"I think you're brushing me off. Which isn't fair because it's still my turn."

"Maybe next time," Paige says softly.

I raise my hands in offered submission, but surrendering isn't part of my game plan. What I want is to know more about this girl. This mix of hurricane and humility that I've never experienced before. She's sassy and self-reliant, tenacious and timid, and beneath her moments of boldness, deep down where she thinks no one can see, this girl is wounded.

Pulling myself to my feet, I reach for her, sliding an arm around her waist. She draws in a sharp breath as my palms press against her lower back and pull her close. The tension in her spine releases, and she tips her head to meet my gaze. I take that as permission and lean in. With my lips just inches from her ear, I whisper, "Next time." Then, as if to seal my promise, my lips skim over her temple before ghosting along her jaw. And as I find my way back to Paige's parted lips, pressing my mouth to hers in a heated kiss, she melts against me.

Releasing a shuttered sigh, she nods in agreement.

# CHAPTER FIFTEEN

## *Paige*

"All right, spill it," Quinn says. "*All* of it."

We left the party at close to two o'clock, and we are now sitting in Quinn's room as she, Sam and Zoey beg for information about Cade. Quinn unloads an armful of snacks that she gathered from the kitchen onto her desk, and Sam quickly rips into a bag of salt-and-vinegar potato chips. I catch Quinn's eye, and she gives me a slight nod, confirmation that she's checked on her mom and all is well. Well, as good as it can be, given what Mrs. Talbot is going through. But I feel better nonetheless.

As I predicted, the girls are eager to analyze what my night with Cade means, in that sort of BuzzFeed quiz kind of way I've come to expect from them.

"He *so* likes you!" Zoey says. "He couldn't take his eyes off you all night!"

"Are you going to see him again?" Sam asks.

I flop onto the soft carpet and stare up at Quinn's ceiling. The image of Cade's dark eyes gazing at me beneath thick lashes as he gave me the sweatshirt off his body is burned into my brain. "He's a nice guy."

A foot kicks me in the leg. "Oh, come on! That's all we get?" Quinn asks. "Uh-uh. I did not sit through that whole party with Gio pawing at me just so you could say 'he's a nice guy.'"

I sit up, and Quinn pins me with impatient eyes. "I thought you said you liked Gio."

"Nooo, I said he was cute. There's a difference. Every time I tried to start a conversation with a college guy, he butted in. It was so annoying!"

"We just talked," I tell them.

"That's it?" Zoey asks, her tone smothered in disappointment. "Just *talked*?"

"Come on, you guys. I just met Cade. And besides, Quinn had me convinced he might be dangerous, so forgive me if I was a little cautious."

"Is he?" Sam asks, her eyes twinkling. "Is he dangerous?"

I laugh. "No. He's—nice."

Quinn rolls her eyes. "Yeah, yeah, yeah. You said that already."

Before I can offer a rebuttal, the three of them launch into chatter, all talking over one another at once. Apparently, they no longer need me for this conversation.

The truth is, I'm not entirely sure what to make of Cade Matthews. I never imagined for one minute that he and I would spend most of the evening together, or that he would be so easy to talk to. But more than that, I never thought I would share so much of myself with him, or that he would open up to me so quickly the way he did. It's all a little strange—and exhilarating at the same time.

"He did ask her to be his partner for beach tag," Zoey reminds them.

"And before they won the game by cheating—yeah, don't think we didn't notice," Quinn says. "They were off together hiding for a long time. *In. The. Dark.*" She levels me with an expectant stare.

"First off, we didn't cheat. Our victory was entirely strategic. And secondly, you three are crazy."

"I knew it, you're blushing! Something did happen!"

"Okay!" I throw up my hands in defeat, pinking up all over again at the memory of Cade's lips on my skin. "There is a good possibility that I like him. Okay? Probably more than I should. So, can we please stop analyzing this? It's embarrassing."

"That's so exciting!" Zoey leans down from her perch on the bed and gives me a contorted, one-armed hug.

"Cade hasn't been interested in any girls at school for a long time, and believe me, he's had plenty of offers. So, the fact that Paige got his attention has to count for something," Sam says. "Unless—" She has my full attention with that one, simple word.

"Unless what?" Zoey asks before I can.

"Well, unless the principal's daughter is just one big conquest to him. Which I'm not saying you are," Sam says quickly. "But maybe—just be careful. That's all."

Is she serious? My eyes shoot to Quinn's for confirmation that Sam's warning sounds as far-fetched to her as it does to me. Her gaze narrows on me in thought, then she shrugs. Great. So much for the reassurance.

Am I just a conquest to Cade Matthews?

"When will you see him again?" Zoey asks, but she doesn't wait for me to answer. "Make it soon. You don't want to give this thing time to cool off."

"Your dad is gonna freak, you know that, right?" Quinn finally asks. "I'm happy for you, but I'm pretty sure you're screwed." Her words silence the room, like a metaphorical mic drop, and their trio of empathetic gazes swing like a pendulum between one another before landing squarely on me. She's right.

I'm still thinking about that when I finally fall asleep close to four a.m., and again on the drive home later that morning. The house is quiet when I unlock the back door. As I reach the top of the stairs, I hear the muffled sounds of a guitar coming from Tanner's room. Leaving my things on the floor outside my own door, I head down the hallway. I'm about to knock when something heavy cracks against the door from the inside. I tap my knuckles lightly against the wood and cautiously push open the door. Tanner sits on his bed, apparently surprised to see me. He immediately puts down his guitar.

"Keep playing," I say. "It sounds good."

He rolls his eyes and snorts. "No, it doesn't. I'm pretty much borderline between awful and suck fest right now."

He didn't invite me in, but I step farther into the room. A music book lies crumpled facedown at my feet, its pages bent from where it hit the floor. The wall above his bed is covered with posters of athletes. Clothes are strewn about, obscuring half the floor, and an assortment of video game boxes and controllers are in a pile by the console next to a small TV on a corner table.

"Cool room," I say, scooping up the music book and placing it on the dresser. This is pretty much what my cousin Tyler's bedroom looked like while we were growing up. Only he had a couple of posters of half-naked super-models tacked up on his walls, much to the dismay of Aunt Faye.

"Is that a Fender?" I ask, motioning to his guitar.

Tanner shrugs. "Yeah. How did you know?"

"I have a friend who plays guitar," I say.

Tanner plucks a string. "I bet she's better at it than I am."

I smile at the thought of Cade playing with his band last night. "Actually, *he's* amazing," I say. "But I'm sure you are, too. Play something for me."

If I've ever wondered what horror looks like on a thir-teen-year-old boy's face, it's staring back at me.

"Oh, come on. I bet you're better than you give yourself credit for. Play something."

I take a seat in the chair across from him. Tanner calcu-lates his options, then sighs and rolls his eyes again. If eye rolling was a measurable job skill, this kid would be destined for success.

Finally, he scoops up the guitar with an exasperated sigh. His dark hair falls over his forehead as he stares down at the neck of the instrument. Placing his fingers just so, he lays his pick to the strings and begins to strum. Not bad. Not necessarily good either, but I remind myself that he's just a kid and still learning. I will, however, give him an A+ for effort. He's concentrating so hard, his scowl deepens each time he plucks the wrong string. When he's finished, he shoots me an "I-told-you-so" look of disgust. "See? Suck fest."

"How long have you been taking lessons?"

Tanner shrugs again. "About a year."

I press my lips into a tight line and nod. "Well, I think you're doing great. It just takes practice."

"I do practice," he says, his words laced with annoyance. "But at this rate, I'm never gonna get to play in a band."

"Is that what you want to do?" He nods. "I get that," I say, and just for the embarrassment factor, I add, "Girls *love* guys who play guitar in bands." I accomplish my mission; his face turns three shades of red. "Look, I think I can help you."

He deadpans, as if I've just told him there's no such thing as bedtimes, homework or video games. "You play guitar?"

"No, but my friend I told you about is incredible at it. I could ask him to help you." I don't know what Cade will think about my offer, but I feel inclined to help Tanner. I've liked this kid since day one. He's not always trying to cozy up to me like his parents.

Tanner's skepticism returns for an encore performance. "He wouldn't mind?"

"I'll ask him. In the meantime, you just keep practicing." Another eye roll. Superb.

When I'm back in my room, I flop down on my bed, and it takes me only a few moments to realize I'm smiling. Smiling at thoughts of Cade offering me his sweatshirt and holding my hand as naturally as if he'd done so a million times. He'd asked me questions in a way that had seemed unobtrusive and yet had been so personal. When Sam's words attempt to creep in and derail my euphoria, I quickly dismiss them. She doesn't know Cade. Well, truthfully, I'm not sure I know him either, but he seems genuine.

The gossip circulating about Cade's past is more salacious and exciting than the truth could ever be, and I'm not surprised that the tall tales have had such a successful shelf life. Rumors are like biting into a doughnut, sweet and gooey, and no matter how many you consume, you always want more. The truth, on the other hand—it's more like kale salad. Everyone knows it's healthier, but it's not nearly as tasty. It upsets me that people in this town judge Cade so unfairly. By his own admittance, he's made mistakes, but we all have. No one is a saint, especially those who try to act like they are. Cade told me that the talk going around about him doesn't bother him, but I don't believe that. Hurtful gossip is difficult to brush off.

Here's the thing: I think I like this guy. I mean, *really* like him. If I had to do tonight all over again—lie to Jay and go to the party without his approval to see a boy he warned me to stay away from—I would. I wouldn't think twice about it. And that's not like me at all.

There's a light tapping on the door. I roll over and sit up. "Come in."

Jay appears in the doorway, a coffee cup in one hand and a folded-up newspaper tucked under his arm. "I thought I heard you come home. Did you have a good time?"

"It was fun," I say. "But we didn't get a lot of sleep."

"Shocking," Jay answers, amused. "How did the studying session go? Were you able to help Quinn?" I wonder if he ever loses that principal-like tone.

"I did my best, but I don't think the Department of Defense will be calling her to help them calculate field coordinates anytime soon."

Jay laughs and takes a sip from his cup. "Well, I'm sure the help was appreciated. Get some rest."

When he's gone, I fall back onto the pillows with a sigh and stare at the closed door. If my mother were here, I wouldn't have to hide anything from her. She'd plop right down cross-legged on the end of my bed and demand I tell her everything. She wouldn't be able to contain her excitement for me, and she'd want to know more about Cade, her blue eyes dancing with anticipation. I would tell her everything, even about the kiss, and I wouldn't be embarrassed about it. I don't want to share any of that with Connie, and definitely not with Jay.

Quinn is right. I am screwed unless I can keep whatever is happening between Cade and me a secret. It's ironic really. Secret-keeping is what landed me here in the first place. My mother kept me a secret from Jay, and now it's all one big mess.

My cell phone buzzes from the nightstand, and I grab for it. I don't recognize the number, but my insides flutter at the words on the screen.

*Meet me at Java Joe's tomorrow at noon. There's something I want to show you.—C.*

Without hesitation, I type *OK* and hit Send.

# CHAPTER SIXTEEN

## Paige

"You want me to get on—*that*?" I stare at the big, silver motorcycle, then my alarm-filled eyes shoot to Cade's, which are bright with amusement.

"Is that a problem?" he asks, holding out a black helmet. "Don't tell me you've never been on a motorcycle before."

I shake my head.

"Then today's your lucky day, Bryant," he says, placing the helmet on my head and fastening the strap beneath my chin with gentle fingers. All at once, the nerve endings in my skin come alive, and I'm hyperaware that someone just painted a thick layer of anxiety down my spine.

"Relax; I'm an excellent driver." He swings a long leg over the bike and settles in, putting on a helmet identical to mine. My eyes scan the parking lot and the windows of the coffeehouse.

Cade's eyes dawn with an unsettling revelation. "Are you afraid to be seen with me?"

My lips part in surprise. "No, of course not. It's just—"

"You're worried that someone will see us and tell your dad, right?"

"No," I say again, but I feel a twinge of guilt at the lie. It's not just the fact that Jay would hit the ceiling if he knew I was about to climb on the back of Cade's motorcycle. It's that I'm no longer convinced this is a good idea. "Where exactly are we going?"

"You'll see," he says with that crooked smile that does something exhilarating to my insides, but absolutely nothing to quell the wave of unease lurking underneath. "Come on, Bryant, trust me. I'll take good care of you. Scout's honor."

"You were a Boy Scout?" I ask, skepticism wrapped around each word.

Cade's mischievous grin is my answer. "Nope." He offers me his hand, palm up, and I stare at it as if there's either an invisible treasure waiting for me or one of those trick buzzers that will send a shock right to my core. I shift from one foot to the other as impulse and reason wage a tug of war inside me. *Oh, screw it, you only live once, right?* I take his hand, and in one gentle pull, he hoists me up onto the seat behind him.

"Hold on to me tight," he says over his shoulder. I do as I'm told as the bike powerfully roars to life, the vibrations shooting through me. Cade pulls out of the lot and onto the road.

When we hit the highway, it feels as if we are flying. I have no idea where we're going, and honestly, I don't care. I wrap my arms around Cade's firm waist like steel clamps as the air whooshes past us and adrenaline bubbles like fizzy soda in my stomach. I've never felt so completely alive. That alone is worth the entire ride. I'm not much of a risk-taker, but right now, I am devouring this sensation of recklessness, of not knowing what's around each bend or where we will end up. I don't care that I have no control over this moment, that it could all end in a heartbeat, in a spectacularly disastrous fashion. All that matters to me at this moment is the guy I'm pressed against and holding on to so tightly he's probably having a tough time drawing a full breath. The connection between us is electric. I have no idea where it came from or what it means, only that I am undeniably addicted to it. And that has me scared out of my freaking mind.

I'm disappointed when Cade slows the bike at a turnoff and steers it up a winding road that leads to a gravel lot. I catch sight of the small entrance sign as we pass: "Devil's Eye Viewpoint."

When he kills the engine, he removes his helmet and runs a hand through his hair. "This is it." I steady my hands on his shoulders as I slide off the bike, then he climbs off behind me and unfastens my helmet. He brushes a strand of hair off my forehead. "Look at that, you made it in one piece."

I take in our surroundings. There are a couple of other vehicles in the lot, parked close to a path that leads into a canopy of trees.

"Where are we?" I ask.

"It's a nature area. You'll love it. It's got a killer view," Cade says, winking at me.

"We're hiking?" I ask, not exactly sure how I feel about that. He nods, releasing a small backpack that's tethered to the rear of his bike and slipping his arms through the straps. I glance down at my impressively white pair of Converses. Not the best choice of footwear for this excursion, but it will have to do. "Okay." I sigh. "Lead the way."

We make our way up the trail, which quickly grows in incline, and my breathing labors as I work to keep up with Cade's long strides. We see a few people on the trail. First, a middle-aged couple with walking sticks is carefully making their way down the damp terrain, and Cade greets them politely as they pass. Then, a second couple, who look to be younger, in their twenties maybe, passes us up from behind. They're moving at an impressive pace. After we've been at it for about twenty minutes, Cade stops.

"Are we here? Is this it?" But that can't be right. We're surrounded by trees, and the amazing view he promised me is nowhere to be found.

"Almost. Just a little farther."

I begin walking again, resuming the ascent up the trail, when Cade snags my hand. "This way." My eyes follow his outstretched arm, but I'm confused to see that the path doesn't veer that way. He smiles. "Trust me." That's the third time in forty-eight hours that he's asked me to trust him. I fall into step behind him as he pushes through some low branches and into the lush greenness. There's a path, but it's apparently not as heavily traveled as the main trail. I'm careful not to trip, stepping gingerly over roots that jut up from the earth and ducking my head to avoid low-hanging limbs.

Finally, I hear Cade announce over his shoulder, "This is it." He pushes away the last branches, and we step out onto a rocky ledge that overlooks the coastline and the vast waters of the Pacific Ocean.

It's just as he promised: spectacular. The sky is the color of a lead pipe, and a web of ferociously dark clouds ring the horizon. But below, the blue-green ocean stretches endlessly, casting a puffy, white foam along the shore as lines of waves roll in almost on top of one another. On a clear day, this spot has to be as close to heaven as you can get.

To my left is the highway, rolling and snaking its way along the sharp, rocky ledges that rise up protectively above it, kissing the coastline in both directions. The cars below look like ants crawling along in broken lines. The crisp, swirling wind mutes the sounds of the surf, interrupted by squawking seagulls circling overhead. I close my eyes and inhale deeply, tasting the sea air.

"I feel so free up here," I say softly, then I gasp when firm hands grab my hips and tug me backward. My eyes shoot open, and I whirl. Cade immediately drops his hands.

"Sorry; you were standing a little too close to the edge."

"I'm not going to jump, if that's what you're worried about."

His eyes sweep the ground, and instead of denying it, Cade shrugs off his backpack, sets it on a rock and unzips it. He reaches over his head and tugs off his sweatshirt, nearly taking his T-shirt along with it. In those few, brief seconds, his lean back is exposed, and I get an eyeful of the long, swirling strands of black ink that snake down his taut skin in an ornamental design, stretching from his left shoulder blade to his waist. As he tosses the sweatshirt onto the ground beside the pack and tugs his shirt into place, I catch a glimpse of another tattoo trailing along the inside of his biceps. There are words inked on his skin, but I can't make them out.

I snap my eyes to the skyline before he catches me staring. "How did you find this place?"

He pulls two bottles of water from the backpack and hands me one. "It was an accident. A couple of months ago, I was hiking to the lookout point when something in the bushes caught my eye. I took a closer look and found this place. I don't think very many people know it's here."

I guzzle the water and wipe my mouth, gazing out at the horizon. "What is this about?" I finally ask.

Cade appears puzzled. "What are you talking about?"

"This." I circle my index finger in the air between us. "Why did you bring me here?"

"Why did you agree to come?"

"Why are you always answering my questions with other questions?" I demand.

"Like you're doing to me right now?"

Oh, good grief. Cade's impossible. I cross my arms over my chest and square my shoulders. "Look, I shared some really personal stuff with you the other night. I need to know if that was just a joke to you."

"Are you serious?" he asks. "In case you've forgotten, I shared some personal stuff with you too."

Oh, I remember, but I'm still not entirely sure why. Then again, there's a lot about this guy that I don't understand. I yank free the hair tie that's wrapped around my wrist and quickly pull my windblown locks into a ponytail. We stare at each other like we're each waiting for the other to make the next move. But honestly, I have no idea what that step is. Only that I don't want to get hurt by this guy.

"I don't want you to kiss me again—if that's what this is about."

Cade lets loose a soft laugh that's filled with astonishment and what I think is a twinge of irritation. "Don't flatter yourself. You did me a favor when you bailed me out after the fight. I thought maybe we could be friends, that's all. But if you're not cool with that, we can leave right now."

"No," I say, the word shooting past my lips before I give it permission. "Forget I said anything. We can be friends. I'm sorry, it's just—"

Cade holds up a hand. "Forget it, Bryant. You don't have to explain. I'm guessing you decided to listen to the gossip after all."

Now I'm irritated. "No, I told you, I don't listen to that stuff. And stop calling me by my last name. I'm not some dude in the locker room. I'm a girl, and my name is Paige." Staring at the churning ocean below, a cool raindrop pelts my cheek. I tip back my head as more drops make contact.

Cade takes my hand and leads me back to the edge of the tree line, where the canopy offers some protection. He claims space on a large rock, motioning for me to do the same just as the sky opens up.

I'm not sure how long we sit like that, but it's long enough that the silence between us threatens to drive me mad. Finally, Cade asks, "Are we cool now?"

I tap my foot and scrub a hand over the back of my neck, kneading at the tension pulsing just beneath my skin. "Yeah, we're cool."

"Good," he says with relief.

"Thanks for bringing me up here," I say, delayed embarrassment making it impossible for me to meet his eyes. "Even though right now you're probably wishing you hadn't."

Cade cocks his head and studies me. "Why are you always telling me what I think?"

"I don't know," I say. "I'm kind of in a weird place right now. Making people uncomfortable seems to be a new talent of mine. I don't seem to make a lot of sense these days."

"You're fine," Cade says.

"Debatable," I murmur to the trees over my shoulder as

I slide off the rock and move to put a little more distance between us. "Okay, enough with the heavy stuff. If you were trapped on a deserted island and you were only allowed to have one item with you, what would it be?"

"That's easy," Cade says. "A boat."

I roll my eyes. "Cheater."

"How is that cheating? You asked—"

"Okay, okay." I hold up my hand. "Chocolate chip cookies or cheesecake?"

"Definitely cookies."

"Romantic comedies or horror films?"

Cade deadpans. "Please. Horror films."

"Soda or coffee?"

"Hmmm," he says, his brow narrowing in thought. "That's tough."

"It's not an SAT question, just pick one," I say.

He shakes his head. "Can't do it. Gotta have both." I let that one slide because, truthfully, I have to agree with him.

"My turn," Cade says. "Dogs or cats?"

As much as Kitty Poppins and I have bonded since my arrival in Mystic, I say, "Dogs."

"Football or baseball?"

I tilt my head from side to side. "I'm gonna have to go with baseball."

"Planes, trains or automobiles?" Cade asks, his eyes twinkling.

"Automobiles."

"And why's that?"

"I've never been on a train," I say, then I make a sour face. "And I'm not a fan of flying." Cade laughs, and I know he's thinking about our debacle in baggage claim. I will never live that down. "But my mom was the queen of epic road trips." Immediately, that familiar ache pinches me deep in my chest, just as it does each time memories of Mom resurface.

"Tell me where you've been." He seems genuinely interested.

A warm smile melts across my lips as I think about the dozens of random destinations the Bryant girls have visited across the country since I could walk. They spill out of my memory bank, and I grab at each one, trying to hold on to it with my entire being. "We took a road trip every summer. My mom liked to visit off-the-map kinds of places. We've been all across the United States. Well, except Alaska and Hawaii. She didn't like to fly either. Besides that, Wyoming and Louisiana are the only other states we never made it to."

"Why not there?" he asks.

My smile falters. "I guess we just ran out of time."

Cade slides off the rock and moves to stand in front of me. The rain has stopped. "Tell me about your mom."

Everything in my body threatens to shut down, as if he just pulled the fire alarm on my soul. "What was she like?"

Unable to look him in the eyes or grasp a cohesive sentence that consists of more than three words, I stare at the dirt and mumble, "She was amazing."

Cade's tenor is soft when he asks, "What made her

amazing?"

"How much time do you have?"

Leaning in, he whispers, "As much time as it takes."

Where did this guy come from? As I contemplate how best to take a chisel to his simple but ginormous question, I know that answering him will require me to share memories I've guarded so tightly. I'm not sure how, but I do it, and something strange begins to fill the space between us. All of a sudden, there are too many words fighting for position on my lips, and each one of them is both endearing and sharp to the touch. I haven't talked about Mom with anyone since I was exiled to Mystic. I didn't want to share my sacred memories—they're the only thing I have left. Until this very moment, I hadn't been sure anyone was worthy of them. I talk, and I share, until that suffocating pang flares in my chest. I inhale sharply at the gut-wrenching sensation that I am teetering on the edge of oblivion. And if I utter just one more word—admit that there are days when it feels like someone reached inside me and scraped my heart right out of my chest with an ice cream scooper—there's a real possibility that I might slip right over the edge and disappear.

No one can truly understand how wonderful my mother was. How could they? The truth is, I didn't even fully understand that until she was gone. And now it's too late. She's gone, and I'm alone, and there are so many things I want to say to her, but I will never have the chance. There isn't a lonelier place than where I am at this very moment.

Cade squeezes my hand, and I blink up at him. "I wish I could have met her."

I slide my hand out of his and emerge from the tree line, walking farther out onto the ledge, but stopping a safe distance from the edge. The chilly wind swirls my ponytail, and I draw my jacket tighter around myself. I can feel Cade behind me.

"When we were on the beach the other night, you said you were only here until graduation. What did you mean by that?" he asks.

*The guy misses nothing.*

"Moving to Mystic wasn't my choice," I say. "For some insane reason, it's what my mom wanted; that's why I'm here. But I'm only staying until I turn eighteen. Then I'll be legally free of Jay."

Cade steps up beside me. "Is it that bad here? With your dad, I mean?"

I avoid his eyes and instead stare out at the churning white caps of the swirling ocean below. "Don't call him that," I say.

"Where will you go when you leave? Back to California?"

For the first time, I realize I don't know what I will do after I leave here. I suppose I always assumed I would return to San Diego, but what's there for me now? Aunt Faye, of course, although I can't live with her forever. Six months ago, I'd planned on a future dancing professionally, but that's no longer an option. Now, I'm lost in the echo of

Cade's question, immediately aware that I have no idea what my future holds.

"I'm not really sure," I say, giving verbal confirmation to my thoughts. Without warning, Cade pulls me close and wraps his arms tightly around me. I expel a breath against his collarbone, sinking into his warm embrace and allowing him to hold me together. When he finally releases me and steps back, I feel exposed, and I wish I could take it all back. I rub at my upper arms. "What? No more questions?"

He shakes his head. "Not right now."

"Then can I ask you one more?"

"Have at it," Cade replies. "I'll tell you anything you want to know."

I guess we'll see if he really means that.

# CHAPTER SEVENTEEN
## Cade

P aige guzzles the remainder of her water and then fidgets with the bottle. "Why do you and Dane hate each other so much?"

I kick at a small rock and send it flying over the ledge. "It wasn't always like that. He was my best friend." Paige blinks back surprise. "Yeah, it's hard for me to believe, too. Seems like a lifetime ago." I smooth a hand down my face, knowing that I owe Paige the same honesty she's given to me. It wasn't easy for her to talk about her mom, and part of me feels terrible that I keep asking her to do it.

"My mom died when I was thirteen," I say. She doesn't react, which confirms that she already knew that. Probably just part of the gossip that continues to circulate about me. "After she was gone, my dad threw himself into his work. A few weeks after the funeral, Macy returned to college in Arizona. She needed to finish the semester, and then she was going to transfer to a school closer to home. By then, my dad was practically living in Portland, where his office was based. I think spending time with me reminded him too much of my mom, and he couldn't deal with it. Because he was hardly ever here, he arranged for me to move in with Dane and his family."

This is harder to talk about than I thought it would be. I shove my hands into the pockets of my jeans, balling them into fists. "My dad was the Sloanes' financial adviser, and the family is really well off, so I'm guessing he was good at his job. What nobody knew was that he was skimming off the top. Had been for years. When someone finally noticed—" I shrug. "My dad went to prison and I was no longer welcome in the Sloanes' home."

Surprise and pity mingle across Paige's face. "What did you do?"

"I slept in back alleys, in unlocked garages, wherever I could find a dry roof over my head. And I found my own trouble," I say flatly. "It wasn't hard. As I said, I got messed up with the wrong people and did a lot of things I'm not proud of." I meet her eyes and see the sympathy in them. "But I paid the consequences. I just lost a lot in the process."

"I'm sorry," she says. "That must have been tough."

"The thing is, I was only fourteen when my dad went to prison. Most of the kids at school don't remember exactly what happened. But even though most of them couldn't tell you what he did, or even what I did for that matter, they're awesome at creating rumors and spreading them around."

"What about Hannah?" Paige asks.

"What about her?"

"Who is she?" She looks both curious and uncomfortable at her own question.

"Hannah is Dane's sister," I say.

Paige's brows pinch together, as if she's trying to comprehend what I just said. "So, did you—? Were you two together?"

"No," I say. "It wasn't like that. Hannah got messed up in her own stuff. But what's the saying—misery loves company? When her parents disowned her, I was really all she had. I never judged her. And even though I wasn't in a good place myself, I tried to help her. But somehow, the whole family blames me for her mistakes. So, let's just say I'm not a big fan of Dane or his lacrosse buddies." I lock eyes with her and firmly say, "If you like him, you and I have no business being friends."

"I don't like him. Not like that," Paige says, and I exhale the breath I'm holding as a surprising wave of relief washes through me. She reaches up and runs a finger lightly across my temple, touching the edge of my eyebrow.

"Where did you get this scar?"

"I got cut in a gang fight." Her eyebrows lift in horror, and she straightens. The girl with the biting comebacks is suddenly speechless. I hold my stoic expression as long as I can, but as her discomfort magnifies, it breaks apart, and I laugh. "Paige, I'm kidding. I fell off the top of my bunk bed when I was six."

I laugh harder when she punches me in the shoulder.

"You're the worst!"

"No, you just have a terrible habit of believing everything you hear, no matter who says it. That's clearly not working for you."

Paige rolls her pale green eyes, but despite her best effort, she can't hold on to her annoyance. She laughs. And then she does something that catches me off guard. Reaching up onto her tiptoes, she cups my face in her hands and pulls me down until her lips press against mine in a firm kiss. When she finally pulls back, I'm dumbfounded, and Paige looks undeniably smug.

"I thought you didn't want me to kiss you," I say.

"You're not kissing me," she clarifies. "I'm kissing you."

I laugh again. "Gotta love technicalities," I say before pulling her against me and pressing my mouth to hers, leaving no doubt that, this time, I'm the instigator. And everything big and heavy that was wedged between us just moments ago—the loss of our moms, the anger I have toward my father and the betrayal of my best friend—somehow dissolves away. I don't think about how broken Paige is, or that maybe I'm not the guy who is capable of fixing her. Here, in this moment with her, none of that matters.

"I want you to do something for me," I say.

"Anything," she breathes.

I stare into her eyes, not sure I should ask the question that pulses on the tip of my tongue. But I need to know if this girl is the real deal. I need to know if she's really in this.

And I need her to know that, despite the rumors she's heard, I'm not playing around. "I want you to tell your dad about us. I want you to tell him we're friends."

Paige's jaw goes slack and her body, which was alive in my arms just moments ago, falls completely still.

# CHAPTER EIGHTEEN
## *Paige*

Things just got complicated in a whole new way.

It doesn't matter what I do or where I go, I can't stop thinking about Cade's request. His harmless-on-paper request that I tell Jay that we're—what exactly? Friends? Hanging out? Dating? But does a game of beach tag and a couple of soul-spilling sessions constitute dating? Well, there was the kiss. *Three kisses to be exact.* The memory of each one is practically burned onto my lips, and yet that doesn't negate the fact that I am freaking out about the thought of telling Jay that I am hanging out with Cade in any way—whether it be dating, kissing or doing the crossword puzzle on the back of the menu at Java Joe's while we wait for our coffee. Under any other circumstances, telling Jay that Cade and I are dating, kissing, crossword puzzling or participating in some other fill-in-the-blank activity like, I don't know, underwater basket weaving perhaps, shouldn't be a difficult task. But because Jay made it clear that he disapproves of me being in any proximity to Cade—that's kind of a problem.

I'm not sure how to handle this, and I've spent an inordinate amount of time thinking about it. What would happen if I did tell Jay? What would happen if I just kind of forgot to share that information? What if I ask Cade to rescind his request and instead ask me to do something a little easier like, say, get a root canal? I'm mulling over all these options the following night when Cade invites me to catch a movie downtown with him and Jared after they get off work at the garage. Quinn tags along because she's become my alibi, and because I want her to get to know Cade and his friends. I need her to see for herself that the rumors floating around about him are not true.

"What's up with you tonight?" she whispers in my ear. At that moment, I realize that, despite the high-speed chase that's unfolding in surround sound on the large screen in front of us, I'm staring down into the popcorn bucket, entirely consumed by my own drama. I shrug her off, and she doesn't question me further.

By the following week, I still haven't worked up the nerve to talk to Jay, even though I've had plenty of opportunities. Somehow, I've managed to convince myself that no time has really been the right time. I mean, springing something like this on him could cause all kinds of problems. He could have a heart condition I know nothing about. Cade has asked me a couple times how Jay reacted when I told him the news, but I just shrugged it off and told him we need to give Jay some time to warm up to the idea. Yup, I'm definitely going to hell on a liar's scholarship.

My guilt is compounded when Quinn and I stop in at Sandpiper Lanes on Friday night to hear Cade's band play. The bowling alley offers live music on the weekends. There's a decent-size crowd, and the guys are killing it. I smile each time Cade catches my eye from the edge of the small stage, but I'm racked with guilt over skirting my promise to him. It's the only thing he's asked me to do for him and yet it feels like he's asking me to step in front of a firing squad.

"If someone had told me that you would be dating Cade Matthews, I wouldn't have believed them. Not for a second," Quinn says, taking a sip of her soda. From her seat beside me, she's studying Cade like he's a life form she's never seen before.

"Why is it so hard to believe?" I ask.

Quinn shakes her head. "I just never pictured you as being his type."

"And what exactly does that mean?" A pang of defensiveness rises inside me at the thought that, in Quinn's eyes or anyone else's for that matter, I might not be worthy of a guy like Cade.

"Relax, I didn't mean to offend you," she says, grabbing a French fry from the basket in front of us. "All I'm saying is that you two come from very different places. You have to know that. And I, for one, never thought I'd be hanging out with Cade and his friends night after night because my bestie has a thing for him."

I want to dispute her words, but I can't. Because I do have a thing for Cade. I'm not entirely sure what to label it yet, but it's definitely sizable. My eyes roam down Cade's tall frame as he plays his guitar beside Jared with a huge smile plastered on his face. "I think Cade and I are more alike than you know."

"What do you guys even talk about?"

"What do you mean, what do we talk about? We talk about—*stuff.*"

"Stuff?" Quinn stifles a laugh, then her twinkling eyes narrow mischievously on me. "Is that what the kids are calling it these days? I'm sorry, but I'm going to need more specifics on that one."

"Nice try, but not happening," I say.

"Fine. But if I ever land some hot guy with a mysterious past, don't expect me to share the steamy details with you either." She snatches another French fry, waggles her eyebrows, and we dissolve into laughter. Because if she lands a hot guy, in any capacity, we both know she will tell me all about it.

✧　✧　✧

On Tuesday, I sleep through my alarm and nearly miss my first class. Then, if that isn't bad enough, I stumble my way through a horrendous pop quiz in calculus in disastrous fashion. And because I apparently can't catch a break, and the morning wasn't already complicated enough, I'm running late for Spanish when Dane corners me at my locker.

"You and I need to talk."

"Excuse me?"

"Matthews. Whatever you're thinking, you need to stop."

I clutch my textbook to my chest. "That's none of your business." I'm less concerned with Dane's temper tantrum and more over who else knows Cade and I are together. We've stayed pretty low key since the beach party. We don't have any classes together, and when I sit with Quinn and the usual crowd in the cafeteria or in the courtyard, Cade doesn't join us. I know darn well it's because of his I-hate-you-more relationship with Dane, so I've taken to spending many of my lunch hours in the library, tucked away at a table in the back corner of the room, where Cade and I can hang out and avoid unwanted attention. And when I say "unwanted attention," I mean Jay's watchful eyes. I am fully aware that *that* pretty much secures me the title of wimp by any definition of the word, but for now, I'm okay with it.

"Look," Dane says, placing an outstretched hand against the frame of my open locker and caging me against the door. He momentarily mutes his tirade as two girls scurry past us just as the bell rings. Late again. *Fantastic.* When they're down the hall, Dane narrows his eyes. "You have no idea what you're dealing with."

I duck under his arm and close my locker, forcing him to step back quickly. I turn to go, but he grabs my arm. "Let go of me," I command, unease prickling along my spine.

Dane immediately releases his hold.

"Sorry," he says. "But Matthews is playing you." I shake my head and glance at my watch. "I don't know what he's told you, but you can't trust him."

*Not this again.* "Save it, Dane. I know all about what happened between you two," I say. "And I know about Hannah."

A muscle thrums along his jaw. "Matthews doesn't know how to tell the truth. You need to watch yourself."

A burst of heat floods my cheeks at his warning. "I'm not listening to this." I turn once more to go, but the dude is fast, whirling and sliding right into my path.

"Get a clue, Paige! You're nothing more than a game to him," he says, his words charged with disgust. "Matthews is just trying to piss off Principal Chapman and stir up trouble. And what do you think is the easiest way for him to do that?"

I level my glare on him. "If I didn't know any better, I'd say you're jealous of Cade."

Dane shrinks back, and his eyes darken. "Don't be stupid."

Stunned, I swallow hard, and this time when I attempt to step around him, he lets me go. I'm both relieved and utterly frazzled by what just happened. I try to shake it off, like his words didn't faze me, but there's wobbling in my knees, and my heart is beating at twice it's usual pace.

As I reach the end of the hallway, Dane calls out, "Don't say I didn't warn you."

✧ ✧ ✧

On Sunday night, Cade invites me over to his house to have dinner with him, Macy and her husband, Shawn. Macy makes a big pot of spaghetti, and we spend the evening playing board games.

"Cade, so help me, if I land on Park Place one more time, I'm going to lunge across this coffee table and hurt you!" Macy warns from her seat on the floor, holding what's left of her Monopoly money in her hand and eyeing all her already-mortgaged properties.

From his spot next to me on the sofa, Cade laughs, holding out a waiting hand for his payment. "Then I guess it's a good thing my hotels have extra security." She sticks out her tongue, which makes Cade laugh even harder. Macy looks to Shawn for help.

"Sorry, babe," he says. "Cade wiped me out ten minutes ago. I don't have a railroad or even any low-income housing to my name." Shawn is what I call strikingly handsome. He's tall, like Cade, but with short, black hair and thick eyebrows that frame dark gray eyes. Cade told me that Shawn and Macy were college sweethearts. He's a paramedic, and just as I'd suspected from our first meeting outside Jay's office, he works at the local fire station.

"Don't look at me," I say. "I'm out, too."

Macy groans in defeat. "Then, I guess—" She rests her forehead on the coffee table.

"Saaaay it," Cade prompts, putting a hand behind one ear and leaning closer to his sister with a wide grin on his face. "Come on, sis, just say it, and this misery will end."

Macy sits up and rolls her eyes. "Fine! You—*win*."

"Yes!" Cade jumps off the sofa, scooping up the boat-load of play money in front of him and tossing it into the air. It rains down all around us. "The queen has been dethroned and there's a new champ in town!" He's having way too much fun at his sister's expense, but finally, her annoyed expression cracks into a smile and she's laughing along with Shawn and me. Cade is lucky to have Macy for a big sister. I can see they have a special relationship, and I wonder if Tanner and I could be that close someday. It seems silly to think about it, because the kid is so shy and doesn't seem to have all that much to say to me.

After Cade finishes his anything-but-modest victory dance, and Macy has tossed every throw pillow she can find at him, we straighten up. Shawn and Cade head to the kitchen to do the dinner dishes and Macy and I stay behind to put all the game pieces back in their respective boxes.

"Paige?"

I pull my eyes away from a framed photo of a much-younger Cade and a dark-haired woman hanging on the wall and turn to see her studying me. "Yes?"

"Are you okay? You look like something's bothering you."

My cheeks warm as I begin to sort the Monopoly money back into the designated slots in the box and quickly try to decide if I should ask her what's on my mind. "Actually, I've been wanting to ask you something."

"Go ahead, ask me anything," Macy says, spreading her arms out wide. "I'm an open book. No pun intended." I fold up the game board.

"How do you… you know… how do you handle the holidays without your mom?" Her face instantly softens, and she puts her arm around my shoulder, giving me a squeeze. "Is that too personal? I'm sorry if it is."

"No, not at all. If there's one thing you and I can talk about, it's that. Cade told me about your mother." I open my mouth, but no words come out. "He tells me lots of things," she says softly. "I'm thankful for that, actually. It makes me feel like I don't have to worry about him so much." She touches my hand. "To answer your question— the holidays without my mom are hard. Even five years later, it's not the same, and I miss her."

"Does it get easier?"

Macy purses her lips. "I'm not sure," she says. "But you will get to a place where you can find joy again. I promise. It's just—different."

It's so hard for me to comprehend what she's telling me. Finding joy without my mom? It just doesn't seem possible. "Cade told me about your dad," I confess.

Her smile weakens as she stares off toward the kitchen. "I hoped that he would. My brother doesn't like to talk about him."

I put the lid on the Monopoly box and sit back on the sofa. Macy takes a seat beside me. "He seems pretty adamant about not wanting to see him. Is your dad nearby?"

I ask.

"He's in a minimum-security facility about two hours from here," Macy says. "I'm guessing Cade told you what he did."

"He said it was embezzlement."

She nods. "But that's such an ugly word if you don't understand the reasons behind it. My dad is a good man, I still believe that," she says, and her soft tone makes me want to believe it, too. "He just found himself in a terrible spot, and I think he was scared." Macy's face transforms, as if bearing the weight of the world, and her eyes sparkle with unshed tears. "When my mom died, he lost his world. Those two were married for twenty-five years, and they were so in love. He was devastated when she died."

Macy fidgets thoughtfully with the delicate gold chain around her neck. "But on top of that, he suddenly had sole responsibility for caring for two kids, one getting an expensive college education, and my mother didn't have life insurance. Cade was too young to know any of that, and my dad didn't talk to me about it. He was in over his head financially, and I think he panicked. Dad was never one to ask for help. He started skimming a little off the top from his more lucrative clients. It took about a year, but they finally caught on."

"I'm sorry." There isn't anything else to say right now that wouldn't sound completely insensitive.

"I keep thinking how desperate he must have been, and he didn't have anyone he could talk to, to help him. I'm not angry with him," Macy says. "I hurt for him. I try to visit him a couple of times a month, but Cade won't go." She glances over her shoulder toward the kitchen again. "He won't even consider it."

"Yeah, he made that pretty clear."

"He's still angry. Cade doesn't understand how our dad could do what he did—risk everything he did and choose money over his family. Not only that, but stealing from people. Cade struggled after we lost our mom, and then he lost Dad, too. That's a lot for a kid to handle."

"But you did okay," I say.

"I was in college. It wasn't the same. I could see the situation differently," Macy explains. "I saw a man who lost his wife and was trying to provide the best he could for his children. I don't support what he did, but I can see how desperate he must have been. Cade only sees an extremely selfish man."

"He told me he got into some trouble after that."

Macy blows out a breath and nods, staring at her hands clasped in her lap. "A lot of trouble. I couldn't seem to find a way to help him. It killed me to see him in so much pain, pretending he didn't care. Paige, I'd give anything if he'd just go see our dad. Just once. It breaks my heart that he won't. I think it could really help him."

"Maybe he'll change his mind."

Macy's smile fills with sadness, but as fast as it appears on her lips, it fades. "The fact that he's willing to talk about it with you has to mean something. Right?" A spark of hope returns to her eyes. "You're good for him, Paige."

"I am?"

"Cade's been different since he met you. He's more centered somehow." I smile, her words warming my insides. "All right, tell me about this watch," Macy says, and I glance up to see that she's eyeing me as I fidget with my watch-band. It's become a habit, and I don't even realize I'm doing it. "I remember seeing it on the plane. It's beautiful."

"My mom gave it to me," I say. "I never take it off."

"Well, it's stunning."

"Wearing it makes me feel close to her, you know? Maybe that sounds silly—"

"No, it doesn't. I completely understand," Macy says. "Don't ever apologize for anything that makes you feel closer to your mom. Ever." She reaches out, and I lean willingly into her hug. She rubs my back, and I close my eyes, thankful once again that our paths crossed that day on the plane.

# CHAPTER NINETEEN

## *Cade*

I'm pressed against the wall inside the kitchen door like an eavesdropping creeper. I told myself that I wouldn't do that, that whatever Macy and Paige talked about in the next room is their business, but when Shawn took out the trash, I couldn't help myself. So, now I'm keeping one ear to the living room and one eye on the back door.

The sadness in Paige's voice when she talks about her mom puts a stranglehold on my heart. I didn't know her watch was a gift from her mother. I've never seen her without it, and she's always touching it, fumbling with the band or rubbing her fingers over the glass. It all makes sense now.

It also nearly kills me to hear the hurt in my sister's voice when she talks about our dad and my refusal to see him. Macy gets nostalgic this time of the year, but the fact remains that the man broke the law. A jury of his peers decided that. And let's not forget, he'd abandoned his family long before the judge's gavel sealed his fate. I don't owe him anything, not my sympathy and certainly not my forgiveness. Macy needs to accept that.

At the sound of Shawn's footsteps, I dart back to the sink, just as the screen door opens. Shawn returns a few items on the counter to the fridge, but he keeps glancing over at me.

"You really like her, don't you?"

"I don't dislike her," I say.

"Well, that's romantic," Shawn quips. "You know, I might use that line on Macy later. *I don't dislike you, babe.* I'm sure that will sweep her right off her feet."

Placing a glass in the top rack of the dishwasher, I say, "Paige is just a friend."

"If you say so," Shawn replies, a knowing gleam in his eye. I flick my hand, splattering him with soapy water. He jumps out of the way, but not before a few drops speckle his shirt. "Okay, okay, take it easy." He laughs. "I'm just saying that she seems like a great girl."

Whether Paige Bryant is a great girl is not a topic for debate. She is, by all measurable standards, a great girl. Which entitles her to be with someone who matches her level of greatness and has something to offer her in return. Do I even qualify for that title? *That* is the bigger question that I can't get out of my head. Am I kidding myself to think that I'm the guy for Paige? I didn't have any doubts until Friday night, when Quinn cornered me at the bowling alley during one of the band's breaks. After Paige excused herself to refill her soda, that bold redhead leaned her elbows on the table and stared me down.

"Are you legit?" she'd demanded.

I'd like to take this moment to declare that never in my nearly eighteen years on this planet has anyone ever asked me that question. And I wasn't entirely sure how Quinn wanted me to answer it. I hadn't spent much time with her before I met Paige—zero time, to be exact. Being that she ran in circles I'd done my best to avoid, it was logical that our paths never crossed. So, having her suddenly up in my face, demanding to know if I was *legit*, had caught me off guard.

Quinn waited expectantly for an answer, but all she got was my confused stare. "You're not allowed to hurt her," she'd said.

"I don't intend to hurt her."

"Yeah, right. That's what people say right before they do what they swore they wouldn't."

"What do you want me to say here?" I'd asked. "Because I'm pretty sure you're not going to believe anything I have to say, even though it is the truth."

Quinn cocked her head to the side and stared at me. "You're a smooth talker." I was pretty sure that wasn't a compliment of any kind, so I didn't respond. I'd just stared back at her and waited for her to make the next move. She was the one with the agenda, after all. "Look, Paige has been through a lot. She doesn't need you taking advantage of that."

"What makes you think that's what I'm doing?" I'd

asked. Look at that: Paige was right. I do have a habit of answering a question with another question. But if Quinn was trying to insult or threaten me, she was going to have to work a little harder at it.

"Just be a decent guy," she'd said softly. "And if you can't do that, then at least have the decency to walk away before she gets more attached to you."

At that moment, in the middle of Quinn's warning that was meant to protect Paige, all I'd felt was a tingly warmth inside me. Paige is attached to me. That made all the rest of Quinn's commands melt away. Those were the only words that mattered.

"How's it going in here?"

I turn as Macy and Paige step through the doorway of the kitchen.

"Almost done," Shawn says, snapping the dish towel playfully at Macy as Paige puts on her coat.

"It's time for me to head home. Will you walk me out?" she asks. I dry my hands and close the dishwasher as Paige thanks Macy and Shawn profusely for a great evening.

We barely make it to her car before I have my arms wrapped around her waist and I'm kissing her like I haven't seen her in hours.

When I pull back, Paige's eyes are closed. "Wowza," she breathes, and I laugh.

"Not sure I've ever reached wowza status before, so thanks for that," I say.

"Your efforts do not go unnoticed—so thank *you*." She

reaches up on her tiptoes and seals her compliment with another quick kiss, so brief that she leaves me no time to linger. Instead, she takes one of my hands in both of hers. "I was wondering if I could ask you a favor."

"Anything," I say, still staring at her lips.

"My brother Tanner is thirteen, and he plays guitar. He thinks he's awful at it, so I was wondering—" She nibbles on her lip. "Would you be willing to help him? You know, come listen to him play and maybe give him some pointers? It's just that you're so talented. And I kind of told him you might be willing to help him. I know I didn't have the right to promise that, so if you're not into it, I totally get it."

I squeeze her hands to interrupt her rambling. Until that moment, I wasn't sure you could make a request and apologize at the same time, but somehow, she just did it. "Of course I'll do it. You don't have to convince me."

"Thank you, that means a lot to me. And I know Tanner will appreciate the help."

"Besides," I say, "I'm looking forward to meeting your family."

Paige's smile falters for a brief second, but then it's back in place when she says, "I'm looking forward to it, too."

# CHAPTER TWENTY

## Paige

I wake on Thanksgiving morning to the sound of rain pelting my window, and I groan when I check the clock and see that it's only 8:13. My cell phone lights up on the nightstand with a text from Aunt Faye. She's at the airport, waiting for her flight. I smile at the screen. In just a handful of hours, Aunt Faye will be here, and I will be able to put my arms around her. Four weeks has been entirely too long for us to be apart.

Unable to fall back to sleep, I roll out from beneath the covers and head downstairs. I find Connie standing at the center island in a colorful Thanksgiving apron, stuffing a huge turkey. A small TV on the counter is tuned to the Macy's Thanksgiving Day Parade. Yawning, I slide onto one of the stools. "Morning," I croak.

"Good morning and Happy Thanksgiving," Connie says in her eternally cheerful voice. I eye two pies cooling on a rack on the counter that were not there last night. This woman has been busy. She puts the large bird in the oven and then washes her hands as I pour a glass of orange juice for myself and return to my perch. Connie busies herself piping filling into the halves of hollowed out hard-boiled eggs.

"Can I help?" I ask.

Pleased by my offer, she passes me the bag of filling and the serving tray, then wastes no time opening the refrigerator and burrowing through the produce drawer to retrieve bags of carrots and celery. "Are you always up this early on Thanksgiving?"

"Like clockwork. There's so much to do," Connie says, brushing stray strands of her blond hair away from her face with the back of her hand. "Every year, I promise myself that I will take it easy and not make so much food, but I can't help it. I have to say, though, I don't usually have company in the kitchen this early. Jay and the kids are still sleeping."

I let loose another yawn.

"How did you and your mom spend Thanksgiving?"

I've come to expect a lot of questions from Connie, but she's usually careful about asking for information about my mother. She's concentrating on slicing the vegetables in front of her on the cutting board, but I can feel her waiting for my answer.

"We usually went to Aunt Faye's house," I say. "My mom wasn't much of a cook. If it didn't have a microwavable option on the label, it really wasn't her thing." I smile at the memory, recalling the Thanksgiving when I was eleven and Mom attempted to prepare the meal all by herself. Although she'd made a valiant effort, we ended up giving thanks over chow mein and egg rolls from The Jade Palace.

"It took me a long time to learn to cook," Connie says. "Now, I love it."

I stare at the TV as a giant balloon of Charlie Brown fills the screen. My mom and I had watched the Macy's Thanksgiving Day Parade every year for as long as I could remember. She'd told me that someday she wanted to take me to New York for the holiday, so we could see it in person. I swallow hard.

"Paige, can you get me the small red platter under the counter over there?" I do as she asks, and she meticulously arranges the carrots and celery into a circular pattern. After covering the entire thing with plastic wrap, she returns it to the fridge and immediately gets to work peeling potatoes. Connie does everything expertly, so precisely that I can't help but wonder how she's dealing with an unplanned disruption like me in her structured world.

When she glances up and catches me watching her, I panic and stammer, "How—how will we eat all this food?"

Connie smiles. "Slowly. And for about the next three days, by my estimation."

We work in silence for a few minutes while I finally finish the deviled eggs and try my hand with the potato peeler.

"Paige, look! It's *The Nutcracker*," Connie says, pointing her peeler at the TV. She turns up the volume, and the announcers are talking about the famous holiday ballet and the "Waltz of the Snowflakes" being performed by children from the New York Ballet. I stare at the young dancers, lithe and graceful, immersed in the very dance that my own two feet have done on various stages since I was eight. Unable to pull my eyes away from the screen, my chest constricts, and white noise slowly fills my ears.

"I just had a wonderful idea!" Connie's voice snaps me out of my trance. "How about I get tickets for you, me and Lily to see *The Nutcracker* in Portland? The Oregon Ballet Theatre puts on a wonderful show every year."

Distracted by both the TV and Connie's words, I miss the potato in my hand and the blade of the peeler slices into my thumb. I squeal, dropping the peeler and the potato as blood colors my skin.

"Oh!" With lightning speed, Connie rips a paper towel from the dispenser on the counter, wets it under the faucet and carefully wraps it around my finger, applying pressure. "I should have warned you, those peelers are sharp."

When I glance at the TV again, the dancers are gone, and instead, an ornate float featuring Santa's workshop has taken their place. I release the breath I'm holding, feeling like an idiot as my thumb throbs with pain. "I'm fine."

Connie wastes no time retrieving the first aid kit from under the sink and disinfecting my wound. She doesn't bring up the ballet again, and I'm thankful. Once my thumb is bandaged, I make an excuse that I want to call Quinn and wish her a happy Thanksgiving. I head back to my room and bury myself beneath my blankets.

✧   ✧   ✧

I'm practically jumping up and down at the living room window when Aunt Faye pulls her rental car into the driveway just after two o'clock.

"We're so glad to have you here!" Connie gushes, welcoming Faye with a hug. Faye presents them with a bottle of wine she brought from her favorite California vineyard.

"That's great, thanks," Jay says, taking the bottle as Connie hurries off to the kitchen to get some glasses.

I don't leave Aunt Faye's side. When we settle into the living room before dinner, I hold her hand. When Connie serves the meal, I escort Faye to the chair next to mine. I know the time I have with her will never be enough, and then she'll leave and I'll go back to missing her. But I can't even think about that right now.

Jay carves the turkey, and we all begin filling our plates. By the time I get through half my meal, I'm thankful I'm wearing my yoga pants. If I were wearing jeans, I'm sure I would have lost feeling to my lower extremities.

"This is really good, Mom," Tanner manages between bites. Lily nods animatedly in agreement.

"You really outdid yourself this year, honey," Jay tells her, refilling Connie's wineglass and then his own.

"Paige was a big help," she says, giving me a wink. "It was nice to have someone in the kitchen with me for a change."

"I didn't do much, really," I say, holding up my band-aged thumb. "This was all you, and it's really delicious." Connie beams at the compliments.

"I told you we'd help, but only if you moved the flat screen into the kitchen so we could watch the football games," Jay says.

"That," she tells him, "will *never* happen."

"Time for thankfulness!" Lily calls, setting down her fork and sitting up as tall as she can in her seat. She has a milk mustache framing her big smile.

"What's that?" Aunt Faye asks.

"It's a thing Mom makes us do every year," Tanner tells her, scooping another forkful of mashed potatoes into his mouth.

"Excuse me," Jay warns. "I think what you mean to say is, it's something your mother *encourages* you to do because it's an appropriate gesture on Thanksgiving."

Tanner looks at Aunt Faye sheepishly. "Yeah, that's what I meant."

"So, what is it?" I ask.

"We go around the table and tell one another what we're thankful for," Jay explains.

"It can be anything, really," Connie adds. "I'll start. I'm thankful that Faye is able to be here with us today and that Paige has joined our family." She smiles so brightly when she says the last part that I divert my gaze to my glass and take a sip of my milk.

Lily begs to go next. She's thankful for the new Barbie

Dreamhouse she got for her birthday. "And I'm thankful for my new sister, Paige. I've never had a sister before. It's fun!" Jay and Connie beam at their polite little girl, who claps her hands together, then sticks her index finger into a black olive on her plate and waves it at me. Aunt Faye squeezes my hand underneath the table.

Tanner is thankful that he's no longer getting a D in science class, and both Jay and Connie nod in agreement. He's also grateful that some new video game I've never heard of is coming out in time for Christmas.

"Tanner," Jay says. "We are giving thanks, not plugging our Christmas lists."

"Sorry. I was just sayin'."

"Paige?" Connie asks. "Do you want to go next?"

I hesitate. Should I be honest and admit that I'm not sure what I'm thankful for after losing so much in the past couple of months? Or is this dinnertime ritual supposed to be for touchy-feely effect only? "I'm thankful for this amazing meal. I think I've already gained five pounds." They all laugh. "And I'm thankful for my new job at the bookstore." I pause, not sure what else to say. Fortunately, Jay steps in.

"I'm thankful for my family. And this year, that includes Paige. I wish we'd had the chance to have more Thanksgivings together."

*But we didn't, because my mother lied to you.*

"The important thing is that you're here now," he says, as if he heard my thoughts. "I'm thankful that you gave us a chance." He takes Connie's hand, and they both look at me as if they're waiting for my reaction. I want to fall into my half-eaten piece of pumpkin pie and disappear.

"Thank you," I say, shifting my gaze to the rim of my plate.

Aunt Faye squeezes my hand again, then dabs the corners of her mouth with her napkin. "As you all know, this has been a difficult season for Paige and me," she says. "I want you to know how much I truly appreciate you all." She turns her gentle gaze on Jay and Connie. "You've been so understanding and—I'm just very grateful. For everything." She takes a sip of her wine as silence falls across the table.

Jay raises his glass. "To family."

"To family," Connie repeats. We all raise our glasses and then clink them with our neighbors, sealing the toast.

After dinner, Jay and Tanner return to their respective couches in the living room to resume their football watching. Lily helps me clear the table and Aunt Faye puts the leftovers away as Connie works on the dishes. When we're finished, I announce that I'm taking Aunt Faye upstairs to show her my room. Connie drops her dish towel on the counter and pulls me into a tight hug. I've accepted that her ambush hugs are part of her method of operation. "Happy Thanksgiving, Paige." When she draws back, her eyes are glossy. I offer her a smile, then tug Aunt Faye away to my room, where we can finally be alone.

"So, how are you—really?" Faye asks the second the door closes.

"Good," I answer, for the fourth time since she arrived. She studies my face, as if she's waiting for some tiny crack to surface. "Don't you believe me?"

"I just worry, that's all."

*And I love you for that.*

I take a seat on the bed while Faye investigates my room. "This is nice. I like the color."

"Connie painted it before I got here."

"She seems sweet," Faye says, then turns for my reaction. I shrug. "You don't like her?"

"It's not that. Connie's just trying really hard. It's a little suffocating, that's all." Like snorkeling without a breathing tube.

"Well, I'm glad she's taking care of you." Faye surveys the bulletin board above my desk, her eyes scanning the photos of Mom and me and her and Tyler, and a crazy picture of all four of us on Halloween four years ago. We dressed up as the Justice League in costumes Mom and Faye threw together.

She laughs. "Oh, I remember that night! Abby insisted on being Wonder Woman. She said any woman who could fight crime and accessorize so well was her kind of superhero." As our eyes connect, her smile falters. Faye takes a seat on the bed and clasps my hand in hers. "How's school going?"

"It's all right."

"Just all right?"

"Well, my classes aren't horrible."

"Have you made friends?"

"A few."

"Any *boys* in that group?" I raise an eyebrow. "What? You used to share that stuff with me all the time." It's true. Faye always loved hearing about my latest crush.

"No one serious," I say. I can't tell Faye about Cade. I can't risk her saying anything to Jay and Connie. That's my job—if I ever find the nerve.

"And how are things with Jay?"

I think carefully about how I should answer that question. Things with Jay are strange. Like that awkward moment in the living room, when I saw a side of him I hadn't expected; when he'd nearly cursed my mother for stealing my existence from him. I'm still not quite sure what to think about that. I mean, he went from detached and aloof the moment I stepped off the plane to experiencing an emotional breakdown in front of me over my baby pictures, then pretending that moment never happened and acting all businesslike ever since.

"It's an adjustment," I say.

Aunt Faye's sigh is troubled. From the phone calls and emails we've shared since I left San Diego, I know she still feels guilty for letting me go and responsible for any difficulty or discomfort I'm experiencing trying to adapt to this new life I never chose. I don't blame her for any of this—not anymore. I still don't understand why my mother did what she did, but I no longer hold Faye accountable for any of it. She'd done what her baby sister wanted, even though it made no sense.

"Would you like me to help you unpack?" Faye asks, motioning to the four boxes stacked against the wall. As promised, she'd brought more of my things from San Diego. "I boxed up what I thought you'd want to have. The rest is in storage for now."

I cross the room, tear off the tape on the top box and pull back the flaps. Inside are DVDs of my favorite movies, more framed photos, mostly of me with my friends from school, and more clothes I couldn't fit into my suitcase.

"If there's anything I forgot, I can always mail it to you," Aunt Faye assures me as she opens the next box. I dive into it and find more clothes, school yearbooks, assorted CDs and photo albums.

"Thanks for bringing all of this to me. I almost—" I freeze as my hands touch something soft at the bottom of the box.

"Paige, are you all right?" Faye's hand is on my shoulder. She peers into the box as my fingers withdraw my pink pointe shoes. I stare at them like I can't identify them, as if they are foreign objects in my hands. The memories that come flying out of the box with them attack me almost immediately. I had some of the happiest and proudest moments of my life in these shoes. But now, in my trembling fingers, I'm swallowed up by a sadness so blinding that my stomach aches.

There's light pressure on my shoulder. "I thought you might want those. Is that okay?"

I can't answer. There are no words, only a torrent of emotions swirling up from my core like a funnel cloud ready to slam down and destroy everything in its path. I shove the slippers back into the box and close it up.

Aunt Faye calls my name, but it sounds far away. I grab up the box and take it to my closet. I drop it on the floor and shove it into the back, against the wall, underneath the clothes that hang there. When I close the door, I turn to find Aunt Faye watching me beneath furrowed brows. The corners of her mouth turn down.

"Sweetie, we need to talk about this."

"No, we don't," I say. "I'll go through that stuff later. I just don't know if I have room for it, that's all."

"Paige, sit down." She motions to the bed, and I know what's coming. I cross my arms over my chest. She gestures to the bed a second time. With a defeated sigh, I lower myself onto the edge of the mattress, my hands folded tightly in my lap.

"Talk to me. I'm pretty sure you're not talking to anyone else, and I'm worried. How are you really feeling?"

"I'm fine," I say, trying to make my words sound light, the same way I do when Mrs. Hopkins asks me that ridiculous question.

"Fine is not a feeling," Aunt Faye replies. I can't count the number of times I've heard her say that over the years. I should have known better.

"What exactly is it you want me to say?" I ask.

"I want you to be honest with me. If you're feeling bad,

I need you to tell me. Even if it's something you don't think I want to hear, I still want you to say it. Keeping things inside will only hurt you more."

I flop back on the comforter and stare up at the ceiling. What's the point of spilling my guts and telling her the truth? It will only make her feel guilty and accomplish nothing.

The mattress bows as Faye takes a seat beside me. She pats my thigh. "I know you miss your mom. I miss her, too. Every day, Paige. But I can't leave here knowing that I could have helped you and I didn't get the chance."

I lay my forearm over my eyes. Even in the darkness, Aunt Faye is watching me. I can sense it. "I told you, it's an adjustment, that's all. Some days are harder than others, but I'm doing the best I can." Silence. I slide my arm from my face. Aunt Faye's eyes stare out into the nothingness of the room around us. As I pull myself to a seated position, she puts a gentle arm around me.

"I know you want to fix this. Fix me. And I wish you could, but—maybe I'm beyond fixing right now." There. I said it. The odd thing is, Faye doesn't react as I expect. I'd imagined a horrified expression, immense guilt, anything but what she's giving me now. She studies my face, then touches my cheek with the side of her thumb.

"There's no question that you're in a difficult situation right now. I wish you could have met your father in some other way, before Abby—while she was still alive. But hopefully, something great will come out of all this."

I close my eyes and sink deeper into Faye's embrace. "I just wish I knew what Mom was thinking. I tried to ask Jay about the time they dated in high school, but I think I made him uncomfortable."

Faye pulls back, and I gaze up at her. "Your mother was crazy about him."

"How do you know that?"

"We used to talk on the phone a couple of times a week before she graduated. I was living in California by then, but we kept in touch."

"She talked to you about Jay? What did she say?" I press.

"They met in science class, and they just clicked. Jay was Abby's first serious relationship." She smiles at the memories. "She fell for him hard. Unfortunately, our father didn't like him."

"Why not?" I recall my conversation with Jay in his office on the first day of school, when I'd tried to extract some morsel of information about him and my mother. He'd mentioned that Martin Bryant didn't like him, but he'd refused to offer details.

Faye shakes her head. "I don't know why. Abby never talked about it. All she told me was that Dad wasn't interested in giving Jay a chance, and he was adamant that she shouldn't either. It was a tough time for her. I'm not sure she ever really got over him."

"I don't understand. If Mom loved Jay so much, why didn't she tell him about me? And if she decided for whatever reason to move on with her life, why would she bring him back into it now?"

Aunt Faye ponders my questions. "I found something that I think may help." She moves to her suitcase, shuffling a few items around before extracting two small books. She brings them to me, and my questioning eyes probe hers.

"These are Abby's journals."

I stare down at them, my hold instantly softening, as if they might explode or simply vanish in a puff of smoke. My words are barely audible when I ask dumbly, "These were Mom's?"

"I found them when I was sorting through her belongings." Her voice cracks. I look at her, really look at her for the first time since she arrived, and I see all the things I didn't see before. Faye's sorrowful, downcast eyes lack their usual sparkle. She's thinner, too, and I wonder if she's eating enough. I think of what the last month has been like for her and shame presses down on me. She's the one who'd had to pack up our home. I knew before I left San Diego that it would have to be sold. Aunt Faye had sorted through closets and cupboards and drawers, finding memories of my mother at every turn. And I wasn't there. She'd done it alone, with no one to lean on.

"I didn't know my mother kept a journal," I say.

"She started writing in high school," Faye says. "Abby said it helped her to think straight, to remember the important things in her life and sort of process the stuff that wasn't so good." She joins me on the edge of the bed again, reaching out and running her hand across the journal closest to her, still resting in my quivering hands. It's a deep turquoise, with a pair of white ballet slippers embossed on the cover. "This is the one."

"And this one?" I prompt, holding up the other journal. It's brown leather, with Mom's initials stamped in gold lettering in the center.

"She started that one about a year ago." Aunt Faye draws a deep breath. "Her last entry was the night before she died." I set down the books beside me on the bed, as if they are alive. "It's all right, Paige. I was just as surprised when I found them. I had no idea Abby had started keeping a journal again."

"You read them?" I ask. She nods slowly. "What's in them?"

"I could tell you that if you'd like, but I think you should read them for yourself."

I nibble on my lip. Part of me wants to open them right now, to push back the covers and read every word my mother had written. But another part of me is scared. What will happen when my eyes see her handwriting? I long to feel that a part of her is here with me again, and yet it seems somehow intrusive to read them. These are her personal thoughts, words she'd shared with no one but herself.

"I don't know what to do right now."

"You don't have to do anything." Faye picks up the journals and places them in the nightstand drawer. "I'll put them in here for safekeeping, and when you're ready, you'll know where they are."

She closes the drawer and returns to the bed, wrapping her arms tightly around me. "I know that a part of you is angry with Abby right now. And that tears you up, because you love her so much. I get that, Paige, I really do. You're not the only one who feels that way." My eyes drop to the floor. "I think these journals might help you understand what was going through your mother's head because we didn't get the chance to ask her."

I want to read them; I'm just not sure I can right now. Had Mom written about Jay on any of the pages? What if the things he isn't willing to share—she can? I stare at the drawer again with both longing and hesitation.

"I miss her so much," I whisper. "So much, I think I might split down the middle."

"I know, honey," she says. "A little piece of her is in those journals. And when you're ready, they're right here for you."

# CHAPTER TWENTY-ONE
## Paige

I tap my fingers on my knees to the rhythm of the clock hanging on Mrs. Hopkins's wall. We stare at each other across her large wooden desk, calculating each other's next move, like we're locked in some intense chess match.

"What frightens you, Paige?"

I blink. "What?"

"What are you afraid of?" Mrs. Hopkins asks again. If there's one thing I've learned during these weekly meetings, it's that this woman is determined to locate my vault of buried feelings, pry it open with her metaphorical crowbar and put the contents under her psychological microscope. So far, her seemingly benign questions haven't cracked me. That has to frustrate her, although you wouldn't know it by the skilled game face she wears.

"I don't know," I say airily. "Spiders, I guess. A pop quiz in calculus. Boys who wear Speedos."

Mrs. Hopkins laughs, propping her elbow on the desk-top and resting her chin in her palm. "You have a wonderful sense of humor, Paige."

I relax back in my chair, pleased that I amuse her.

"But I'm not talking about spiders or unbecoming swimwear. I want to know what *truly* frightens you." She leans in and gives me that analytical sizing up she does so well. If it were possible, I feel like Mrs. Hopkins would jump at the chance to peel back my skin and crawl right inside me, just to get an up-close look at what's really going on in my mind. "I'm talking about the kind of fear that reaches deep and wakes you up at night. Do you have fears like that?"

I retract my previous comment about her question being benign. I should have remembered who I'm dealing with. As always, Mrs. Hopkins has an agenda. "Why do you want to know?" I ask. "If I do, does that mean there's something wrong with me?"

"No, of course not," she says. "Everyone experiences fear on some level, Paige. But if you can identify what truly frightens you, you can take back some of the power and make things less scary. So, what are you most afraid of?"

Honestly? That something else bad is going to happen. Isn't that what they say, that bad luck happens in threes? Maybe it's that celebrities die in threes. Whatever, the point is that three is a very precarious number. And it's a little too close for comfort. I've lost my mom, been forced to give up my home—what's next? I'm not sure I'm capable of surviving another blow to my life.

"I'm not afraid," I say, shifting in my seat.

Mrs. Hopkins's shoulders deflate just a smidgen, but enough that I can see her disappointment. However, as always, she will not be derailed. She flips through the pages of that familiar folder on the desk in front of her. One of these days, I'm going to get my hands on that folder and find out just what it is she knows about me. "Okay, let's talk about something else."

Yes, *please*.

"How old were you when you started dancing?"

I choke on my gum, and Mrs. Hopkins wastes no time retrieving a bottle of water from the mini fridge behind her desk. I sputter a couple more coughs, then grab for the water and down a few swallows.

"Are you all right?"

I nod, putting the cap back on the bottle and place it on the desk. Our eyes lock once more in their familiar standoff. Mrs. Hopkins is itching to call checkmate, and I'm determined that I will destroy the playing board of whatever twisted game this is before I will ever let that happen.

"I'm guessing that you started dancing when you were quite young. Is that right?"

"I'm guessing that the answer to that question is in my file," I counter.

Sympathy lays claim to the fine lines around Mrs. Hopkins's eyes. She closes the folder and sits back in her chair. "You're right. I know quite a bit about you, Paige. On paper anyway. But I'd like to hear it from you."

"Why?"

"Because I think it will help."

"I disagree."

"And why's that?"

"Because talking about my life doesn't change it," I say.

"Doesn't change what exactly?" she asks. I shake my head, forcing her to switch tactics again. "Can you at least tell me why it's so important for you to keep everything inside?"

"Why is it so important to you that I put everything out there?" I keep waiting for Mrs. Hopkins to throw up her hands and declare defeat, to finally admit that even with the fancy diplomas framed on her walls, my mind is no match for her mad skills.

Mrs. Hopkins returns her pen to her desk drawer, then clasps her hands together on the desktop. "Grief is a natural reaction to loss, Paige. But it doesn't feel natural, does it? It probably feels overwhelming, like everything is out of your control."

I stare down at my watch.

"Grief can also be frightening, and it may seem like the best way to handle it is to bottle it up inside where you can control it," Mrs. Hopkins says. "But I'm here to tell you, Paige, that holding in your grief doesn't make it better. It makes it dangerous. And when it does finally break free, because it will eventually, you won't be able to control it. I don't want that for you. Please let me help you. Talking about it is the first step."

"Fine. You want to know something about me that's not

in your file? I started dancing when I was four. I love it because it makes me feel free. Because I'm good at it and it's—" I can't finish. My insides feel like they are on fire, like someone lit a match inside me and the powder keg buried deep is about to blow at any minute. And if it does, there will be no survivors.

"It's what?" Mrs. Hopkins asks.

I twist my watchband harder, the leather creating slow-burning friction against my skin, mirroring the heat inside me. "It's all I've ever known, okay? It's the one true connection I have to my mother, and I can't bring myself to do it anymore."

"Tell me why." Her words are soft, but they hit just the right pressure points.

*Nope, not happening.* I shake my head, refusing her question and trying desperately to hold in my next words, where they can't be heard—where they can't hurt me.

"I've seen some videos of you online. You're a magnificent dancer, Paige, and you clearly love it. Why would you choose to give that up?"

I shrug. "Because."

"Because why?"

Those two words are the tipping point, and without warning, my resolve splinters, propelling me out of my chair. "Because it's not fair for me to feel that kind of happiness when my mom can't!" Something invisible squeezes my throat and I can't breathe. I collapse forward, my clenched fists digging into my thighs and my face hot with shame. Well, look at that—Mrs. Hopkins got her checkmate after all. Guess her crowbar finally worked.

Unable to retrieve my confession, I pull my sweater tightly around myself and eye the door. Mrs. Hopkins immediately stands. "Paige, please stay."

I lunge for the knob, throwing open the door. I fly past Karen, who glances up from her computer, and rush into the hallway before either she or Mrs. Hopkins can utter a word to stop me.

I feel jittery, like I'm drowning in a thousand cups of coffee and there's nowhere to hide. As I rush down the hallway, I bump into two students. One drops her books, and I apologize, but I don't stop. I have no destination; all I can think about is Mrs. Hopkins at her desk, scribbling my revelations into that damn folder. I round the corner and nearly slam into Cade.

"Hey, hey, hey." He places his hands firmly on my shoulders. "What's going on?"

I press the back of my wrist to my mouth, preventing myself from blurting out something ridiculously embarrassing. Instead, I wrap my arms around Cade and exhale my relief when he pulls me in tight and cradles me in his arms. I don't bother looking around to see who's watching. Because I don't care anymore. "What happened?"

I shake my head violently against his chest. I can't tell him the truth, that I am precisely what Mrs. Hopkins thinks I am—more frightened than I can ever allow myself to admit. And I can't tell him that what terrifies me more than

218

anything is that I'm falling for him in a big way. I'm risking everything for a guy who has the power to break my heart just by changing his mind and deciding that I'm not what he wants, that maybe I'm too broken to be worth the trouble. Forget spiders and pop quizzes and cringeworthy visions of the boys' swim team. Losing Cade is my worst fear of all. Because he just might be the only thing that's holding me together.

# CHAPTER TWENTY-TWO
## *Paige*

On Friday night, it seems as if the entire population of Mystic Shores stops what it's doing to take part in the town's annual holiday festival, and Connie is practically bursting with excitement to show it to me.

Downtown looks like Christmas on steroids and could easily be the backdrop for a Norman Rockwell painting—if you don't count the McDonald's on the corner, decked out in thousands of white twinkle lights, or the coffeehouse across the street, advertising peppermint mochas and eggnog lattes on its very modern reader board. At McGrath's Pharmacy, Kris Kringle and his reindeer are the focus of the window display, each figurine perfectly placed to create a winter wonderland. And all the mannequins in the front display case at Myna's Fashion House are clad in red and white Santa hats to accent their festive party dresses and elegant suits.

Pop-up tents staffed by various civic groups line one block of the main drag, each selling holiday wares to support their various causes. Quinn, Zoey and Sam are working the dance team's booth, selling poinsettias, wreaths and garland. We stop to say hello, and with the skills of a slick used car salesman, Quinn works her powers of persuasion on Connie. In no time at all, Connie has her checkbook in hand and is placing a large order before Jay manages to pull her away. I hug Quinn and promise to call her later.

"So, what do you think?" Jay asks as we stroll the bay-front, weaving in and out of people on the crowded sidewalk. A group of carolers joyously sings from the street corner. Everywhere I look, I spy the wonders of the season and feel the thick holiday cheer like an extra layer of clothing. It's all very peace on earth, good will toward men, and—I can't help but think how much my mom would love it. With that one simple thought, the familiar sadness that's undeniably become a permanent part of me, like another limb on my body, squeezes me tight.

Connie loops an arm through mine as we stroll along. "What do you say we get some hot chocolate?" I still haven't figured out if Connie is so attentive to me because she really wants me to feel comfortable here, or if she's merely doing it for Jay's benefit.

There's a tug on my sleeve, and I look down into Lily's big blue eyes. "Paige, let's go see Santa. I have a lot to tell him." The little girl has definitely been swallowed up by the magic. Jay, Connie and Tanner head off in the direction of Java Joe's, in search of hot chocolate, while Lily and I walk half a block to stand in line at Santa's Village. As we wait our turn, we have a perfect vantage point to see the big guy. He's sitting in a large, ornate chair, trying to wrestle his beard away from a screaming toddler who doesn't seem to care one bit if she lands on the naughty list. Not to mention, she's completely uninterested in the photographer, one of Santa's elves who's waving frantically and trying so hard to get the little girl to look at the camera that he appears to be trying to land a jetliner.

I can identify, almost with certainty, which kids are here past their bedtimes. There are several full-on tantrums in progress, and I'm not sure who's crankier, the children or their mothers, whose hopes for the perfect holiday photo are quickly fading.

Unlike the other children, Lily stands patiently at my side holding my hand. As we make our way forward in the line, I ask, "What are you gonna ask Santa for this year?"

"I can't tell you," she says, smiling so big I can see where she lost a bottom tooth last week. "It's a secret."

"I don't even get a hint?" I ask, feigning disappointment. She giggles, tightening her hold on my hand.

Five minutes later, Lily is on Santa's lap, and I'm standing close enough to see that she is giving him an earful. I can also see that the guy in the Santa suit looks like he's been through the wringer. If someone has to pay the price to keep the magic of Christmas alive, it's this poor dude.

Lily's small hands gesture wildly at the dimensions of the toy she's describing. If I had to guess, I'd say it has something to do with Barbies. Everything in her world usually does. Maybe a swimming pool to go along with her new dreamhouse.

"He's a fraud."

I turn, and I'm pleasantly surprised to see Cade. "Hey!"

"That's the same guy who plays the Easter bunny at the community center every spring. Don't be fooled by the beard."

I laugh. "Noted."

He reaches out and takes my hand. "Aren't you a little too old to be sitting on Santa's lap? I'm sure you'll make his day but—"

"That's my little sister up there," I say, nudging him in the ribs. I glance back at Lily, who is still talking, while the worn-down Santa continues to nod. "And by the looks of it, her list is pretty long." The smile he gives me melts my insides like a marshmallow over an open flame. "What are you doing here? Is Macy with you?"

"She's at the bookstore. I spent the last two hours helping her hang Christmas lights. Not high on my list of what constitutes a good time, by the way. But I think it turned out okay."

"I'm sure it looks awesome." I lean my head on Cade's shoulder and squeeze his hand a little tighter.

Lily hops down from Santa's lap and gives him a wave before she prances over to where we stand. "I hope he was listening," she says, her forehead creased with tiny lines of concern.

"Oh, I'm sure he was," I assure her. "Santa has an excellent memory."

Lily gazes up at Cade. "Hi."

"Lil, this is Cade. I work for his sister at the bookstore." I almost say *this is my boyfriend, Cade,* but quickly stop myself. There are some things a five-year-old doesn't need to know.

"Are you going to see Santa?" Lily asks. Amused, I wait for his response.

"Already did," he says.

"Whaddya ask for?" she prods.

"Can't tell you. It's a secret."

Lily smiles and nods with understanding.

"There you are!" I turn at Connie's voice, and I release Cade's hand as if a bolt of electricity just zapped my palm. Connie offers me a white cardboard cup with a lid before leaning down and wrapping one arm around Lily. "Did you see Santa, sweet pea?"

"I sure did!" Lily gushes.

"They had quite the conversation," I say, folding my hands around the warmth of the cup.

"And who's this?" Connie eyes Cade curiously.

"This is Cade." Right on cue, he reaches out and shakes her hand.

"Nice to meet you, Cade, I'm Connie Chapman. How do you two know each other?"

*Oh, please, no.* "This is Macy's brother," I blurt out. "And she needs to see me at the bookstore right now, so can

I catch up with you guys later?"

Connie tosses me a knowing look, but she plays it cool. "Sure thing. We're going to watch the tree lighting. Don't be too long; you don't want to miss it."

"I'll be there soon." When Connie and Lily head off down the sidewalk, I sigh.

"Sooo—I'm just Macy's brother? What's with the lying? Santa frowns on that this time of year."

"That was an evasive maneuver to save you, actually," I lie again and start walking toward the bookstore. Cade falls into step beside me. "She was about to launch into a million questions. I thought I'd save you the interrogation."

"Wait." Cade reaches for my hand and pulls me to a stop. "She doesn't know about us?" I stare intently at a crack in the sidewalk. "I thought you said you told your dad."

"I said I will," I assure him. "It just hasn't been the right time—"

"When?" he presses. He has every reason to be upset with me, but he delivers that one simple word with unwavering patience.

"This weekend, I promise," I say, and I pull him along down the street.

We stop on the corner across from Macy's shop. Red and white lights frame the windows and door. "Nice job," I say, gesturing grandly at his work.

"What can I say? I'm gifted." He leans down and presses his lips to mine in a lingering, toe-curling kiss. *Yes, he most certainly is.*

Once inside, we visit with Macy while Shawn rings up customers' merchandise, looking the part of a jolly old elf with a jingle-bell hat and pointy ears. I offer to help, but Macy dismisses me with a wave of her hand, followed by a quick hug, and she tells me to go have fun. Cade walks me out and kisses me goodnight under the mistletoe hanging above the doorway, and I'm all but floating on air as I head back toward the big Christmas tree in the square to find Connie, Jay and the kids. They're right where she said they'd be. The lights on the tree in the center of the plaza are aglow, and colorful ornaments are hanging all over it, all the way to the top, where a giant star twinkles against the black, marbled sky.

"Paige is back!" Lily squeals, and she skips to my side.

"Oh, Paige, you missed it!" Connie exclaims.

"Sorry," I say, fishing quickly for an excuse. "I was helping Macy at the shop. She's busier than she expected."

Jay studies me, his brow furrowed. "Connie said you were with a kid named Cade. Was that Cade Matthews?"

*Just be honest.* "Yeah," I say. "Is there a problem?"

"Paige, I don't want you hanging around him," Jay says flatly.

Defensiveness inches it's way over my skin, tightening the muscles in my shoulders. "He's a nice guy," I say. "And I work for his sister."

"And I appreciate that she gave you a job, but her brother runs with a different kind of crowd," Jay says, an edge of sternness to his words. "I don't want you getting mixed up with them."

I should tell Jay I know all about it. That I've met this *different crowd* that Cade hangs out with, and that Jared, Zeke and Ash are nice people, too, and I like them. I could also tell him that he doesn't have the right to dictate who I can and cannot hang out with, and that I will make that decision. But the words die on the tip of my tongue and, as usual, I say nothing.

"Are you hearing me? That kid's been in some serious trouble."

"People change," I say.

"And some people don't." Jay shakes his head. "This isn't open for discussion. Stay away from Cade."

"Please, don't ask me to do that."

"I'm not asking."

"So—that's an order?" I demand, waiting for him to admit that he's overstepped and to back down. He doesn't. Jay doesn't even blink.

"Yes, it's an order, but for your own good," he says. "And I expect you to follow it."

I glance down the street in the direction of the bookstore. I should have known better than to tell Jay the truth. When I turn back to him, I nod. *Liar, liar, pants on fire. Again.*

To no one's surprise, Lily talks the entire ride home. I've never heard a kid rattle on so intently about their discussion with Santa without revealing any specifics about the conversation. And I can see Connie is trying hard to extract the details, so she'll know what to buy for Lily to unwrap on Christmas morning.

"How do you even know you're on the good list?" Tanner asks her, his devious and calculated line thrown into the conversation at just the right time to horrify his little sister. "You broke my video game controller."

"It wasn't my fault! You left it on the floor."

"And you stepped on it!"

"I'm sure Santa knows it was an accident," Connie says.

"I don't know," Tanner says with a skeptical sigh. "I just know he's got people to write those things down."

"*Moooom!*" Lily wails.

"All right, enough," Jay says as he turns the SUV onto the highway.

"I'm sure your sister is not on the naughty list. But you, mister—" Connie points her finger over her shoulder. "You might want to be careful." Tanner laughs.

It's close to nine o'clock when we get back to the house. As I stand at the bathroom sink brushing my teeth, I think about Cade. I've liked guys before, but this time is different. When I'm with him, I somehow feel whole. Hopeful. Like the frayed edges inside me seem to magically mend themselves, and he makes me believe that maybe, one day, I will find a way to put the pieces of my world back together.

The girl in the mirror rises up on her tiptoes, her arm instinctively following, extending gracefully from her side. I stare at her, my toothbrush still against my lips. Immediately, I drop my feet flat to the floor as my shoulders deflate.

*This will be a hard habit to break.*

Quickly, I rinse my mouth and run my toothbrush beneath the faucet before placing it back in its holder on the counter. After taking one more look at the girl frowning back at me in the mirror, I flip off the light and head to my room.

# CHAPTER TWENTY-THREE
## Cade

"If you put any more ornaments on that tree, you won't be able to see the branches," I say, just as Macy affixes a small, glass angel to the heavily decorated Douglas fir lit up next to the bookstore's front counter.

"Back off, little brother. This is one of my favorite parts of Christmas. Plus, I keep finding these cute ornaments." She turns and swats my leg. "Don't you have something better to do than sit on my counter and bother Paige? Get down!"

I slide off the counter and catch Paige biting back a smile. She's concentrating a little too hard on pricing the stack of books in front of her.

"There! What do you think?" Macy asks, stepping back and admiring the tree.

"It's perfect," Paige says. "Probably the best-decorated tree in town."

Macy beams. "I can't believe it's less than a week until Christmas. I still have so much to do."

"Can I help with anything?" I offer, praying she hasn't found more lights to be hung.

"Well, since you asked—" She draws a deep breath as she moves an ornament from one branch to another. "I'm going to see Dad in a couple of weeks. Will you come with me?"

The muscles in my jaw clench. "No."

"Come on, Cade," Macy says. "We don't have to stay long."

"I said no," I repeat, and I notice that Paige has inconspicuously slipped out from behind the counter and is dusting the shelves by the window. "We've been through this a hundred times. I have nothing to say to him."

My sister and I stare at each other, and I'm pretty sure she thinks that if she holds eye contact with me long enough, she'll wear me down and make me change my mind. Not going to happen. Finally, Macy breaks our connection and glances at the floor, shaking her head. "Will you just—please consider it? For me? Just this once?"

Macy always resorts to some form of guilt when she can't get me to bend. It hasn't worked in the past, and it's not working now. "I'm not going. And there's nothing you can do to change my mind."

With a small, disappointed shake of her head, she picks up the empty ornament box on the counter and heads into the back room, leaving me with a sourness in my stomach that I've disappointed her again.

I lean my hands on the counter and hang my head,

unleashing a frustrated sigh. When I feel warm hands on my back, I straighten. Paige wraps her arms around me, and I pull her close, resting my cheek on the top of her head, her soft hair tickling my nose.

"Are you okay?" she asks.

"It wouldn't be the holidays if she wasn't trying to get me to visit my dad. It's no big deal," I say, attempting to lighten the mood.

Paige tilts back her head and her gorgeous green eyes flecked with gray gaze up at me. "Can I ask you something?"

"Always," I say, giving her my standard answer to her frequent question.

"You told me that your dad has been sending you letters for years, but that you've only read the first one. What did he say in it that made you not want to open the rest?"

I lean down and brush my lips against her forehead. "He said he was sorry." Paige looks confused. She can't make sense of how an apology sounds unreasonable.

"That's it?" she asks.

"No, that's not it," I say. "Saying he's sorry doesn't fix what my father did. He destroyed our family because money was more important to him. He abandoned us. When my mom died, and I needed him more than anything, he *chose* not to be there. Simply saying he's sorry will never make up for what he did." Paige's arms tighten around my back as the anger builds inside me to the point of eruption. Gently, I push her away and step out of her embrace.

"That's why you refuse to see him." Paige's face fills

with sympathy.

"I have nothing to say to that man."

"But it's the holidays," she points out. "The holidays are all about being with family."

"Macy and Shawn are my family. They're all I need."

Paige leans her back against the counter. "Aren't you even a little curious? I mean, don't you want him to explain why he did what he did? I would kill to be able to ask my mom why she gave custody of me to Jay. But I'll never have that chance."

I shake my head. "This isn't the same thing."

"I know," she concedes. "I just thought—"

I cut her off with an outstretched hand. "If you're trying to figure out how a father could abandon his son like that, don't waste your energy. I've been trying to figure it out for years, and there's no explanation for it that doesn't make him an asshole. There's no way in hell I'm gonna give him the chance to hurt me again. *Never* again."

The door to the back room opens, and Macy returns with a small, wrapped package in her hand. "I have something for you." She refuses to make eye contact with me and instead holds out the package to Paige. "I was going to wait until Christmas Eve, but what the heck! Open it."

"I'd do what she says if I were you," I say, giving Macy a light nudge with my hip, hoping that weak gesture conveys that I'm sorry. I don't like arguing with my sister, especially about our dad. I don't ever want him to come between us. "She gets pretty bossy when it comes to Christmas."

Macy makes a face, her way of acknowledging my wordless apology. Paige laughs and gently tears away the paper to reveal a white box. She removes the lid, and her breath catches as she withdraws three silver bracelets, all decorated with tiny moons. I recognize them immediately, and so does Paige, because her eyes snap to Macy's wrist to see that some of her bracelets are missing.

"Macy, I can't…"

"Yes, you can. I want you to have them. You've told me several times how much you like them and, well—" Macy pauses, taking the bracelets and slipping them over Paige's hand. "I believe in fate and that everything happens for a reason. You and I were supposed to meet on that plane. I'm absolutely sure of it."

"How do you know that?" Paige asks, her eyes never leaving the bracelets.

"I wasn't supposed to be on that flight," Macy says.

Confusion settles on Paige's face. "You weren't?"

Macy shakes her head. "I always fly into the Eugene Airport, but instead, at the last minute, I decided to book my flight into Portland so I could do a little shopping and visit some bookstores. Visiting Powell's Books is my secret shame." She laughs. "That's why I was on that flight, and that's why I was sitting next to you. And because of that, you and Cade met in baggage claim."

Paige doesn't look convinced that any of what Macy just said was proof of divine intervention, but she smiles when my sister gives her a hug. "You were meant to come into our lives, Paige. I'm sure of it. You make my brother happy in a way I haven't seen in a long time." Macy smiles at me, and I'm at a loss for a response. She's right about that part. Paige is clearly overwhelmed by my sister's words.

"I don't know what to say" is all she can manage to get out.

Macy hugs her tightly a second time and whispers in her ear, "Just say Merry Christmas."

Paige hugs her back. "Merry Christmas."

This is all the family I need.

# CHAPTER TWENTY-FOUR
## Paige

Christmas morning arrives early, with Lily banging on our doors and yelling that Santa has come. Despite her determination to stay up late and surprise the jolly old elf as he descended down the chimney, the little dynamo passed out on the sofa just after midnight and Jay carried her to bed.

Lily doesn't seem the least bit disappointed as she practically drags me by my hand down the stairs. I'm yawning when she pulls my staggering frame into the living room, and my bare feet stop in their tracks. The Chapmans' Christmas tree, fully decorated from the sparkly gold star at the top right down to the tree skirt, was transformed sometime in the night and is now bathed in piles of presents, all wrapped in beautiful paper, shimmering ribbons and brightly colored bows.

"See, Paige, I told you Santa was here!" Lily squeals.

I fall onto the sofa and curl up as Connie and Jay come into the living room in their robes. Tanner is already digging under the tree to see which packages have his name on them. He reads the tag on each gift and, with unwanted help from his little sister, they hand out the presents. To my surprise, I'm surrounded by gifts when they're finished. I look up at Connie, and her wide smile nearly mimics Lily's.

"Go ahead, Paige. Open one."

At those words, the kids dig into their own piles of presents. To his delight. Tanner gets the video game he wanted. In addition to a swimming pool for her Barbie dolls, Lily also unwraps the Pet Shop she'd spent the last month begging for. I laugh as she starts ripping into it before she bothers unwrapping the rest of her gifts.

Connie gasps when she opens a small box with an emerald ring inside. She flings her arms around Jay's neck. "It's beautiful! Jay, I love it!" Both the kids and I look away when the kissing starts.

I pick up one of my larger presents and carefully tear back the paper. As I lift the lid of the box inside, I stare down at an incredible pair of boots. They're tall and made of soft brown leather, adorned with brass buckles down the sides.

"Do you like them?" Connie asks. I didn't realize she was watching me.

"They're amazing." They really are, and I can't wait to put them on. "Thank you so much."

She claps her hands together. "Open another one, Paige."

By the time our present-opening session is over, it looks like a gift-wrapping factory exploded in the living room. There is wrapping paper everywhere, and I'm surrounded by clothes and makeup and numerous other surprises that I hadn't expected but love nonetheless. Lily adores the clothes I gave her for her dolls and Tanner seems excited about the iTunes gift card I bought for him. Jay thanks me for the gift certificate to Opal's Restaurant.

"Connie told me it was your favorite place to eat," I say.

"It is," he replies, reaching out and taking Connie's hand. "Maybe that's where we should go on New Year's Eve."

"Are you going out?" I ask.

Connie glances at Jay and then at me. "Actually, we wanted to ask you if you could watch the kids that night. Unless you already have plans."

I shake my head. "No, nothing special. I don't mind."

"I don't need a babysitter," Tanner says, his eyes never leaving the remote-controlled airplane manual he's studying.

"No, you don't," Connie says. "But Lily does." She meets my eyes once more. "Are you sure, Paige?"

"What do you say, Tanner? We'll eat a bunch of junk food and watch the ball drop on TV." He shoots me a scrutinizing look, as if he has other options to consider, and then shrugs.

"I want to stay up until midnight!" Lily announces.

"We'll see about that," Connie replies.

"Thanks, Paige," Jay says. "This means a lot. I don't think Connie and I have been out on New Year's Eve since Lily was born.

"I'll make reservations tomorrow." Connie claps her hands. "I can't wait!"

After helping clean up, I excuse myself to my room so I can call Aunt Faye. When I snatch my cell phone off the nightstand, there's a text waiting.

Cade: Merry Christmas.

I send him a GIF of SpongeBob Square Pants wearing a Santa hat and dancing a crazy jig. Because it's cute. And because I can. His response is immediate.

Cade: Is that what you look like this morning?

I smile at his winky face emoji.

Me: Exactly. Adorable, right?

Cade: Definitely. Can I see you later?

I type yes in as many languages as I can think of. Besides English, I only know three. French: Oui. Spanish: Sí. And German: Ja. But I'm sure he gets the point.

Cade: When can I stop by?

My joyful Christmas buzz fizzles. Oh, boy.

Me: How about I stop by your house after lunch?

There is no response, so I quickly type, "I have gifts for you and Macy. I'd love to see her." I hold my breath. The truth is that I still haven't told Jay that Cade and I are dating, and now it seems like forever since I promised him I would have that conversation. *You are such a coward*, I scold myself.

Cade's response finally appears: When do I get to come to your house?

I stare at the thinking face emoji and rack my brain for a response. I glance at the door and then back at my phone as I type.

Me: How about you come over on New Year's Eve?

# CHAPTER TWENTY-FIVE
## *Paige*

When New Year's Eve rolls around, it takes Connie and Jay what seems like forever to leave the house.

"Where are my keys? We're going to miss our reservation," Jay says, searching frantically around the living room, under the magazines on the coffee table and in between the couch cushions.

"They're right here," Connie calls, coming into the room jingling the key ring in her hand. She's wearing a red dress that hugs her curves and superhigh black heels. Her thick, blond hair is swept up into a loose twist, and her coat is hung over one arm.

"Wow," Jay says. "You're gorgeous."

Connie smiles wide. "Thank you, kind sir."

"He's right," I say. "You look amazing."

"Thanks, Paige. And thanks again for staying with the kids tonight. If anything comes up, call us. We're just going to dinner," she explains.

"And then we're going dancing," Jay announces.

Connie's face lights up like the Christmas tree still adorned in the corner. "Really?"

"Yes," he says, then turns his attention back to me. "So, unless the house catches fire or someone needs medical attention, I give you full authority to handle any problems yourself."

"Understood," I say, giving a mock salute. "Have a good time and don't worry about anything. We'll be fine."

About a half hour after Jay and Connie leave for dinner, Cade knocks on the front door. He's smiling, looking freshly showered, with the tips of his hair still damp. He wears a hooded sweatshirt under his leather jacket, and his guitar case is slung over his back.

"Come on in," I say, stepping aside. As Cade enters, he leans over and gives me a kiss, and right on cue, my heartbeat comes alive like the final number in a Broadway musical.

"Your dad knows I'm here, right?" he asks.

"He and Connie went to dinner, and then they're going dancing," I say.

Cade's expression grows serious. "That didn't answer my question."

My lips part just as Lily bounds down the stairs with a pink plastic guitar in her hands. "Hi!" she says to Cade. "Can you teach me to play guitar?"

Cade glances at me, his eyes alight with amusement.

"Lily, go away," Tanner says as he rounds the corner. "You don't play guitar." He gives her a light shove.

"I could if someone would teach me," she tells him, one hand on her hip as her eyes land sweetly once more on Cade.

"Cade, you've met Lily. And this is Tanner. Tanner, meet Cade."

They nod at each other. "Can't wait to hear you play, man," Cade says. "Paige tells me you're pretty good."

We move into the living room, where Tanner has his guitar waiting. Cade slips off his coat and unzips his case. When he pulls out his own guitar, Tanner exclaims, "Whoa! That's an awesome axe!" I stifle a laugh and scoot Lily off to the kitchen to fix a snack. They aren't going to get anything done with her and her pink guitar there to distract them.

After delivering a plate of Connie's homemade chocolate chip cookies and two cans of soda, I wrestle Lily back to the kitchen to play a game of Chutes and Ladders, but I'm still close enough to listen in on their conversation. I've always considered Tanner to be relatively shy, but to my surprise, he peppers Cade with questions, demanding to know what it's like playing in a band and whether he's played with anyone famous. When he asks how many girlfriends Cade has had, I nearly fall out of my chair straining to hear the answer. Cade just laughs and says, "Why don't you play me a song and let's see what you've got?"

For the next couple of hours, I listen to them rehearse. Some of it is good, and some of it definitely needs work. Cade talks about chords and notes and demonstrates different techniques. At nine o'clock, I put Lily to bed, despite her impassioned protests to stay up just a little while longer.

"*Pleeease*, Paige. I'm not tired. I want Cade to give me a guitar lesson, too!"

"Maybe next time. Tanner needs his help right now."

"But why can't I stay up until midnight? I'm five; I can do it."

"Your mom's orders." Lily doesn't like that, but I manage to wrangle her onto her bed and under the covers. Three storybooks later, I reach over to turn off the light on the nightstand, and she wraps her arms around my neck, pulling me into a tight hug. I'm enveloped in the aroma of berry-scented shampoo.

"You're the best babysitter ever," she whispers.

I smile and pull back. "Good night, Lily. Sweet dreams."

By ten o'clock, Tanner heads toward the stairs with his guitar and the new sheet music Cade brought for him.

"Hey," I call. "I thought we were gonna watch the ball drop."

"I'll come back down later. I want to work on this song," he calls over his shoulder.

"Okay. I'll give you a shout when it gets closer to midnight."

We settle onto the couch, and Cade slips an arm around my shoulder. "Thank you so much for doing that," I say. "I've never seen Tanner so energized about playing his guitar. The last time I got him to play for me, he was so frustrated, he threw a music book across the room."

"He's a cool kid," Cade says. "Although he sure was desperate for me to tell him if playing the guitar will make him a chick magnet. I think he asked me that question at least four times."

I clear my throat and confess, "I might have told him that girls like guys who play in bands."

"Well, that explains it, then." Cade fingers a strand of my hair, and my cheeks warm.

"How long have you been playing?" I ask.

"About eight years."

"Do you play any other instruments?" He gazes past me and jerks his chin toward the baby grand piano in the corner. I stand, taking his hand and leading him to the piano. He slides in next to me on the upholstered bench. With a quick wink in my direction, he places his long fingers on the keys, and they move over the ivory as fluidly as they take to the strings on his guitar. Soft, harmonious sounds float up from the piano as he plays a song I don't recognize. When he finishes, he turns and flashes me a smile.

"I'm no Bach, but I can hold my own."

"Where did you learn to play?"

Cade drops his hands into his lap, and his gaze rests on the keys. "My mom taught me."

"I'm sorry; I didn't know."

"It's fine, don't worry about it. She was a great teacher. I don't play much anymore, but when I do, I think about her." His eyes lock with mine, and they sparkle like broken glass, reflecting the sharp remnants of loss. "What about you? Do you play?"

I quickly shake my head. "Oh, no. Not unless playing 'Chopsticks' counts. That's the only piano playing these fingers can do."

Cade takes my hand in his and he raises it to his lips, kissing my fingertips and subsequently snatching the breath from the back of my throat.

"What time will your dad be home?" he whispers in my ear.

I clear my throat. "Jay and Connie don't get out alone much. They won't be home until after midnight."

Cade raises a questioning eyebrow. "How come you don't call him your dad?" he asks. "I mean, you have no trouble calling Tanner and Lily your brother and sister. That doesn't make a lot of sense. Isn't it kind of the same thing?"

It isn't the same thing at all. And what confuses Cade makes perfect sense to me. It's one of the few pieces of my life that actually does fall into some recognizable pattern that my brain understands. "Because Tanner and Lily don't expect anything from me," I say. "Their titles are harmless. There are no expectations with having a brother and a sister."

"But having a dad—that comes with expectations?" Cade asks. He's trying to figure me out. "Am I being stupid for not getting this?"

"No, of course not," I say. I stare at the family portrait framed on the wall above the fireplace. It was taken a couple of weeks after I arrived in Mystic. Connie had insisted on it and made the arrangements. She even had the photo professionally framed. I study each of the five faces in the photograph. *Which one of these doesn't belong?*

"Finding out I suddenly had a father, and trying to figure out exactly how that's supposed to work, is a lot to handle. I've had so much to deal with over the past three months. I'm just not there yet, I guess."

He nods. "And how are you doing dealing with everything else?"

"I wish I could say it's getting better, but honestly, I'm not sure it ever will."

"It will. Trust me," Cade says, playing a series of soft notes, then stopping abruptly. "It just won't happen as fast as everyone around you wants it to. I think that was the hardest part of losing my mom. Everyone wanted to help me through it, but they didn't get it. It takes time. Years. Maybe forever, I don't know. I don't think I'm really there yet. And sometimes, when people think they're helping, they're not."

"What do you mean?"

"You know, when people offer you words of comfort that aren't the least bit comforting? Like—when I was at my mom's funeral, and my uncle put his arm around me and told me that I should be happy that my mom is in a better place." Cade's voice tenses at the memory. "She's in a better place? What the hell was I supposed to do with that? She was in a perfectly fine place with me when she was alive."

I squeeze his hand, and he releases a deep breath, tipping back his head to stare at the ceiling. "I know now that he was just trying to comfort me in the best way he knew how, but—at that moment, and for a long time afterward—I was so angry at him for saying that to me. I get that it wasn't intentional, but those words made me feel small, like my grief was something I would get over and move past."

I nod as a tightening in my chest begins to grow. "Yeah, I've had my fair share of that. If one more person tells me that everything happens for a reason, I might lose it," I say. "I mean, what reason could there possibly be for a drunk driver taking my mom's life? I feel so helpless when people say that to me. There's nothing I can do with a comment like that. It's useless."

He raises our entwined hands and places another soft kiss on my knuckles. I move my free hand to his arm, sliding a finger down his biceps to the edge of his T-shirt sleeve, where just a fragment of black ink is visible on his inner arm. "What does your tattoo say?"

Without a word, Cade draws back his sleeve to reveal three words: *Live Every Day.*

"These are the only words that matter," he says. "Forget what others say. What's important is what you say to yourself. But you have to be louder than the rest of them."

I stare at each letter, tracing them with my fingertip, my voice lost somewhere deep inside me. I lean in, wrap a hand around Cade's neck and pull him toward me. I kiss him. Oh boy, do I kiss him—softly at first, but then something powerful shoves the docile me aside and consumes what's left. The fierceness of our connection grows until both my arms are wrapped tightly around his neck. His warm, gentle lips are so soft and willing against mine. His arm tightens around my waist, and with that one movement, I feel secure and wanted. Cade sees me in a way that most people don't, like there's more to me on the inside, and even though it's buried deep, under a mountain of crazy at times, he's willing to make an effort to search it out. And for some unexplainable reason, the openly flawed, emotionally wrecked, baggage-laden me doesn't scare him one little bit. He should get some kind of a medal for that.

I breathe in the scent of him, a hint of soap mixed with whatever he put on after his shower, and I want to drown myself in it. After watching him earlier tonight with Tanner, so patient and attentive, I like him even more. He gave up his New Year's Eve to help a thirteen-year-old kid learn to play the guitar. Who does that? There are so many better ways he could have spent his evening. I stroke his cheek with my fingertips. He's a good guy. A good and honest guy—and he wants to be with me. If this is a dream, I never want to wake up.

"What the hell is this?"

I fly off the piano bench so fast, I would have knocked it over if Cade hadn't been there weighing it down.

Jay stands frozen in the entrance to the living room, his

cheeks a light crimson and his eyes narrowed accusingly on us. Connie stands right beside him, her eyes wide with surprise.

"Damn." Cade exhales under his breath. The legs of the heavy wooden bench scrape against the hardwood floor as he slowly stands, the hard lines of his face shutting out all the gentleness that was there just seconds ago.

Damn is right. This is not going to be good. Not by a long shot.

# CHAPTER TWENTY-SIX
## Cade

I should have been prepared for this, but I honestly didn't see it coming.

"What are—what are you doing here? I thought you were going dancing," Paige sputters.

"Connie wasn't feeling well, so we came home." Mr. Chapman's voice is nearly a growl, and his icy gaze is cemented on me. "What the hell is going on here?" His wife grabs his arm.

"I'm outta here," I say.

"No!" Mr. Chapman points an accusatory finger at me. "You stay right there until someone gives me an explanation."

"It's no big deal," Paige says. "I asked Cade to come over tonight."

"Jay," Mrs. Chapman warns, tightening her grip on his arm. "Calm down."

"Paige, I made it perfectly clear that I didn't want you hanging out with him. And now I come home to find you *sneaking* around? In my home?! Where are the kids?"

"They're upstairs. And we're not sneaking!" Paige protests. "Cade came here tonight because—"

He cuts her off with an outstretched palm. "Save it. You were supposed to watch Tanner and Lily, not—"

"Not what?" she demands, her cheeks reddening, and I want to say something to defend her, but I don't.

Mr. Chapman shakes his arm free from his wife's grasp and steps into the living room, his fists planted on his hips. "How could you defy me like this?" he demands of Paige while pointing his finger at me. "I told you, he's trouble."

Paige's mouth gapes in horror as my fingers clench into fists. There's so much I want to say right now, but there's no point in it. I will never get a fair trial in front of this man. Instead, I step past Paige, grab my jacket off the back of the couch and sling my guitar case over my shoulder in one swift movement. I glance back at Paige, but the wave of disappointment shooting through every nerve ending in my body prevents me from forming even a single word. All I can do is shake my head in defeat.

Paige lunges forward, clasping my wrist in her trembling fingers. "Please, don't go. Cade, please," she begs. "I know I messed this up. Please, just—explain!"

I twist free from her grasp. "It's pretty clear what's happening here. I don't have anything to say." And I don't. I just want to get the hell out of this house. Now.

"Cade!" Paige calls after me, but I'm out the door and down the front walk without another glance behind me.

What did I think was going to happen? That Mr. Chapman would accept me? Welcome me into his family with open arms? I'm an idiot.

"Cade, wait!" Paige calls from the door, and she races after me, catching my elbow just as I reach the sidewalk in front of the house.

"I'm sorry! I'm so sorry I didn't tell him about us. I know I promised you I would, but I didn't and—I'm sorry!" Her glossy eyes are wide and panic marinates her words.

"Who does he think you've been hanging out with the last two months?" I demand. Her lips part and her gaze drops. "Why didn't you tell him about me?"

"Because," she says frantically, "I was afraid Jay would stop me from seeing you, and I couldn't do that. I just couldn't. You are so important to me. Please, Cade, you have to know that. I can't lose you, too."

"If I were that important, you would have said something to him. The only thing I ever asked you to do was to stand up for me. But you didn't. Dammit, Paige, I've had enough people in my life lying to me. I didn't think you'd be one of them."

"Let's go back in, right now," she says, tugging urgently on my arm. My feet remain firmly planted on the concrete. There's no way I'm stepping foot back in that house.

"I'll tell Jay what happened. He can't blame you for this. None of this is your fault. It was me, it was all me!"

"Just forget it." I turn to go, but her desperate grasp on me tightens, her fingers digging into my flesh. "Please stay!

Why won't you let me talk to him?"

I lean in but stop short, just before our foreheads touch. We're close enough that I can smell her body spray and yet, at this moment, it feels like we're miles apart in so many ways. I sigh as frustration and disappointment collide in an elite-caliber wrestling match inside me. With a two-second pin, defeat wins out, and I say, "Because he expects this of me, not you."

Never have truer words been spoken. After all, I'm the one with the reputation for being irresponsible and defying authority. A total disregard for the rules—that's my specialty. I will never be welcome in this house. Maybe it's better if Paige figures that out now.

"Please, let me fix this!" she begs.

I shake my head. "Just let it go. It's not worth it."

"Don't say that," she whispers, pressing a hand to her stomach as if she's going to be sick. I want so badly to wrap my arms around her right now, but maybe this is for the best. I mean, who were we fooling? I will never be able to outrun my mistakes. Because there's always someone there to remind me where I've been. If it's not Mr. Chapman, it'll be someone else. And I can't deny that they're right—Paige shouldn't get mixed up with me. I'll only drag her down, and that's not fair to her. She has enough problems. She shouldn't be expected to carry mine, too.

I brush my lips against her forehead, lingering for a few seconds just to feel her skin against mine one more time. Even though it kills me to see the agony on her face, the torment glistening in her eyes, I step away from her and head for my bike. I slip on my helmet and kick-start the engine into a snarl, grasping every ounce of willpower I have not to turn back. If I meet her eyes, I'll break, I'll give in, and that's not what she or I need right now. I need to put some distance between us before I say something I'll regret.

# CHAPTER TWENTY-SEVEN
## Paige

I'm not sure how long I stand on the curb, staring out into the blackness and praying with everything in my being that Cade will come back. When the sprinkle of raindrops hits my cheeks, I reluctantly head back toward the house. With each step, fresh anger reignites inside me. It percolates until, finally, it explodes, and I slam the door behind me and storm into the living room.

"I hope you're happy," I seethe. "Cade's gone, and he probably wants nothing more to do with me!"

"I don't think that's a bad thing," Jay says, more reserved than he was just a couple of minutes ago. He's taken off his coat, but Connie still stands in the same spot, wearing hers. She hasn't even set down her purse.

"Why did you have to be so mean to him?" I demand. "He didn't do anything to deserve that. He came here tonight to coach Tanner on the guitar." I fling a hand at the ceiling. "Your son is miserable right now because he thinks he's awful at it. Cade helped him."

"I'm going to go check on the kids," Connie announces, and I'm not sure I've ever seen anyone leave a room so quickly. When she's gone, I turn my accusatory eyes back on Jay.

"You barely know that boy, Paige."

"So?"

"That kid has been in a lot of trouble. He spent three months in juvenile detention."

"When he was fourteen! I know all about it. He told me."

Jay snorts. "And you honestly think he's told you the truth? Don't be so naive. People with something to hide are never what they appear."

*You would know.*

"You're just as bad as everyone else. It's no wonder the rumors about Cade refuse to die," I say. "But you don't know him like I do."

I'm just getting warmed up, preparing to make Jay feel some kind of remorse for being so awful to Cade, but my perfectly planned monologue dissolves on my lips when he says, "That boy vandalized the school. Did he tell you that?"

I stare blankly, my mouth agape.

"I'm guessing by your reaction that that topic of conversation never came up. Can't say I'm surprised." Jay's words are drenched in disdain, and that ticks me off even more.

"And when exactly did this alleged crime take place?" I demand. As far as I know, there's been no incident at the school. And with the way gossip flies around that place like a witch on a broomstick, I'm pretty sure I would have heard about something that big by now.

"Three years ago," Jay says. "A group of kids broke into the school through the roof. Cade was with them. They didn't realize they tripped a silent alarm. By the time the police got there, they'd done nearly ten thousand dollars in damage."

"You're lying," I accuse, shaking my head in an attempt to deflect his words, but I can't shake the dread curling in my stomach. Cade told me that there were a lot of things in his past he regretted, but he's never shared any of them in detail, and he certainly never mentioned vandalizing the school. That one I would have remembered.

A new swarm of unanswered questions buzzes wildly through my mind. Is Jay making this whole school thing up? Would he do something like that just to keep Cade and me apart? And if what he's telling me is true, why didn't Cade tell me himself? I feel sick, like I'm stuck on the tilt-a-whirl at the fair and there's no way off.

"I don't want that boy in this house. And I want you to stay away from him. Do you hear me, Paige? He is no good for you."

Jay's words slice deep gashes into my heart, and maybe, under other circumstances, this is where I would fall to the ground and surrender, but my good old pal anger refuses to let me tap out and let Jay win. Instead, I narrow my eyes and take aim. "Cade is not mixed up in any of that anymore. He's a good student. Check his attendance records, *Principal Chapman*!" Jay grimaces. "I thought that you, of all people, would be open to second chances, but instead—" I dig deep into my arsenal for something that will wound him. "Instead, you're treating Cade exactly the same way my grandfather treated you!"

Jay's face drains of color. "That's enough."

"My grandfather didn't like you, you said so yourself. Aunt Faye confirmed it. What did you do to deserve that?" I taunt. Jay doesn't respond, but I can see I've struck a nerve. "How does it feel to be the bully on the other side?"

The muscles in Jay's jaw tighten. "It's my obligation to protect you, Paige."

"Is that all I am to you? An obligation?" I say it like it's a dirty word.

"That's not what I meant," Jay huffs. "It's my responsibility to look after you. To protect you."

"Why even bother?"

"Because I'm your father, whether you like it or not."

"No!" I shake my head. "You are my warden. But fortunately for both of us, that won't be the case for much longer."

I bound for the stairs, taking them two at a time up to the second floor. I expect to hear footsteps behind me, but there's nothing, not even a hint of movement from the living room, where I left Jay with his mouth ajar, brought up short by my sharp words. Deceit pounds in my veins, fueled by Jay's hateful accusations. I'm practically itching to pack my bags right this minute and forget everything about this house and the people who live here. But beneath the anger lives a sadness so thick, it nearly chokes me. I'm not sad for myself or for my own unfortunate circumstances. That I can deal with. What nearly suffocates me is that Cade was hurt in all of this. The look of disappointment in his eyes tonight racks me with guilt. How did I let this happen? It had started out as such a perfect night—and it had imploded in the blink of an eye.

I bury myself beneath the blankets, not even bothering to turn on the lamp beside my bed. The room is dark, and my one hope is that it will swallow me whole, leaving nothing behind except the sheet over my head.

*Mom, I need you.*

The doorknob turns, and my body stills. Slowly, I peek out from under the blankets. The hallway light streams in through the crack of the open door, and I can make out Lily's silhouette as she slips inside.

"Paige?" Her small voice beckons as she slowly moves to the foot of the bed. "Are you sad?" She must have heard the terrible exchange between Jay and me in the living room. Does she know what a terrible person I am?

"I'm fine," I say, ready to send her away and return to my solitude. But before I can get the words out, to tell her to go and not to worry about me, she pads over to the bed in her footed pajamas and crawls up under the blankets. I adjust quickly to make room for her, and she nestles into my chest, wrapping her small arms around my body. I tug the blankets up around her chin and slide back on the pillow.

I'm not sure how long we lay like this. An hour? At one point, Lily's breathing slows, and I know she's fallen asleep. I stare at the ceiling, unable to close my eyes. In the faint distance, I hear the clock in the living room chime. It's midnight.

So much for a happy New Year.

# CHAPTER TWENTY-EIGHT
## Paige

Cade and I haven't talked in three days. I'm too embarrassed and ashamed to call him. I can't seem to figure out how I would even begin that conversation. And it's not a good sign that Cade hasn't bothered to call or text me either.

To make matters worse, Jay and I aren't speaking. We had one conversation on New Year's Day, and it was just long enough for him to ground me for a month. As punishment, I must ride with him to and from school, and I'm only allowed to drive my car to work and straight home. He made a rookie mistake when he took away my cell phone for only two days, but I wasn't about to bring that up. That phone is the only lifeline I have left until my sentence is sufficiently served.

"Are we clear, Paige?" Jay's face was a stern mask as I sat stiffly on the couch trying not to roll my eyes.

"Crystal," I'd said flatly. Jay had sighed in frustration as I'd retreated to the solitude of my room, where I've spent most of my time since.

Pressing my hands to my bedroom window, I peer down into the backyard, my vision slightly distorted by the pelting rain against the glass. I imagine myself washing away with the water on the other side.

How in the world did everything get so messed up? I miss Cade so much, although I don't blame him for being angry. I let him down when I didn't stand up for him. And my biggest fear is that I won't be able to fix it.

My mother would know what to do. For starters, she would put her arms around me and tell me that regardless of how bad I feel right now, the earth will not shift off its axis and everything will be okay. But she's not here. I clutch my shoulders as a cold emptiness begins to seep into my veins, just like the outside rain pooling on the patio beneath my window.

Without another thought, my hand reaches for the nightstand drawer, and in one fluid movement, I withdraw my mother's turquoise journal. I trace the embossed ballet slippers on the cover, my heart racing as if it could bust free from my chest at any moment.

Am I ready for this? *Yes. No. Maybe?* All I know for sure is that I need my mom, and if I'm only able to have her words, I will take them; I will drink them in and try to get as close to her as I possibly can. I sink onto my bed beside Kitty Poppins, who's stretched out in the middle of my comforter. Ignoring the cat's growl of protest, I flip open the book.

My mother began dancing when she was four years old, just like me, and by high school, when she'd started this journal, she was well on her way to dancing professionally. It was her dream. Just like it had been mine. I still feel robbed that someone took all that away from us in a matter of minutes. It's not right or fair or anywhere close to okay, and I don't know how I'm supposed to move on from that.

I lower my head, and my eyes take in the words scrawled so beautifully in blue ink. My throat grows thick and I scrunch my eyes tight, trying to slow my breathing against the pounding jackhammer behind my rib cage. I can do this. I want to do this. I need to feel that a sliver of my mother is here with me, to wrap myself in her thoughts and words, to finally know what it was that she thought about when she was my age. But most of all, I'm hoping she will tell me what happened between her and Jay. I'm desperate to know how love can go so horribly wrong and lead to— whatever this is that's happening to me now.

I open my eyes and begin reading. The first entry appears to have been written just hours after Mom and her friends returned from seeing Janet Jackson in concert. She gushes over how they were starstruck and singing at the top of their lungs when the pop icon performed their favorite songs. The energy in her description puts a wide grin on my face. Mom had a couple Janet Jackson CDs in her car that she always insisted we listen to on long drives. She may have mentioned seeing her in concert, but if she did, she certainly wasn't as animated about it as the girl writing this journal.

I quickly find myself lost in each page turn, reading through numerous entries about friends, school and her dreams for the future. My breath catches when I get to the first entry about Jay. They met in biology class, just like Aunt Faye told me. Mom describes how another girl had been after him, but she'd snagged him first.

*He's so cute,* she wrote. *He asked me to the movies on Friday night.* I recall the picture in Jay's office of him in his football uniform. He did look good back then. He still looks good, only now he looks like a principal, all authoritative and serious.

I'm not going to lie—it's a little awkward reading about their first kiss, and she describes it in surprisingly vivid detail. I remind myself that these are the poetic words of a girl who is on the brink of falling in love. I know what that feels like. It's blissful and mystifying and exciting, all rolled up into a gooey ball that hovers on the edge of exploding from the inside out—until it all goes wrong. The moment thoughts of Cade surface, I dismiss them and refocus on the journal, which, I remind myself, isn't any better. My mother's feelings for Jay would be incredibly sweet if it weren't for the fact that they were about to plunge headfirst into a relationship destined for destruction. Call it the ultimate spoiler alert.

Mom wrote about the evening she took Jay home to meet her father for the first time. I sit up straight as my eyes scan her words. She'd been so excited to show off her new boyfriend to her family, but her excitement fizzled to disappointment when the introduction turned out to be a dismal failure. I pull the journal closer.

*Dad doesn't like Jay. He told me he's not good enough for me, and that I should be with someone who's going places, not with a guy who doesn't have two nickels to rub together or an ounce of ambition to stand on. That's what he said. I'm so mad at him right now. He's being a complete jerk.*

I reread each sentence. My mother's discouragement is palpable in every stroke of the pen against the page. What in the world had created a dislike so strong, and after just one meeting, that Martin Bryant would use such hurtful words to crush his daughter's excitement? I hope for my mother's sake that she was able to talk to my grandmother about all this, but there are no entries, at least so far, to indicate that she had.

It's strange to think that Mom was my age when she wrote in this journal. Stranger yet that I'm literally watching her love for Jay grow from one page to the next, while a rift begins to grow between her and my grandfather. I wish I could ask Jay what exactly happened back then, but if I do, I will have to show him the journals, and I don't want to do that—not yet anyway. My hands grip the edges of the book tighter. This is a special connection between my mom and me, and I'm not ready to share it with anyone else.

I'm surprised when something falls from between the pages and lands in my lap. It's a photograph of Mom and Jay. They're wearing blue caps and matching gowns, each clutching what look to be their diplomas. I raise the picture closer, so my eyes can study every inch of it. Jay's arm is around Mom, and he looks proud. My mother's smile is a mere shadow in comparison. My eyes trail back to the journal in search of answers to this new piece of evidence.

*I graduated today,* Mom wrote. *And now I'm more scared than I've ever been. I'm planning to tell Jay everything tonight. I still don't know if I'm doing the right thing. My dad doesn't want me to say anything, but I just can't take it anymore. Jay has a right to know, and I can't keep secrets from him anymore. If he freaks out and breaks up with me, I don't know what I'm going to do. I don't think I can do this on my own.*

My heartbeat pounds everywhere in my body all at once, ricocheting into my ears and throat. With my mouth suddenly bone dry, I reach to turn the page, surprised when I notice that my fingers are shaking, the anticipation electric as they quiver against the paper. This is it. This is what I've been waiting for. I know how it ends, and yet I'm still hoping there's something I missed, something within these pages that makes all of this somehow less devastating. I'm not prepared for the next words I read. My eyes widen. In a shaky hand, Mom has scrawled, *Dad talked to Jay before I got the chance. It's over.*

The following words and sentences come at me in a torrent of angry, heart-crushing strokes of her pen. In utter disbelief, I stare helplessly at the words as they hit hard. Reading and rereading the awful sentences, I search this page, and the next, for something that will tell me this isn't what it is. I'm desperate for anything—a word or a sentence that will take it all back, confirm in some small way that Martin Bryant is not the monster he's morphed in to on the pages of this journal. And Jay—he'd sworn to me he'd loved my mom, but the words from her own hand confirm that's a bald-faced lie. An odd sound escapes my throat as my eyes freeze on the next sentence. The journal shakes in my white-knuckled hands. *What the—?*

Shock, disbelief and denial collide, and the book slips from my fingers and onto the hardwood floor at my feet with a thwack. Frozen on the edge of the bed, I'm unable to pick it up, paralyzed against any movement at all. My heart pounds out a frantic jig, as if it's trying to break free from the confines of my body, and I gulp in shallow breaths. The room around me is loose and fluid, my vision pitching from side to side, and deep down in my center, a wave of nausea swirls like a tornado of knives. I drop my face into my hands as the cold, hard truth sinks in, delivering the final blow and crushing my heart into tiny splinters.

How could he do that to her?

# CHAPTER TWENTY-NINE
## Cade

"I don't know what's eating at you, son, but if you slam down one more of my tools, you and I are gonna go outside and have some words."

"Sorry," I mutter, picking up the wrench and returning it to its place on the wall. Even with my back turned, I can feel Mac's heavily critical eyes. I focus on my work, careful to give the tools the gentle respect they deserve. Mac closes the hood of the minivan he's been working on and, just as I predict, he's beside me at the workbench.

"Is there something you want to talk about?"

"No," I answer, wincing when he claps a heavy hand on my back, his subtle way of informing me that my disinterest in having a conversation isn't a factor in this equation. Mac wants to talk, and even if it's a one-sided chat, my presence is required.

"I think I'll get a cup of coffee," he announces. When he doesn't move, I glance up. Mac juts his stubbly chin toward the break room, and I have no choice but to follow his silent command. I will, however, take a moment to acknowledge the irony in all this. The last thing I've been able to catch lately is a break in any form.

Joe and Brian, the two mechanics working nearby, at least have the decency to pretend they weren't watching our exchange. When I glance their way, they're both focused on their work, but not Jared. He just shakes his head, like I should have known better than to bring my problems to work.

Once we're in the break room, Mac grabs his usual mug off the shelf and tips the coffeepot into it. "Spill it, Cade."

"Spill what?" I ask, leaning my hands on the back of one of the chairs.

"Whatever it is that has you so riled up that you're taking it out on my equipment." Mac lowers his tired body onto a chair with a grunt. "We've got a lot of work to get done and only a few more hours to do it, so take a seat and give it to me straight."

I sigh and drop into the chair across from him. Despite my reluctance, I rehash the details of my fallout with Principal Chapman on New Year's Eve. I tell Mac everything, right down to how he looked at me as if I had no right to breathe the same air as his daughter. And then I share the worst part of that night. It wasn't Mr. Chapman's accusations, although enduring that was no picnic. What was most disappointing is that Paige hadn't told him about me—that she hadn't wanted him to know I was part of her life. That hurt worse than anything Mr. Chapman could have thrown at me.

"Let's just say it was a real shit show."

"Language," Mac warns.

I roll my eyes. "Fine. It wasn't exactly how I planned to ring in the new year," I correct.

"Did you try to talk to Mr. Chapman and explain what was really going on?"

I shrug. "No."

"Why not?" he asks. I have a bucketload of reasons *why not*, but not a single syllable makes contact with the air before Mac says, "Seems to me that maybe you should have stood up for yourself, and for Paige."

"What's the point? Mr. Chapman will never accept me."

"Not if you don't give him a reason to. Look, son, you've got a lot to offer this world. But you've got to start standing up for yourself. Yes, you've made some mistakes. But part of being a man means stepping up and showing the world that you've learned from those mistakes and that you're a better person for doing so. When you don't defend your character, when you let gossip and rumors circulate without injecting the truth when and where you can, you're part of the problem."

"That's easy for you to say, but—"

"Not so fast," Mac says. "Cade, I don't give you advice just to hear myself talk. I've been right where you are. Believe me when I tell you that I've made my fair share of mistakes. Some big ones. And I wallowed in them for a while, until I realized that if I wanted things to change, I was going to have to get off my butt and make that happen."

"Maybe there are some mistakes you just can't outrun," I say.

"I don't believe that. And I don't want you to believe it either." Mac runs a finger along the rim of his mug. "I think what's complicating matters here is that you love this girl."

"*What?* No, I like her, but..."

"All right, take it easy," Mac says, but the smug look on his face tells me he thinks I'm full of crap. "The point is, Paige is important to you. If she weren't, you wouldn't be this upset. But when things get tough, you run because that's what you've always done."

I start to protest, but Mac holds up a grease-stained hand. "I don't fault you for that, Cade. I used to be a runner myself when I was younger. But I've learned a few things since then, and the most important one is this—at some point, you've gotta stop and face your problems head-on. I think you need to consider going to see your father."

I slap my palms on the table and shoot out of my seat. "Not gonna happen," I say.

"Hear me out before you tell an old man to go to hell."

I bite down hard, sealing in the heated words filling my mouth. Mac takes a drink and motions for me to sit back down. "Look, Cade, forgiving your father doesn't mean accepting that what he did to you was okay. Not at all." Mac raps his knuckles on the table to get my attention. I raise my eyes to meet his. "Forgiving means you give yourself permission to let go of the feelings that are poisoning you. Until you do that, all this hatred is going to continue to eat you up. Choose to let it go."

Silence fills the room as Mac's words settle around me. I hear what he's saying, and all of it makes sense on paper. Forgiveness equals peace and love and happily ever after. And that sounds really good. In reality, it would be easier and much less painful if he asked me to jump in front of a train.

# CHAPTER THIRTY
## Paige

Saturday is a slow morning at the bookstore. Two hours into my shift, Macy appears in the doorway of the back room, where I'm organizing boxes of inventory. I use the term "organize" loosely because Macy has a pretty good system for keeping everything in its place. She eyes the room and says, "You should take off."

"Really?" I ask. I've never been sent home early before.

She rests her hands on her hips and studies the clock. "Yeah. I'm not expecting things to pick up. I've got some bookkeeping work to do, so I can hold down the fort. No sense in both of us being here on a beautiful day."

She doesn't have to say it twice. Within fifteen minutes, I am out of the store and in my car, wondering what I'm going to do with myself for an entire Saturday. I'm not going home, that's for sure. I don't care if I'm grounded; I can't stand being in that house with Jay. I can barely look at him, now that I know the truth about what a terrible human being he is.

I consider calling Cade but quickly dismiss the idea. I haven't yet figured out a way to grovel for forgiveness that doesn't end with him blocking my number. After our New Year's Eve fiasco, I'm what one would call a chicken. A scaredy-cat. A wimp. Or just a plain old baby. Yup, *that's* how I've spent my time, looking up alternatives to the word "coward" in a thesaurus I found on a shelf in the back room.

I want to make things right with Cade, more than anything. I miss him. But I think I may have jacked things up beyond repair this time. Part of me hoped he would be the one to reach out and put me out of my misery, that he would drop by the bookstore today like he always does on Saturdays, but he's apparently gone off the grid. Or he's just really good at avoiding me.

I tap my fingers on the steering wheel. I know what I want to do today. I stop at a nearby convenience store, filling my gas tank and grabbing a large fountain drink, readying myself for my first solo road trip since arriving in Mystic. I pull up the Maps app on my phone, plug in my destination and hit the highway. When I reach the Eugene city limits, I call my cousin Tyler, and he gives me directions to campus.

As I carefully maneuver my car along side streets looking for a parking spot, I can't wait to see Ty. I didn't realize just how much I've missed him until he was so close. Tyler and I share a bond that I don't have with anyone else. He's the only person who hasn't tried to get me to open up about losing my mom. He's always been there for me, no matter what, to make me laugh or to give me a shoulder to lean on when I just want to be quiet.

Fifteen minutes later, after I've essentially hugged the crap out of him, Tyler and I are seated in the student union sipping steaming lattes. Apparently, Tyler's been up to his eyeballs studying for a political science test, so my call was a pleasant surprise.

"This is a spontaneous trip," he says, raising a questioning eyebrow.

"It was slow at work today," I answer. I meet skeptical eyes, so I add, "I wanted to see how the frat boys live. How's the food here?"

Tyler gives his abdomen a contented pat, intentionally sticking it out to make it appear stuffed. The truth is, he's in excellent shape, and I'm pretty sure a person could scrub laundry on his washboard abs.

"And how goes the rest of college life?" I ask.

The corners of his lips turn up, confirming what I'd already guessed—college life is excellent when you're as attractive as my cousin. Long stares from passing females only serve to validate my theory. Tyler notices them also. Occasionally, his eyes linger on a leggy blonde or an athletic brunette, but his eyes always return to me, along with his attention to our conversation.

By the looks of us, you can't tell that we're related. Ty was blessed with the sparkling blue eyes of the Bryant clan, just like my mother. Inconspicuously, I take in his broad jaw, high cheekbones and the curve of his chin and decide those must come from his father's side of the family. Uncle Trevor and Aunt Faye split up when Tyler was eight years old. I don't remember Ty's dad very well. Mostly what I remember is that he traveled a lot, and Faye and Tyler were often on their own.

"Look, Paige, I love that you came to visit me, but I think there's another reason you're here." He takes the last swallow from his cardboard cup and chucks it over my head and into the trash can behind me.

"Impressive," I say. "The basketball team is missing out."

"Actually, there's a group of guys from fraternity row who get together for pick-up games at the rec center twice a week. I'm their secret weapon." He grins and pats my knee. "Come on, let's take a walk."

We stroll across campus, with Tyler pointing out the buildings where he has classes. But to my dismay, he hasn't forgotten that I've dodged his question about my visit twice now. He asks me about it again. We wander past the library before I finally say, "Things are bad, Ty. I just don't fit into my life in Mystic. At all."

"Are the Chapmans making things hard for you?"

*Jay lied to me.* That's what I want to say, but I don't.

"Are you not getting along with their kids?" Tyler prods.

"No, they're fine," I tell him.

His brows furrow. "Then what's the deal?"

It seems like such a simple question. But it's not. It's complicated in so many ways, and the thought of dredging it all up for Tyler exhausts me. "I just feel like I should never have gone there. It's like I'm an intruder and their lives can't really get back to normal until I'm gone."

Tyler's eyes remain trained on the path in front of us, his expression unreadable. "Sounds to me like you don't want to fit," he finally says.

"What does that mean?" Tyler picks up his pace, forcing me to do the same. "Hey! You can't just say something like that to me and keep walking." I have to grab the hem of his jacket to get him to stop.

"Sorry, I shouldn't have said anything."

"Well, you did, so now explain yourself." I cross my arms over my chest.

"Look, Paige," Tyler sighs. I can tell he's struggling with how to phrase his next sentence. "Your world has been completely turned upside down. I can't even begin to understand how you feel." I appreciate him acknowledging my feelings, but before I can say so, he continues with, "But at some point, you've got to right it. You're the only one who can."

This time, I'm the one who starts walking. I have no idea where I'm going, but I know Tyler is following me when I hear him say, "Hey, guys" to two people passing by on my right. One of them, a tall guy with blond hair who's wearing a green sweatshirt with a yellow "O" on it, winks at me.

"Frat brothers," Tyler says as he falls into step with me. I refuse to look at him. "Come on, I'm sorry. Don't be mad."

"You're saying that I'm making this situation harder than it needs to be. That *I'm* trying to make sure it doesn't work. That's what you're saying, isn't it?"

Tyler's silence is deafening. I'm not exactly sure what is happening right now. One minute we're drinking coffee and talking about college life and the next I'm having to defend myself to a guy who hasn't seen me in more than three months and doesn't have a clue what I've been dealing with.

"Come with me," Tyler says. "There's something I want you to see."

Reluctantly, I follow him across the sprawling lawn of the library, and we make our way to a scholarly looking brick building. After climbing three flights of stairs, I'm just about ready to tell Tyler I've had enough. That's when he stops and leads me over to the railing. We look down into an ample space with shiny hardwood floors, wall-to-wall mirrors and about a dozen people in dancer's attire moving to music coming from a piano I can't see.

From our vantage point, the dancers are oblivious to us, gliding about the floor in beautiful, graceful performance. An icy chill shoots from the base of my skull straight down to my toes as an enormous lump forms in my throat.

"Why did you bring me here?" The hollow, empty words tumble from my numb lips.

"Mom says you refuse to dance since Abby—"

I shove myself away from the railing as if it's searing-hot

metal biting into my palms, and I back against the wall, far enough away that the dancers are out of sight. "I don't want to talk about this."

"That's the problem, Paige. You don't want to talk about it, but you need to. Shutting out the world, the people who are trying to be here for you and the things you love isn't gonna bring her back."

"Stop." I clasp my hands behind my neck and shake my head repeatedly.

"Look, I didn't say anything before because you don't need a million people giving you advice, but you need to hear this," Tyler says, placing his firm hands on my shoulders. I stare at his shoes.

"You love to dance. And your mom was a huge part of that. You can't just give it up because she's no longer here, Paige. Abby wouldn't want that. You know she wouldn't."

The lump in my throat doubles in size, threatening to choke the life out of me. Tyler takes my arm and gently pulls me back to the railing. "Look down there. *That* is what you should be doing. You love it, and you're amazing at it." I pry at his fingers, but his hold is firm. "You know I'm right. Just admit it."

Again, I'm shaking my head, and I feel sick, like I'm about to lose everything inside me—my latte, my sanity, everything.

"Not dancing isn't gonna bring her back."

"I can't do that without her!" I yell, the echo of my unexpected outburst slicing through the empty space around us, startling myself and Tyler. In one quick movement, I manage to yank my arm free and push myself away from him. He can't possibly know how this feels. He isn't the one who lost the center of his world. He isn't the one who found his life instantly turned upside down and every plan he'd made for his future suddenly so far out of reach, it literally paralyzes him with fear. "You don't get it."

"Then help me understand," he begs.

"I didn't come here for a lecture, Tyler!"

"I'm not lecturing you, Paige. I love you. You're acting like your life is over, but you are still here. Don't throw away a God-given talent that makes you happy."

I don't say goodbye to Tyler. I bolt down the stairs and out of the building, running as fast as I can across the campus to my car. And with each step, I feel more alone than I have ever been in my entire life.

# CHAPTER THIRTY-ONE
## Cade

I read Paige's text for the third time, just to make sure I didn't imagine it. She asks me to meet her at the jetty, and it takes me only a handful of seconds to respond and tell her I'll be there. It's been the longest week of my life, and at this point, I've replayed that awful night at her house so many times, it's all become an ugly blur, and I'm not really sure who should be angry with whom anymore.

Paige is waiting in the parking lot when I pull in. She jumps out of her car and throws her arms around me, nearly knocking me off balance as I climb off my bike.

"Hey!" I laugh. "Take it easy."

"I didn't think you'd come." She pulls me down for a kiss. I go willingly, and she knots her fingers through my hair, drawing me closer with undeniable desperation.

When she finally allows me to pull back, I'm breathless. "What was that?"

"That's me saying I'm sorry. I'm so sorry about every-thing! You are so important to me, and I handled things badly with Jay. Please forgive me. You *have* to forgive me," she begs. The green flecks in her eyes blaze with regret, and they melt away any remaining strife between us. The brisk wind whips her long, dark hair and I smooth back the wayward strands from her forehead. I've missed being able to touch her like this.

"There's nothing to forgive," I say. "It wasn't all your fault. I shouldn't have left the way I did the other night, and I'm sorry about that." Paige wraps her arms around my waist, drawing me into another tight hug, and she's shaking. I hold her against my chest, rubbing her back until she begins to relax and her shallow breaths even out. "What's going on?"

Without a word, Paige takes my hand, and we walk down onto the beach, which is fairly deserted for a late Saturday afternoon. There's a family with two small children playing by the water, a couple walking their dog and a man who looks like he's scouting for seashells. We move past all of them to the south end of the beach near the jetty. When we're finally alone, Paige pulls me into another long embrace.

"I've been pretty lost without you this past week," she says. "Jay and I aren't talking."

I expel a long breath, not surprised by that piece of information, but bothered by it. "I never wanted to cause problems between you and your dad. That wasn't my intention."

"Jay and I have a lot more problems than I realized."

"I think he just wants what's best for you." She expels a derisive grunt, and I narrow my eyes. "Why do you do that?"

"I'm so tired of people telling me what they think is best for me," she says, then she recounts the last four hours of her day and her trip to Eugene to visit her cousin. She rehashes the whole unpleasant conversation between the two of them, and when she finishes, she looks to me for my reaction. I know what she wants me to say, but instead, I chew on the inside of my cheek and divert my gaze to the rolling shoreline.

"Do you think I overreacted?" she asks. "Do you think Ty was *right*?"

I have two choices here. I can tell Paige that her cousin had no right to talk to her like that, given what she's been through, and that whether or not she decides to dance again or hang it up for good is no one else's business. Or I could tell her the truth—that I think Tyler *is* right. He and Paige are close—she's told me that on numerous occasions—which means he probably knows her better than anyone else, certainly better than I do. I've never had the opportunity to see Paige dance, and maybe I never will, but I know it's been a considerable part of her life and I don't think her cousin would risk his relationship with her by saying those things unless he knew it was important that she hear them.

"None of us gets to choose what happens to us," I say. "But Paige, you can choose how you respond. Maybe you should have heard him out."

"Not you too!" she huffs, drawing back.

"I'm sorry. I'm trying to help you."

"Are you? Are you really?" she demands. "Because, quite frankly, *helping me* means being on my side."

"No, it doesn't," I correct.

"Well, it sure as hell doesn't mean lecturing me." She throws up her hands. "You're just like Tyler!"

Two minutes ago, her arms were wrapped around me like she couldn't get close enough, and now—she's pissed. Even though I know I'm not the direct source of her anger, that it's a residual response to her conversation with her cousin, it doesn't erase the fact that she's shooting daggers at me. "I wasn't lecturing you," I say calmly, reaching for her hand, but she pulls away. "Come on, don't be like that."

"You can't possibly understand what I've been through. You don't get it."

My eyes widen. "What exactly don't you think I get?" She doesn't say a word, but the silence between us speaks volumes. Her cold eyes hold my gaze, then drop away, her unspoken words pummeling me with realization.

I blink hard. "Are you—are you saying what I think you're saying?" I open my palms as if I'm expecting reason to drop from the sky and back into the space between us at any minute. "You really think that because my mom died of cancer and not in a horrific tragedy like yours, that I can't possibly feel her loss the way you do?" Never have so many unspoken words struck me so hard. A simple shrug of Paige's shoulders is all I get in response, but it's all the confirmation I need. Astonishment seizes hold of my entire body, and I blanch as her absurd accusations fully register. "I cannot believe you would think that." She still refuses to respond or meet my eyes. A new wave of disappointment rolls through me, and the mere two feet of space between us grows expansive and icy cold. "I lost a piece of my world the day my mom died. So don't you dare tell me that *I don't get it.*"

"But it wasn't your fault!" she cries. Paige tilts her head skyward and gulps in air like she's been searching for eternity for just one pure breath. "You couldn't stop what happened to your mom," she says, pressing the heels of her palms to her eyelids as if to suppress the agony swirling inside her. "You couldn't save your mom—but I could have saved mine."

# CHAPTER THIRTY-TWO
## *Paige*

If I were a supervillain, my evil power would undoubtedly be wounding people with my thoughts. I don't need words. The hurt I've inflicted on Cade is unmistakable, radiating in his hard, brown eyes.

Cade was thirteen when he'd lost his mom. She'd been sick. There wasn't anything he could do about it, but he'd known it was coming. He'd had *time*. He'd had days, weeks, even months to say everything he'd needed to say, to hug and kiss her over and over. He'd had time to say the goodbyes that I would have sold my soul to have with my mother—to have just one more day, a handful of minutes at the very least. It wasn't Cade's fault that I'd been cheated out of more time with my mom, but without even allowing the words to make contact with the air, I'd managed to dismiss his pain like it didn't matter as if it pales in comparison to mine. I've cut him deep, and that isn't fair. That doesn't give me supervillain status—it just makes me a brat. A brat who just revealed something I haven't shared with anyone else until now.

"How could you have saved your mom?" Cade asks.

I can't look at him. I drop to my knees in the sand, no longer able to shoulder the full weight of everything I've kept inside me all these months. If it all ends here, I might as well go out with a bang. I swallow hard. "The night my mom died—it shouldn't have happened. I could have stopped it." Shame burns in each syllable.

Cade kneels beside me, his hand brushing my wind-blown hair away from my face so that he can peer into my eyes for some sort of understanding. I turn away, my hair slipping through his fingers and falling forward to shroud the view between us.

"You said a drunk driver hit your mom. There's no way that could have been your fault. You didn't do anything."

I shrink in on myself as his words form tiny bullets that lodge deep in the fibers of my heart. "You're right, I didn't," I say, twisting my watchband back and forth. "I didn't do the one thing I should have done. And that's why she died."

"Wait. What?" His forehead creases, as if he's trying to solve an equation without all of the information.

He doesn't understand. Because how could anyone possibly comprehend how a daughter could be so selfish, so wrapped up in herself that she would make a decision that would cost her mother her life? If I could cry right now, I would, but the tears still refuse to come. Maybe that's my punishment, that I will carry the burden of this white-hot guilt inside me for the rest of my life, deep in the essence of my soul, as eternal penance for my sins. It doesn't quite seem like enough.

"C'mon." Cade reaches for my hand, but I pull back, quickly standing and turning away. I can't have him this close. There is comfort in his touch, and I don't deserve that. I don't deserve to be in the arms of this incredible guy that I just seem to keep hurting. "Talk to me. Why do you blame yourself?"

The waves bash against the jetty with measured force, stabbing down onto the large, jagged rocks and mirroring the sensation churning inside me. "I'm a terrible person."

Cade's warm hands are on my shoulders, and he gently turns me around to face him. "No, you're not." Concerned eyes swallow me up, and I want to fall into him, beg him to hold me just one more time and forget everything that's happened in the last three months. Instead, I pull back the lid on my secrets. He deserves to know the truth.

"My mom shouldn't have been on the road so late that night. We were at our ballet studio, and she was helping me prepare for a big audition. It could have been my big break. Mom was so excited for me." I pause, attempting to swallow the memories that feel like cotton in my mouth. "Did I tell you that my mom danced professionally for about ten years?" Cade shakes his head. "She'd loved it, and she wanted me to have that experience." I close my eyes for longer than a blink. "I wanted it, too."

Cade takes one of my shaking hands and holds it in both of his. This time, I let him, because this might be the last time he has any desire to touch me. And the thought of that—of losing him for good—shatters me from the inside out.

"I was under a lot of pressure," I manage. "The ballet company that I was auditioning for rarely considers offering apprenticeships to dancers my age. The audition was just a couple of weeks away, and we'd been working so hard." My mind catapults back, rewinding the months until I am right back in the studio that night with Mom. The room unfolds around me in vivid detail, so clearly that it draws a sharp, unsettled breath from my lungs. Mom stands in front of the mirror, showing me an eight-step combination. She is as graceful as ever, vibrant and beautiful in her movements, talent pouring from each limb. I loved to watch her dance.

I shake my head and clear my throat, releasing the memory before I'm utterly lost in it. "Mom was choreographing my audition piece, and she wanted it to be unforgettable. She was a stickler for perfection. But we'd been at it for hours, and I was so tired."

Cade squeezes my hand.

"She wasn't happy with the end of the dance; something was off." I cast my gaze upward, blinking against the patchwork of cottony clouds in the bright afternoon sky. "I wanted to go home. I had a math test I needed to study for, but she said we had to get it right, that there was so much riding on this audition." My eyes settle on the middle of Cade's chest. "Every muscle in my body was exhausted, and I didn't want to continue. Finally, Mom told me to go home and she'd stay and finish up on her own. There were a couple more changes she wanted to work on."

I force my eyes to meet Cade's, and I search them for a spark of realization. But all I find in his face is more confusion.

"I still don't see how any of it is your fault."

"Don't you get it?" I cry out. "*I left her!* I went home, and she stayed to work on my audition piece. She stayed to make sure everything was perfect for *me*. I should have made her come with me. I should have told her not to worry about it, that we could work on it the next day." My voice rises. "If I'd made her leave with me, she wouldn't have been on the road, and she wouldn't be—"

His arms are around me in an instant, constricting me in a fierce hug as I struggle to get free. I don't deserve his comfort. I need him to yell at me for being a stupid, selfish girl.

"It isn't your fault," he breathes in my ear, but I shove his chest with my palms to force distance between us.

"It is my fault! I wasn't thinking about her. I was only thinking of myself. If I hadn't been so wrapped up in what I wanted—this never would have happened!" Cade takes a step toward me, but I take two steps backward.

"That's what moms do, Paige. They do what's best for their kids. She probably wouldn't have gone home with you, no matter how much you begged."

"Then I should have stayed with her. At least then she—" The harsh, unavoidable words fizzle into oblivion.

"She wouldn't have died alone." Cade sighs as my face crumples. Now, he knows everything, and my shame is exposed. "Is that why you don't dance anymore?"

Nearly drowning in disgrace, I cup my elbows to hold myself together. "I can't. Every time I walk into a dance studio, I fall apart."

I brace myself for Cade's reaction. I'm expecting revulsion, disgust, or at the very least disappointment. But that's not what I get from him. Not even close.

"Come on, Paige, that's ridiculous," he says softly.

Surprise sprouts inside me, and at first, I'm struck dumb by his response. But it's quickly edged out by irritation. "What do you mean, *that's ridiculous?*"

"I just mean—" He hesitates, as if he's weighing his next words. "I think that's a cop-out. Dancing made your mom happy. She was proud of you, and you said yourself that she had dreams for you to dance professionally, and that's what you wanted, too. Why in the world would you stop trying to make those dreams come true?"

Disbelief and dejection wrestle for control, but they're lost somewhere inside me, among the thousands of puncture wounds from Cade's words. This is not how this was supposed to go.

"I'm not saying you haven't lost a lot," he says. "You lost your mom, and that's devastating. But as far as the rest of it goes—come on, Paige, you didn't lose it. You gave it up."

"Go to hell."

"Look, I'm not trying to be a bastard. I know what it's like to feel sorry for yourself. I've done it for a lot longer than you have, and you know where it got me? Nowhere. And nowhere is a really lonely place to live."

I shake my head. "You just don't get it."

He throws up his hands. "Not this again. What don't you think I get this time?"

"All of it!"

"Fine. Think what you want, but I am truly sorry you had to go through any of it. I really am, and if there were a way that I could take all of it off your shoulders so that nothing hurtful ever touched you, I would. But that's not how things work," he says regretfully. "And if it makes you feel better to be mad at me because of that, be mad. Be as mad at me as you want. But the truth is—Tyler is right. At some point, you have to decide to look up. Take a look around at what you have left. Because that's what matters. I'm sorry if that's not what you want to hear; I'm just being honest."

"Oh, so now you decide to be honest with me?" I demand. "Good to know. But if I were you, I would have led with the part about you vandalizing the school."

My words blindside him, and he steps back, raising his hands as if to bring this conversation to a halt. "You know about that?"

"Yeah, I do. Jay told me, right after I made a fool of myself trying to defend you, trying to convince him that you've changed," I say, feeling the wounds inside me rip open just a few more millimeters. "But I think you're missing the point. Why didn't *you* tell me?"

"Because I don't like to talk about it," he says. "And it's not what you think. I didn't vandalize the school. I'm just the one who got caught and took the brunt of the blame." Now it's my turn to look dazed and confused. With a worn sigh, Cade turns his back to me and trains his eyes on the surf. "It happened just after I'd been kicked out of the Sloanes' house. I was hanging out with a group of guys I'd met on the streets. They're the ones who did the vandalism. I didn't even know what they were up to; I was just supposed to keep an eye out. By the time I figured it out, the cops were there. The guys took off, and I got caught."

"Is that why you served time in juvenile detention?"

He nods. "It was the last straw. And it's the reason your dad can't stand the sight of me."

I pace back and forth while Cade's eyes remain trained on me. "Is that why you wanted me to tell Jay that you and I were together? Because you were trying to get back at him? That's what Dane said. Is he right? Are you just playing me?" I demand, barely able to stomach the sickening reality of my words.

Cade's entire demeanor transforms. His momentary surprise takes an immediate U-turn and disintegrates, and he levels me with a look I've never seen before. "Since when do you believe anything that prick says about me? You know what, forget I asked. Believe whatever you want, Paige. I wasn't trying to get back at your dad; I was trying to make amends. I thought that being honest with him about us was a good place to start, that maybe if he saw you giving me a chance, saw that I was important to you, he'd be willing to give me a second chance, too. I guess I'm the idiot here."

"No. You're a hypocrite." Okay, so maybe I should feel slightly bad that a part of me considered believing Dane's accusations, and yeah, maybe I jumped to conclusions, but I'm not ready to apologize yet. I'm not done being mad. "You want Jay to give you a second chance when you refuse to give your own father one?"

I hit a nerve. Cade's eyes narrow, and the muscles in his jaw flex, his cheek twitching in agitation. "Don't do this, Paige."

"Why? Because it's okay for you to judge me for my actions, but you, Mr. High and Mighty, are above such criticism? I don't think so."

"You've been given a second chance with your dad, Paige. He never abandoned you," Cade says. "Yeah, he never knew about you all those years, but that's not the same thing. He's here now, with an entire family who wants you, but you refuse to accept them." He rakes his fingers through his hair and huffs out a breath. "All I'm saying is that you have people who love you and want what's best for you, and you're shutting them out."

My body shakes as irritation pulses through me with every word he exhales. And apparently, he's not finished.

"You got a raw deal; I get that. But you can't stop living

your life and give up your dreams because you feel guilty. You lost your mom because of unfortunate circumstances, not because you did anything wrong. Don't punish yourself for something you had no control over."

I'm not sure which hurts worse—that the boy who has been on my side no longer is, or that he's belittling my feelings, making light of the guilt that not only consumes me but is close to destroying me once and for all. Well, two can play at this game. Ignoring the small voice in my head that's begging me to shut up, I let the words fly. "Have you ever given your father a chance to explain why he did what he did? Open the damn letters!"

"I said don't," he warns, his voice low and on the verge of snapping, but I wave him off.

"Maybe he had a reason for what he did, maybe he didn't, but how will you ever know when you refuse to give him a chance? You weren't the only one who lost someone, Cade. Did you ever think about that? He lost his wife!"

Cade turns to go, but I grab his wrist. "No! You don't get to stand there and tell me to grow up when you refuse to do it yourself. Do you honestly think that throwing this selfish tantrum is gonna teach your dad a lesson? Guess what? It won't! The only person you're hurting is yourself—and your sister."

He's still when the last, awful sentence vomits from my mouth, and I drop my hand from his wrist, well aware that I just crossed the point of no return. Cade and I have never argued like this, and the chasm between us now is vast and bottomless. My heart aches with regret. How in the world did we get here? Maybe this was bound to happen. Maybe two messed-up souls can only coexist for so long before they begin to dig at each other's brokenness, just to make themselves feel whole. Or maybe I'm still being a brat and he's taken as much as he can handle.

"Macy loves you, Cade," I say. "And this divide between you and your dad is tearing her up."

He shakes his head. "Are you listening to yourself? Yeah, I know I'm far from perfect. I'm well aware of that, because I'm reminded of it every day of my life. But *this*—this is all about you. So don't you dare tell me how to handle my crap until you're prepared to accept and handle your own." And with that, he turns and trudges off across the sand toward the parking lot.

And I'm alone. The wild roar of the ocean drowns out everything else around me except for one small thing—the ever-so-faint cracking of my heart.

# CHAPTER THIRTY-THREE

## *Paige*

I don't know how long I sit crumpled in the sand, the gravity of Cade's words heavy on my shoulders. When I finally manage to pull myself back to my feet, the sun is dipping low and beginning its slow, spectacular melt into the horizon. The magnificent wash of pinks and yellows streak across the sky, like Quinn's photograph, as if God himself has drawn a paintbrush across it in long, swift strokes.

I gaze out across the surf, but I don't see beauty or serenity. Two critical pieces of my world have been stripped away from me in a single day, and I am destroyed.

I don't recall the drive home. I don't know how I pulled myself from the car and up the staircase to my room. I don't remember pushing open my bedroom door—but I will never forget what I see on the other side.

Connie sits ramrod straight on my bed, so still that I'm not sure she hears me come in. She stares blankly at the wall in front of her, and for a moment, I think something might be wrong. Then I see what she's holding in her hands, and I throw my purse on the bed, shattering the silence. My wallet and phone spill out onto the comforter, and Connie shoots to her feet, an explosion of panic across her face.

In her trembling hands are my pink pointe shoes. The same shoes I'd shoved into a box deep in my closet. "Paige, you scared me, I—"

"What are you doing in here?" I demand, lunging straight for her before I even know I'm moving. I yank the slippers out of her hands so hard, Connie stumbles forward.

"I'm sorry. I was putting away your laundry." She motions to the half-empty basket on the bed. "And I—well, I—"

"You just thought you'd paw through my belongings while you were at it?" I wave the shoes in the air as my voice grows an octave. Blood pulses behind my ears. "You have no right!"

Connie raises her hands and takes a step toward me, then abruptly stops. "You're right, Paige. I didn't mean to snoop, I just—I just want to help you. To try to understand you a little better."

I shake my head. "You went through my things. How could you do that?"

"Please, listen to me. I–I know you're angry. It's just—" Connie stammers, trying to find her words. "You don't talk about your mother or how you're feeling, and I just thought—"

"You just thought you'd go through my stuff and try to

figure me out?" I'm seething at the betrayal, wishing at that moment that I could shoot lasers from my eyes. She would be dust by now. I'm nanoseconds away from unleashing more angry words on her when I notice Connie's eyes are rimmed in red. Had she been crying before I came in? Over me? Over the loss of my mother? The anger inside me instantly magnifies, and my hands reflexively tighten, squeezing the silky pink fabric of the shoes. It's nearly unbearable to me to think of this woman trying to measure my pain, to initiate some sort of feeble attempt at sympathy over my loss. She has no right to do that.

"From the moment I got here, you've been trying to figure me out. All of you. Just because I have to be here doesn't mean I want to share anything with you!" Venom coats every word, and Connie bristles.

"Please, listen," she says.

"No! *You* listen. You are not my mother, so stop acting like you are. I don't need your sympathy or you telling me that you understand what I'm going through. I don't need you hugging me to make yourself feel better about whatever it is you think I'm dealing with. You know nothing about me!" My chest heaves, and I think I might actually throw up. First Tyler, then Cade, now Connie—I don't know how much more I can take.

Connie sucks in her bottom lip, and her eyes drop to the floor. She stands frozen for a few moments, then she turns and picks up the laundry basket from the bed. When she reaches the door, she turns, and her face is filled with pain. In a sad, strained whisper, she says, "I'm truly sorry, Paige."

Just as she steps into the hallway, Jay appears and touches her arm. She shakes him off and moves past him.

The look Jay shoots me sends a chill down my spine. He's angry, and I instantly know without asking that he heard every accusatory word I hurled at his wife. I don't feel remorseful, not one bit, but I swallow hard when he steps into the room and shuts the door behind him.

"I don't want to talk to you either," I say. "I want to be left alone."

"I don't really care what you want," Jay says, surprisingly calm despite the hard look on his face. "You're not calling the shots anymore, Paige."

"When have I ever called the shots around here?" I ask, confounded by his choice of words. Jay crosses his arms over his chest. As his eyes bore into me, my instinct is to look away. But my fierce stubbornness refuses to bend, so I hold his gaze and cross my arms, mirroring his stance.

"You and I seem to have a communication problem," he says. We have a lot of problems. If he wants to label them individually, who am I to stop him? "In case you've forgotten, you are grounded. That means you come straight home after work."

"I'm here, aren't I?" I say, stretching my arms out to my sides.

"And where were you earlier? Because you certainly weren't at the bookstore. Were you?" My arms slowly lower as a new realization surfaces. Jay holds up a hand. "No more lies, Paige. I know you were at the university."

"How did—? How did you know that?"

Jay's eyes drift to my cell phone laying on the bed.

"You're tracking my phone? So now you're spying on me?" Astonishment collides with betrayal inside me and my stomach twists.

"I'm trying to keep you safe, Paige. But that's hard to do when you insist on being reckless. Like driving to Eugene without telling anyone where you were going. What if something had happened to you?"

Forget astonishment and make way for fury. It shoots through me, welling my hands into fists at my sides. "You don't trust me."

"I want to," he says. "But you've made that pretty difficult. Sneaking around with Cade Matthews? Running off to God-knows-where when we think you're working? What else have you been doing?" I grit my teeth and stare at the floor.

Jay runs his hands through the top of his hair and releases a slow, labored breath. "Do you have any idea what it took on Connie's part for you to come live here?"

Here we go again. Jay isn't interested in anything I have to say. This is going to be a lecture. One more to add to the day's inventory.

"She had no right to go through my things," I say, waving the shoes. They're crushed satin, beaten into submission by my own hands to get them to fit just right, and then from all the hours I've spent wearing them. I cross to the dresser, yank open the top drawer and shove them in, slamming the drawer shut. When I turn back, and we lock eyes once again, Jay's expression hasn't wavered.

"You have no idea the painful memories she relives every time she looks at you."

Is he for real? How is this all of a sudden about Connie? I'm the one who's lost everything. She fixed up the guest room, cooked me a few dinners, big deal. How did my uprooting become such an inconvenience to her? I'm not amused.

"I didn't ask her to let me come here," I remind him. "I never wanted to be here in the first place. You should have just left me in San Diego; we all would've been better off." I've wanted to say that for so long. There's no sense in faking diplomacy anymore.

"Be. Quiet," Jay warns, his face pale, his green eyes darker than I've ever seen them. Any ounce of sympathy or patience he'd pretended to show me over the last several months is long gone, replaced with disgust. Jay Chapman has a limit to what he's willing to take, and I know I'm about to push it. I take the cue and press my lips together.

Jay crosses to the window, leans a hand against the frame and stares out through the glass. He keeps his back to me for a long time, and the air humming up through the heating vents in the floor is the only sound in the space between us.

I wait, studying a copy of *Us Weekly* magazine resting

atop the dresser. Who are the best and worst dressed celebs? I'm about to compare Beyoncé's red leather number with Taylor Swift's metallic mini when Jay turns his attention back to me. I draw a deep breath. Jay inhales one also.

"I wasn't sure I wanted to bring you here at all," he finally says.

Oh, that's good. Bring out the big guns and try to make me feel worse than I already have for months. I suppress my urge to interrupt, although that's most likely what Jay expects me to do. Instead, I decide to let him finish his speech, his miscalculated attempt to try to make me loathe myself for not giving his precious wife a chance.

"When the lawyer called me—let's just say I didn't know what to think. Shocked is an understatement. I had a teenage daughter I never knew existed." Jay walks around my room as he talks. "Suddenly, she's mine, and I'm her sole guardian. And because of her mother's final wishes, I'm to take responsibility for her?" Jay dissects the story as if he's talking to no one in particular. When he finally stops, turning his eyes back to me, he's ashen. "Are you kidding me?" Jay all but shouts. He takes another deep, labored breath, trying to regain some composure. "I'll tell you, Paige, that scared the hell out of me. I mean, you didn't know me from Adam. I had no clue who you were or how you'd been raised for seventeen years. I had no trouble convincing myself that bringing you here would be the worst thing I could ever do."

Thank you! He's finally making sense. I never wanted to

come here. I knew it was a bad idea from the start, too. If only he'd followed his gut, we wouldn't even be having this horrible conversation—

"But," he says, interrupting my silent tirade, "it was Connie who convinced me to step up and accept the terms of Abby's will."

My eyes narrow and I see red. Connie's the one! She's the one who'd opened her big mouth and convinced Jay to mess with my entire world. Connie is to blame for me having to leave my home, being separated from the only life I've ever known. That's perfect. Just. Freaking. Perfect.

"There's something you don't know about her."

"I don't want to know," I begin, but he cuts me off with a sharp wave of his hand.

"You're not going anywhere until you hear this. I want you to understand what she gave up for you."

What could Connie possibly have sacrificed so I could become an outcast in her family? I wait to see which ridiculous words are next to fall out of Jay's mouth.

"Connie and I had a little boy."

"Yeah, Tanner. I've met him," I say in an attempt to hurry the storytelling along.

Jay's stern tone returns with less patience than before. "Sit down. And be quiet." I sink onto the edge of the bed. "Not Tanner," Jay corrects. "His name was Nathan. Nathan James Chapman." There's a sad longing in his voice. "Not too many people know what I'm about to tell you. It happened before we moved here."

I sit stiffly, my hands tightly clasped in my lap. Jay rubs at the back of his neck and clears his throat with a cough.

"We were living in Seaside. I'd just finished college, and I was teaching at the high school there. Connie and Nathan were coming home from her mother's house in Astoria. They'd gone there to visit for the weekend." He coughs again, as if trying to coax out his next words. "They were just about home when a trucker fell asleep on the highway and crossed the center line."

Out of the corner of my eye, I'm immediately aware that Jay is as still as the fixtures in the room and my insides feel as if they are suddenly melting. "They were trapped in the mangled car for two hours while the paramedics worked to free them."

*No. No. No, no, no.*

"I don't know how, but miraculously, Connie had only a few broken bones." His voice cracks like plaster and an odd sound escapes from the back of his throat.

I'm spinning, like clothes in a dryer, and before I can fully grasp the sensations that are swirling through me, I'm falling—plummeting into my own memories. They come at me fast and furious, pulling me under in a wicked riptide. The empty halls of the hospital. The cold waiting room. My hands clutching desperately to Aunt Faye as we prayed. Each memory is a crystal of ice piling up inside me and freezing me into place.

I should never have loosened the lock on my memories and shared them with Cade. I'd kept them shut away for so long for a reason, and now, because I trusted him, because I unhinged the latch and let him in, they are so fresh under my skin that they close in all around me, squeezing me so tight I can't breathe. Despair stabs viciously at every nerve in my brain, shooting down my spine and directly and unmistakably into my heart.

"Nathan?" I ask, my voice barely audible.

Jay's eyes brim with tears, and he shakes his head. "He was only a year old."

In that split second, my entire body is alive with panic, like I hit a trip wire and I'm about to implode. I need to get out of this room any way I possibly can. "I didn't know," I hear myself say.

"You didn't care to know," Jay says quietly. "When Connie looks at you, she sees what you've lost. She feels it. That mother-child connection is powerful. Taking it away is like losing a limb, and she feels that, too. Every day, Paige."

I want to correct him, tell him it's like losing your heart, your soul and your purpose all in one awful, unforgettable moment, but I can't seem to find my voice. It evaporates as my skin prickles and a sheen of perspiration forms across my forehead.

"We're trying to make this work. We want to make this work." Jay looks me right in the eyes when he says that. And that's when I manage to retrieve my voice.

"No," I say, shaking my head. "You don't."

"What did you say?"

"You don't want this to work," I repeat. "You may think

you do, but you never wanted me in the first place, and it had nothing to do with Connie."

"Paige," Jay says, but I cut him off.

"You never wanted my mother or me."

"That's not true." Jay steps toward me, but I lunge off the bed and out of his reach. "Your mother never told me about you."

"You're right, she didn't," I agree. "But you didn't stick around long enough to give her the chance."

Confusion washes over Jay's features. "I don't know what you're talking about."

"If you loved my mother so much, how could you possibly have left her?" I demand, a new sensation welling inside me. This one pushes down the hurt that was there before. This one is scalding hot, growing out of the glowing embers of anger still alive deep in my core.

"We've been through this." Jay sighs. "Abby and I were seventeen. We were kids who didn't even know what life was all about yet. I had to leave so she could have a chance at reconciling with her father. I didn't want to be the one to stand in the way of that."

"But you said you loved her."

"I did," he softly says. "I honestly did."

"People who love each other don't leave," I accuse. "Unless there's something they want more." The anger now bubbles inside me, unleashing something new: courage. At that moment, I'm strong enough to tell Jay that I know everything, to shout in deafening volume that he can't hide behind the lies anymore and accuse me of not being honest with him. He's been misleading me all along.

"You're not making any sense."

"I believed you," I say. "I actually believed you when you told me you left my mom for the right reasons. It sounded good, almost noble. But that's not what happened."

"Paige, please. You don't know what you're talking about," he says, stepping toward me. "I left for your mother's sake."

"You're a liar!" I yell, shoving him away. "You left because my grandfather *paid* you to leave!" It all spills out then—the bitterness, the rejection and the heartache that has pooled together for so long inside me. "He wrote you a big, fat check to get out of my mother's life for good. Isn't that right?"

Jay goes white, panic filling his eyes. "How did you know about that?"

I stalk over to the nightstand and wrench open the drawer. I scoop up the journals, the last, tangible connection I have to my mother, and I hug them close. Scrunching my eyes tight, I finger the smooth leather. *I love you, Mom.* Spinning on my toes, I slam the journals into Jay's chest. His arms fly up to catch them. "I know because my mother told me!"

I storm out of my room and down the stairs. Slamming the door to my car, I turn the key and the engine roars to life. Without a second thought, I back out of the driveway and barrel down the street. The look in Jay's eyes as my last words hit him are burned into my brain. He'll read the journals. Of course he will. He won't have a choice, and then he will know how much my mother loved him and how much it had killed her when he left. He will see his betrayal in her words. With every stroke of her pen, he will finally be exposed to the hurt she'd lived with for so many years.

As for me? I don't know where to go. Everything is so screwed up. In less than twelve hours, nearly every semblance of a relationship that's been instrumental to my existence here has been severed. What's left now? I could go to Quinn's, but honestly, I don't want to rehash my whole afternoon with her, and I'm not interested in any advice she's sure to give me. The bookstore is closed now, and while a part of me wants to see Macy, to cry on her shoulder, I can't tell her about my fight with Cade. It's too personal, and it hurts to think about how he walked away from me.

There's no way I can possibly call Aunt Faye. I'm too ashamed and still too angry over my fight with Tyler. Besides, I'm sure he will tell her soon enough. The fact that she hasn't called or texted me yet is a pretty good indication that he hasn't contacted her. But I know he will; it's just a matter of time.

There isn't much light left in the sky. I drive all the way to the edge of town before I finally know where I want to go—where I need to go. A place where I can be alone, just me and my miserable, wretched thoughts.

I put the car into Park and stare up at the trailhead in front of me. The parking area is deserted, and it will be dark in no time at all. Cade's words of warning not to hike up there alone echo in my head, but I dismiss them quickly. Just like he'd dismissed me.

Climbing out of the car, I grab the flashlight Jay put in the glove box for emergencies. Zipping up my hoodie, I survey the forested hillside. There's something up there I desperately need—clarity. Up there, everything is somehow unobstructed and uncomplicated. I can breathe in a way that I can't down here.

I move quickly, climbing up the main trail. There's no one on the path, and that's both comforting and slightly unnerving at the same time. Darkness falls beneath the canopy of trees, but I'm not afraid. The idea of being alone calms me. There are no prying eyes here to condemn me for my outbursts, no one to chastise me for my selfish thoughts. But it's nearly nightfall, which explains why no one is coming up or down the trail. Everyone else is probably smart enough to know that hiking at night is dangerous. But I forge ahead, quickening my pace.

The cold air burns in my lungs with the increasing incline, but I'm more determined than ever to continue. The problem is, I can't quite remember where Cade took me from here. We'd broken off from the main trail, that much I recall, but as I glance to my left and to my right, shining my flashlight on my surroundings, there's so much overgrowth, I can't tell for sure where this alternate path begins. Closing my eyes, I listen for the distant sound of the ocean. Trusting my instincts, I veer into the black tree line on my left with only the small, white glow of light to guide me. I manage to find the weak indentations of a pathway and fall in step with it, hoping that I'm going in the right direction.

When I woke up this morning, all I'd hoped for was a quiet day at work with Macy. Never in my wildest nightmares had I suspected that my world would unravel stitch by stitch. But it had. So incredibly quickly.

I push through the last branches and, to my great relief, step out onto the familiar outcropping. I found it! All by myself, with no help from anyone. I inhale a deep, victorious breath and peer out at the now-dark ocean spilling out for miles below me. The last rays of sunshine have evaporated, taking with them the mesmerizing glow I'd hoped to see ringing the skyline. This time, things are different up here. It's colder, for one, the midday temperatures falling away with the light. I wrap my arms around myself as I step toward the ledge, careful not to get too close. I stare down at the ominous, rolling waves, the perfect arc of the black water chased by the fluid surf crashing onto the beaches below.

I inhale the cold, salty air and it hangs in the back of my throat before pulsing down into my chest. As I slowly exhale, I concentrate on banishing all the hurt and despair of the day from my body. I imagine it leaching away and dissolving into the night air. Below me to my left, cars wind up and down the highway in glowing red and white dots. All of them have somewhere to go—and I don't. The wind rustles my hair, sending a chill down my spine and unleashing goose bumps over me like a second skin.

The last time I came up here, I had Cade to keep me warm, and this space offered me the freedom I desperately needed. But something's changed. This once wide-open space is undeniably empty. I close my eyes, willing my nerves to release the grip they have on me. As I tilt my head skyward, I hold my arms out wide, ready to embrace what it is I want, but the tranquility I'm searching for isn't here.

I shift my weight from one foot to the other and take another cleansing breath, opening my lungs wide to the offerings of the night air, trying again to purge all the hurt and disappointment that is tightly binding my insides. If I'm going to survive this and pull myself together, I have to find a way to separate myself from everything that just happened, to disengage at least long enough for me to formulate a plan. If I can't find a way to leave it all behind, high up on this cliff where it can't follow me back down, then I'm sunk.

I try as hard as I can to find my center, to clear my mind, to push aside any thoughts of this horrible day. Complete stillness consumes me as I wait to see if the night will comply with my wishes.

I get my answer. A sharp, ear-shattering crack jolts me back into the moment. The ground beneath my feet quakes and my eyes shoot open, a split second before I make the terrifying realization that I am no longer standing.

I'm falling.

# CHAPTER THIRTY-FOUR

## Paige

Everything in my body hurts. Unforgiving heat sears into my muscles and bones, as if someone lit a match inside me. The flames multiply until they consume every ounce of me, leaving agony in their wake.

I blink hard, my eyes straining to bring the view above me into focus. Squinting into the darkness, my brain struggles to bring the swirling view to a halt and make sense of what just happened. When my vision finally settles, horror seeps in. I'm staring up at the spot where, just moments ago, I was standing.

Slowly, one by one, the scenes drop into place. What I'd assumed was stable ground beneath my feet had crumbled, and I'd fallen right along with the rocky pieces of the hillside. But instead of plummeting to certain death in the ocean, I'd slammed down onto this rocky surface below.

Burning flares again in my back and bites at my right shoulder, a jarring reminder that I'm alive, but not in good shape. I concentrate on moving my left hand and feel a rush of hope when it complies. Gingerly, I inch my fingers toward the pocket of my jeans, willing myself to find the one thing that could save me. My heart sinks the instant I realize my pocket is empty. I don't have my cell phone. I'd left it on my bed when I'd stormed out of the house because I was so angry at Jay for using it to track my whereabouts. My flashlight is also gone, lost somewhere in my fall. My body constricts against the waves of burning pain as I shiver uncontrollably against the cold ground.

I'm alone. Not even the sounds of the ocean waves crashing against the shore below me break the isolating silence. *Don't panic. You're okay. You're going to be okay.* The voice of reason inside my pounding head tries desperately to maintain control as I take a quick inventory. I can't move without excruciating pain stabbing at some part of my body on my right side; my shoulder, my back, my hip. I'm also intensely aware I'm growing colder by the minute. It's a short list, but long enough for me to know that I'm in trouble.

"Help!" I muster every ounce of sound I can make to shout that one, desperate syllable into the night, only it's too weak to carry far before drowning away. I draw a deep, painful breath and try again. "Can anyone hear me?" My voice cracks as my lungs pain at the effort. The only answer are the sounds of the night closing in around me, the relentless whistle of the wind and the churning ocean below. There's nothing else. Warm wetness rolls from the corners of my eyes, dampening my wind-bitten cheeks.

Is this some sick joke? After everything I've been through and after convincing myself that my messy life couldn't possibly take another cruel turn? A wave of pure, ice-sharp terror floods my veins, temporarily numbing the fire inside. *No! No. No, no, no!* The voice inside me screams against my skull. It can't end like this. Not here. Not alone. Not after I've messed things up so badly and hurt the people I love.

Gritting my teeth, I attempt to sit up, but sharp, knife-like stabs of pain hold me hostage against the uneven ground. Even if I could manage to move, there's no way I can climb back up there. There's definitely something wrong with my shoulder. A broken bone? Maybe several? My head pounds as if someone cracked it open with a hammer, and a series of small explosions ignites somewhere behind my right temple. Carefully lifting the one hand I'm able to move, I touch my forehead, and I'm met with something warm and sticky.

It's cruelly ironic. I came to this spot to be alone. And on any other day, it would be the perfect place to gather my thoughts, to see things clearly. That's all I'd wanted. To be able to think, to figure out my next move—what to do now that my world is crumbling at its foundation. But the solitude I'd convinced myself I'd needed has cost me in the worst possible way.

What I want right now is a do-over. I want to do it all over again, to erase the last several months and start from the beginning. To go back to that day on the plane knowing what I know now. But this mess is too large for a do-over. What I've created for myself isn't a game or a silly argument that can be fixed with such a simple declaration. I've dug a hole too massively deep for such an uncomplicated solution.

*Mom, I've messed up so badly.*

My chest aches, but it's not from the pain that consumes the other parts of my body. This hurt, this talon-sharp regret, cuts so much deeper.

The warm tears from my eyes now trickle into my ears, but I don't wipe them away. The last time I cried, I was in the cemetery, standing beneath a steel-gray sky and watching as my mother's casket was lowered into the ground. That will forever be the darkest day of my life—the day that life as I knew it ceased to exist. After that, I'd shut off the tears and managed to seal away the crux of the pain I'd endured, walling it off into the recesses of my soul where no one would get to it—where no one would be able to comfort me.

Well, damn. Mrs. Hopkins had been right after all. She'd warned me that someday there would be a breaking point, that despite my efforts to disengage from my feelings, my body and mind would eventually be unable to hold the immensity of all that I'd shoved away, and they would betray me.

*Aunt Faye.* I don't think I've fully appreciated how big a part of my life she's encompassed. I blamed her for not doing enough to keep me. Somehow, I'd convinced myself I'd forgiven her, but I hadn't. Not entirely. I'd unjustly accused her of giving up too quickly, of not loving me enough, only nothing had been farther from the truth. She's done nothing but love me, love me so much that she did what she believed was best for me, despite her own needs and wants. She didn't want me to go, but she'd respected the fact that it wasn't her decision to make. She'd done what she'd had to do because that's what my mom had asked of her. I know that now. Honestly, I think I knew it then. So why didn't I tell her that I understood? Why didn't I tell her how much I loved her for loving me and wanting to do the best she could for me?

The pressure in my chest intensifies as I process the hurt I've inflicted on the people I love. Mom is gone, and I will always carry the guilt of that horrible night with me. It wasn't her choice to leave me, but somehow, deep down, I'd blamed her, too. I'd blamed her for the lawyer and those awful papers that surrendered me to a stranger. To a man who'd been offered money to walk away—and had taken it. At that moment, the wall inside me cracks and shatters into a million irreparable pieces.

Gut-wrenching sobs spill violently from my insides, shaking me so hard, I'm sure it will be only a matter of seconds before I split in half. The physical pain that consumes me turns to daggers, stabbing down again and again as my body spasms against the rolling waves of emotion gushing out of me. My shrieks howl into the night, uncontrollable, ugly and raw.

I can still see the look on Jay's face when I threw my

mother's journals at him. I'm not sure I'll ever forget it, no matter how hard I try. I'd stunned him. He never thought his ugly secret would see the light of day. I close my eyes, and burning behind my eyelids are my mom's devastating words.

*My dad told Jay about the baby. Then he offered him $10,000 to walk away and never contact me again. I can't believe Jay took it.*

That's where the journal ended. My mother never wrote another word about Jay Chapman or how he'd destroyed her. Any remaining hope that Mom and Jay could be a family had ended before it had a chance to begin. Jay betrayed her. And so had my grandfather. How could a man who claimed to love his daughter stoop so low as to offer cash for a person's silence? And worse yet—what kind of a man takes it? Why did Jay do that? And why in the world did he allow me into his life now? Guilt? Maybe attempting to be my father is his shot at redemption. That thought sickens me. But what hurts most of all—is that I wanted him to be my dad. Not at first, and not when he told me to stay away from Cade, but there were other times, the times when I was able to see a small spark of the man who appeared to care about me. There, in those moments, the small ones, when he'd been genuinely interested in me and regretful that he'd been denied the opportunity to be my father so many years ago. I'd wanted that, too. I couldn't admit it because I didn't fully realize it at the time. I'd convinced myself that I didn't need a father, and I'd fought it. I'd fought Jay's attempts to be part of my life, but deep down—I want a dad. I want someone to *want* to be my dad. It was my mother's secrets that brought Jay into my life, but it was his own lies that ruined anything good that could possibly have come from that.

And Cade.

At that moment, he's all I can see, all I can think about—the guy who makes every trouble I've ever had melt away just by putting his arms around me. He's the most fantastic surprise I've discovered since I came to this town. And I hurt him. So many people warned me to stay away from him, but the truth is—they should have warned Cade about me. His only wrongdoing was trying to get me to see the truth, even when it hurt. He's been more honest with me than anyone I've met since I came to Mystic, and I'm the one who pushed *him* away. I wounded him with my nasty words and broke his heart. What if I never get the chance to take it all back?

I'm so stupid. Cade told me not to come up here by myself, but I disregarded his warning. He'd explained, in no uncertain terms, that this was rough terrain and all the crisscrossing trails can cause trouble for even the most experienced hiker. Why didn't I listen? *Because you're stubborn.* The words press against my brain.

No one can hear my cries, and no one knows I'm here. And when they finally realize something is wrong, they won't know where to start looking. For all Cade knows, I'm at home, and Jay knows I am angry and will try to be anywhere but near him. He probably thinks I'm somewhere cooling off. Somewhere safe. If I can just get myself to move, I might have a chance. Biting down against the pain, I try once more to pull myself off the cold ground. Once again, I fail.

I cry out in frustration, a fresh wave of hot tears streaming from my eyes, stinging as they collide with the wind. I've wasted so much time. I've spent months swallowed up by grief—so consumed by the loss of my mom that I didn't bother to see anything else. And by doing that, I surrendered all thoughts of my future. I gave up on my dreams and pushed people away. And for what? I close my eyes and wince at the unrelenting ache deep in my chest.

Did I *choose* to be unhappy?

Maybe it doesn't matter anymore. How cold can a body get before hypothermia sets in? I try to remember if we studied that particular fact in health class, but the thick band of fog pressing against my mind prevents it from retrieving an answer.

My heavy eyelids slide closed. I no longer know which pain is physical and which is emotional, only that they are working in tandem, in a slow, calculated attempt to suck me under.

And they are winning.

# CHAPTER THIRTY-FIVE

## Cade

I stare out the kitchen window, seeing nothing but my reflection against the darkness outside. The guy in the glass is wrecked. I can almost see the regret and anger piled up on his shoulders, and I want to tell him he's an idiot. He's an idiot for picking a fight with the girl he would do anything for. All Paige had wanted was a shoulder to cry on, but instead, she'd been abandoned by the guy she'd counted on.

"Try leaning over the sink instead of dripping water all over my clean floor," Macy says from the doorway, jarring me from my stupor. The plate I'm holding slips from my hand and plunges into the basin, spraying the front of my shirt with soapy water.

I swear under my breath, grabbing for the dish towel on the counter.

"What is with you tonight?" she asks, grabbing a second towel and mopping up the puddle on the floor. "You've been out of sorts since I got home."

"I'm fine."

She studies my face with narrowed eyes. "I'm not buying that. Want to try again?" I shake my head. "Here, let me do it," she says, nudging me aside.

Macy gets right to work scrubbing the lasagna pan, occasionally side-eyeing me as if she's waiting for me to make the next move in this conversation. When it's clear that's not going to happen, she asks, "What's eating at you? And don't tell me nothing, because clearly, it's something. And by the looks of you, I'm guessing it's something big."

I sigh. "Paige and I had a disagreement."

"A disagreement?" she repeats.

"An argument, okay?" I confess. "I'm not even sure how it started. One minute she was telling me about a fight she had with her cousin, and then she was saying how she thinks her mom's death was her fault, and before I knew it—" I throw back my head and growl at the ceiling. "I said some things, and she twisted them around. It turned into one big mess, and I stormed off."

Macy's incessant scrubbing halts. "Why does Paige think her mom's death was her fault?"

"It's a long story," I say, not wanting to rehash it. Besides, it's not my story to tell. Paige told me that in confidence, and I won't disrespect her by sharing it without her permission. "The point is, we both said some pretty hurtful things. Honest things, but still hurtful. And now I don't know what to do."

"Have you tried calling her?"

I shake my head. "I'm the last person she wants to talk to right now."

"You won't know that unless you call her."

I lean against the counter, mulling over Macy's words while she resumes her dishwashing. Staring at the ceiling tiles, I replay our argument. Maybe I shouldn't have been honest with Paige. Maybe I should have just let her get everything off her chest and not insisted on injecting reason into the conversation. She clearly hadn't wanted that. She just wanted me to be on her side, to offer her empathy and tell her she was right. I could have done that, but instead, I'd opened my mouth, put her on the defensive and set our impending demise into motion. I pace the kitchen floor as I consider my options. When I realize that the only way to fix this is to reach out to her, I slide my cell phone out of my pocket and dial her number before I can change my mind. My shoulders deflate when the call goes to voice mail.

"I'm sorry," Macy says as I drop into a chair at the table. "Maybe she just needs a little time to come around."

"You weren't there. It was bad, Mace."

She wipes her hands on the dish towel and takes a seat next to me. "Things always seem worse in the moment. Give her some time to cool off. One argument isn't going to change her feelings for you."

I'm not so sure about that. Macy pats my hand as the doorbell chimes. My head shoots up, and Macy smiles. "See? I bet that's Paige now. I told you she'd come around."

I slide out of my seat and practically run out of the

kitchen, slowing my steps when I hear two male voices down the hall.

"Is Paige here? Is she with Cade?"

As I round the corner into the foyer, Shawn turns expectant eyes on me. Mr. Chapman stands in the doorway, worry heavy across his face. He straightens when he sees me. "She didn't come home this evening. I didn't know where else to go. Have you seen her?"

I shake my head. "Not since late this afternoon, when I left her at the beach." The words are thick with guilt. "She didn't come home at all?"

"She was home, but she left at about five." Mr. Chapman's brows furrow. "We had an argument and she—left."

"Did you try Quinn's house?" I ask. It's hard for me to look Mr. Chapman in the eye. All I've ever seen in them is condemnation. But tonight, there's unease in his usually authoritative gaze. Maybe even a hint of fear.

Mr. Chapman shakes his head. "She's not there. Quinn says she hasn't talked to her all day. I tried some of her other friends, too, Zoey and Samantha, but no one has seen her. She left her phone at the house; I can't reach her. I don't know what else to do." He scrubs a hand over the back of his neck, a muscle ticking along his jaw. He looks awful.

Macy appears, and she quickly reads the temperature of the room. "Is there something wrong?"

"Paige is late getting home," Shawn explains. "Mr. Chapman was hoping she was here."

"Can you think of anyone else she might be with?" His

intense eyes plead with me. "Cade, I'm really worried, so if you know anything at all, please tell me." I shove my hands into the pockets of my jeans as Macy wraps a gentle hand around the back of my arm.

"I don't know, maybe—" I blow out a full breath, and although it's difficult, I say, "Try Dane Sloane. Maybe he knows something." Hope sparks in Mr. Chapman's eyes, but I'm sickened by my words. I don't want to think Paige would turn to Dane after our fight, but the two of them have obviously been talking. She told me earlier that he'd warned her I was playing her. Maybe Paige talks with him more than I know. She has the right to speak to anyone she wants. The important thing right now is that Mr. Chapman finds her and that she's okay.

"Thank you, I'll contact the Sloanes," he says, turning to go.

I step forward. "You might also try the movie theater. Or the bowling alley."

Reading my expression, Shawn offers, "We could check out those places if you like and help you cover more ground quickly."

Mr. Chapman nods. "I would appreciate that."

"I'll check the bookstore," Macy offers. "I don't know if she's there, but she has a key. If she wanted to be alone, that's a good place."

Another nod from Mr. Chapman. "Thank you."

They exchange cell phone numbers. "We'll let you know if we find her," Shawn says. When Mr. Chapman heads for his car, Shawn glances at his watch, then grabs my coat off the hook by the door and tosses it at me before retrieving his own. "Let's get going."

✧   ✧   ✧

An hour later, after we've checked the cineplex, the bowling alley and a half dozen other places, including the spot near the jetty where I'd left Paige earlier, I'm at a loss. There's no sign of her. I was hopeful that we'd find her at the city park next to the library, but she's not there either.

"Dammit!" I scrub a hand through my hair, tired and frustrated that we're nowhere closer to finding her. "This is all my fault."

"Don't say that," Shawn says.

"What about the police? Maybe they can find her."

"Take it easy. Let's not jump to conclusions. Is there anywhere else you can think of that Paige would go? Think hard, Cade."

I shake my head and take a seat on one of the swings. Paige loved this spot, that's why I thought she'd be here. I brought her to the park for the first time about a month ago, after we'd gone to the movies with Ash and Zeke. It was late, so the area was deserted, and we were alone. I got Paige all to myself, and she got the opportunity to swing like she was eight-years-old again. I'd pushed her for nearly an hour, and she'd pumped her legs until she was swinging as high as she could go. Just that simple act put a childlike smile on her face. She'd told me a long time ago, shortly after we met, that she likes heights, that being up high makes her feel free. *Height*—I roll the word around in my brain. "She felt free."

"What did you say?" Shawn asks.

I lean my forehead against the cold metal chain. "Paige told me she likes heights—because elevation makes her feel free," I say slowly. I shoot off the swing. "I know where she is." I take off for the truck in a dead sprint.

"Cade, wait!" Shawn calls. He's right behind me when I reach the truck. "Where are we going?"

"Devil's Eye Viewpoint," I say. And for the first time tonight, I hope I'm wrong.

# CHAPTER THIRTY-SIX
## Cade

When we pull into the parking area at the trailhead, I'm both relieved and concerned to see Paige's car. It's the only vehicle in the lot, ringed by the soft yellow glow of the light post it's parked beneath.

"It's locked," Shawn announces after checking all four doors and shining his flashlight in the windows.

I stare into the tree line as Shawn retrieves his two-way radio and his first aid pack from the truck. Panic floods my chest as I absorb the reality of his actions.

"Just in case," he says, and he barely gets the words out before I'm heading for the path, my cell phone flashlight in hand.

"This way," I shout, and Shawn quickly falls into step behind me.

"How far up?" he asks.

"About twenty minutes," I say over my shoulder. Aside from the snapping of twigs beneath our feet and our labored breathing as the path grows steeper, silence consumes our hike. I try to focus on what's in front of me, but my mind keeps retreating to the argument I had with Paige. That stupid, ridiculous argument. I shake away the memory, only to have it return moments later as if it's on a revolving playlist along with the rest of my punishing thoughts. Each time it creeps back in, I hike faster, no longer concerned whether Shawn is keeping up. I have to get up there. I have to find her.

Even with the light from my phone and the beams coming from Shawn's flashlight behind me, the darkness is disorienting. I'm having a hard time gauging my surroundings and identifying where to break from the main trail. I'm forced to slow my pace so I don't miss it. My heart soars when I locate the familiar side trail, marked only by a couple of broken branches.

"Through here!" I call. "Watch your step." I impatiently swat my way through the wayward branches, stepping carefully over the underbrush as the churning ocean grows louder. As I emerge from the trees onto the outcropping I know so well, horror replaces every ounce of triumph and satisfaction that sprouted just moments before. It's not what I see but what I don't see that brings me to an abrupt halt. Not five feet in front of me, the ground has crumbled and the edge—is gone.

Within seconds, Shawn is beside me, the bright light of his flashlight illuminating the space, and that's when the gravity of the situation lands squarely on top of me like a pile of bricks. I ease forward to get a better look—and I spot her.

"Paige!" Her name shoots from my mouth in both a plea and a prayer. The earth has fallen, and Paige is crumpled on the ground below, maybe ten feet down. She's not moving. *Oh, God, she's not moving.* Panic explodes inside me.

"Get back!" Shawn orders. "We don't know how stable the ground is." Immediately, he's on his radio, calling for help.

I disregard his command and instead, I lunge forward until I'm on my hands and knees.

"Cade, don't!" Shawn's sharp warning echoes into the night, but I'm already over the edge, frantically trying to secure my footing on the rocky earth beneath me. I lose my grip and slide, pain slicing across my stomach and chest, and I shout out, clawing at the rocks to regain my hold. Beams of light rain down from Shawn's flashlight, along with more shouts. Warnings? Instructions, maybe? I can't concentrate on that. My sole focus is getting to Paige as fast as I can without loosening any more rocks and sending them showering down on top of her. The night wind is biting and relentless, beating against my back and cutting chills down my spine.

When my feet reach the ledge, I carefully crawl my way toward Paige. She's bleeding from a gash on her forehead and several cuts along her cheeks. I lay two fingers on the side of her neck and relief shoots through me when I feel her pulse. It's weak, but it's there. I place an ear to her chest.

"She's breathing!" I shout.

"Don't move her!" Shawn yells. "Help is on the way."

"Open your eyes," I plead, but there's no response. "Come on, Paige. Wake up. Look at me." Her skin is like ice. That damn wind! I shake out of my jacket and cover her with it, consumed by helplessness that I can't do more for her. I stretch out next to her, ignoring the sharp rocks cutting into my side and the pain burning across my chest. Gathering her in close, I shelter her with the warmth of my body. And I pray.

"Come on, Paige. Stay with me."

# CHAPTER THIRTY-SEVEN

## Cade

The waiting room in the ER is unnervingly quiet. A woman with an inconsolable infant was just taken back through the large double doors, leaving only one couple in the far corner, huddled close together and holding hands.

Mr. and Mrs. Chapman were called back to see Paige about a half hour ago. I'm hoping that's a good sign, but I'm not family, so the nurse at the desk refuses to give me any information on her condition.

After Shawn alerted the Coast Guard, a helicopter rescue team was dispatched. Once Paige was stabilized, they'd hoisted us both to safety, where an air medevac team transported her to the hospital. Shawn called Jay, told him what had happened and instructed him to get to the hospital.

I stare at the clock on the wall, then close my eyes. I'm physically exhausted but mentally wired. A nurse patched up the cuts and scrapes on my stomach and chest while Shawn spent nearly fifteen minutes on the phone with

Macy, trying to convince her that I was okay, that she didn't need to come to the hospital and we'd be home soon. I wasn't surprised when Macy showed up thirty minutes later and hasn't left my side since. Shawn is outside, talking with an ambulance crew from his station that transported another patient about twenty minutes ago.

"Why is it taking so long to hear something?" I ask, leaning my elbows on my knees.

Macy gently rubs my back. "I don't know. I'm sure they'll tell us something soon. I'm going to get a drink from the vending machine down the hall. Do you want anything?" I shake my head, and she kisses my cheek. "I'll be right back."

Without Macy there to distract me, my mind replays everything that's happened, and my thoughts quickly turn to all the ways I could have prevented tonight from happening. If only I'd handled things differently, Paige wouldn't be hurt, and I wouldn't be blaming myself for it. I scrub a hand down my face and stare at a cracked floor tile at my feet.

"Cade?"

I lift my head and meet Mr. Chapman's stoic but tired eyes. I quickly stand. "How is she?"

"They're still running some tests, but they think she's going to be all right." His smile is guarded, but it's there, lifting the corner of his mouth ever so slightly.

I release the breath I didn't realize I was holding. "That's great news."

"We're not sure how long she was exposed to the elements, but long enough that she suffered mild hypothermia. The paramedics say it would have been worse if you hadn't been there." Mr. Chapman dips his head, and his eyes sweep the floor. "Thank you for that. To you and Shawn—I never would have found her on my own."

I nod.

Mr. Chapman scratches the back of his head and clears his throat. "I owe you an apology."

Did I hear him right? Maybe my exhaustion has somehow morphed into delusion, and my mind is somehow manipulating the words coming from his mouth.

"My daughter accused me of jumping to conclusions and not giving you a fair shake. As much as I would like to deny it, she was right." He rubs at the back of his neck. "I was hard on you, Cade, and I apologize for that."

I nod, and my inclination is to say, "That's okay," but I manage to swallow my response before it can escape. Because it's not okay how Mr. Chapman treated me, and it's time that I retire those words for good. I think Mac would call that progress.

"Paige is sleeping now, but they should be moving her to a room upstairs soon. You're welcome to visit her," he says. "I'm sure she'll want to see you."

I never thought I would hear him speak those words to me—to issue an invitation. And while that should fill me with relief and with the hope that his acceptance is also implied, I'm drained. "I should probably get going. But I'm glad she's gonna be all right."

"Would you like me to tell her anything when she wakes up?" he offers.

My eyes stray to the closed doors. The man just gave me permission to see his daughter. It's the only thing I've ever wanted—but I can't take it. Not now. Not after so much has happened.

"No, thank you," I say. "No message."

# CHAPTER THIRTY-EIGHT
## *Paige*

A soft, rhythmic beeping draws me slowly back to the surface. My eyelids are heavy, as if someone glued them shut, and it takes me a few moments to blink them open. When I finally do, I squint up at white lights glowing down from the ceiling above me. I'm no longer cold, that much I know instantly. The sharp ground beneath me is gone, replaced by something soft and warm. The pain radiating through my body, once sharp and deep, is now a dull, throbbing ache.

I search for the source of the beeping, locating several machines to my left, their monitors blinking red, green and white, with numbers I can't understand. A clear bag of liquid hangs from a hook on a long metal stand. My eyes trail along the tube attached to it and discover that it's connected to my arm.

Then I see Jay. He's slumped in the chair between the machines and my bed, his elbows on his knees, his eyes closed and his hands fisted against his lips.

A weak moan escapes from the back of my throat as I try to swallow and find my voice. Jay's eyes shoot open, and he straightens. "Paige?" His voice lowers into a guarded tone. "How are you feeling?"

"It hurts," I manage, realizing for the first time that my right arm is in a sling.

"I know," Jay says, scooting his chair closer to the bed. "You dislocated your shoulder, and you're really scraped up and bruised. But nothing's broken, thank God."

"My head's pounding," I tell him, my voice raspy against my dry throat. I raise the hand that's attached to the tubes and wince when I touch my forehead.

"Easy there. You have a nasty cut. Took twelve stitches to close it up," Jay says, his brow creased with concern. "Do you remember what happened?"

I think about that, but all I see are random, swirling images. I close my eyes and concentrate, trying to get them to slow down and fall into some recognizable pattern that makes any kind of sense. Pain beats against my skull. "I remember falling," I say, recalling the searing pain that had devoured me like flames. I cough, and a blast of agony tears across my shoulder and shoots down my back. Jay lunges forward in his chair and lays a hand on my unencumbered arm.

"Are you okay?" His face is a mask of tension. I exhale sharply and relax against the pillow with a small nod.

"I'm going to get the nurse," he says, turning for the door.

"Please, don't go," I say. I can handle the pain, but it will be unbearable if he leaves me alone right now. Jay hesitates before sliding back into his chair and gripping the edge of the bed.

"What were you thinking, hiking up that mountain by yourself?"

"I don't know," I whisper. "It wasn't my best decision."

He runs his hands through his dark hair and clasps them behind his neck, staring at me like he hasn't seen me in weeks. "We could have lost you, Paige."

What can I say to that? He's right, and there's no debating it. I was dumb and reckless, and it ended badly. I stare down at the sling and the tubes and sigh—then I see it. I mean, I don't see it. My watch. Where is it? I glance at the table beside the bed, then frantically scan the room. "Where's my watch?!" I nearly shriek. The machine beside the bed beeps faster, and I wince at the pain as I sit forward, spurred on by my panic.

"Take it easy," Jay says, standing and leaning forward to calm me, but realizing there isn't anything he can do.

"Where is it?" I demand again, taking another scan of my left wrist as if I might have overlooked it the first time.

"I don't know, let's see." Jay moves toward another chair on the other side of my bed and begins to dig through a large plastic bag. "They put your clothes and belongings in here." He pulls out my jeans, my sweater and my shoes, even the bangles Macy gave me, which become a permanent fixture on my wrist. But my watch isn't there.

"Maybe you weren't wearing it," he suggests, showing me the empty bag.

"I was wearing it!" I say. "I never take it off. Mom gave me that watch. We have to find it!"

Jay shakes his head helplessly. "I'm sorry, Paige, it's not here."

Tears press against my eyelids as a new pain takes hold of me. I sink back into my pillow as wetness slides down my cheeks. This hurts so much worse than my shoulder or my head. This hurt radiates from my heart. The tears drip onto my hospital gown.

"I'm so sorry," Jay says again, circling around to the other side of the bed and placing a comforting hand on my forearm. There aren't enough I'm sorries or sympathy on earth to make this better.

With his shoulders hunched in exhaustion, Jay reaches for something on the floor beside the bed. He gently places my mother's journals in my lap, careful not to disturb the tube in my arm.

"I never took the money," he says. "I need you to know that."

A white envelope peeks out from beneath the pages of one of the journals. I open the book and hold it up. It's addressed to Jay. "What's this?"

Jay's quiet for a moment, his eyes resting on the envelope. "That's a letter from Abby."

"What?" The skin on my arms tingle. "Where did you get this?"

Jay clears his throat. "From the lawyer. After he contacted me and told me about Abby's will—he sent it to me." I stare down at it, running my finger across Jay's name scrawled in my mother's familiar handwriting. "I know you don't understand why Abby did what she did. I thought maybe this could help. You're welcome to read it."

I stare at Jay before flipping over the envelope and pulling out the letter. My hands are shaking.

*Dear Jay,*

*I'm not quite sure how to start this letter, so I'm just going to write down everything I'm feeling and hope it makes some kind of sense to both of us when I'm finished.*

*First, let me apologize for the lawyer. I can only imagine how shocking it must have been to get that phone call. By now you know that something has happened to me, and because of that I'm reaching out to you on behalf of our daughter, Paige. Oh, Jay, she's incredible, and she's grown into quite an amazing young woman. I think you would be proud to know her, and I'm hoping that you will take this opportunity to do so.*

*I never imagined that there would come a day that I wouldn't be there for Paige, but if I've learned anything over the last several years, it's that time is fleeting, and things often change without warning. I need to know that I gave Paige the chance to get to know her father—if that is something you both want.*

*I used to think that Paige didn't need a father in her life, that I could offer her all the guidance and love that she deserved. I think I've done a fair job, but over the years I've often wondered if perhaps I made a mistake by not reaching out to you and offering you a chance to meet her. Life is too short, which I now fully understand. I regret the years I wasted being angry at my father and resentful towards you for all the things that happened so many years ago. I can't imagine what my life would have been like without Paige. Despite how things ended, you gave me the best part of my existence. I will forever be grateful to you for that.*

*I realize that I am asking a lot of you. I'm aware that you have a family and obligations that might make it difficult, if not impossible, for you to invite Paige into your life. Please know that you are under no obligation to care for her. But if you have thought about her over the years or wondered if there could be a place for you in her life after all this time, know that there is. I hope you will consider it. And if not, I won't begrudge you that.*

*I hope that life has been good to you and that you are surrounded by happiness and love. We all deserve that.*

*Abby*

I run my hand slowly over the letter and blink at Jay through watery eyes. His expression bleeds remorse.

"It's true that your grandfather tried to pay me off to leave your mother alone. But he never told me she was pregnant. I swear to you." Sadness fills Jay's face, darkening his eyes. He holds my gaze for a long moment. "Martin asked me to go away so Abby could pursue her dancing. He said she was never going to truly focus on that if she thought there was still a chance she could be with me. But Paige, I never took the money."

Jay slowly paces at the foot of my bed, his hands on his waist and his head hung low as he sorts through his thoughts. "My father was an alcoholic, and he struggled to hold down a job. My mother worked three jobs to make ends meet." He stops and tilts his head toward the ceiling. "I hadn't planned to go to college. I wanted to work, so I could help my mother and relieve some of the burdens on her. When I told Martin that I wasn't going to college, he was done with me. He told me there was no way his daughter could ever be happy with someone who would never be able to adequately provide for her—and he couldn't risk letting her be with someone who would probably turn out just like his father."

My heart aches at the harshness of his words, and I imagine what it must have been like the first time Jay heard them. "But you did go to college," I say.

He nods. "My mother insisted. But by then, things were over between Abby and me. Her father made it clear that he was never going to accept me."

"That's why you left?" I ask, wiping at my eyes. I'm seized unexpectedly by another round of sharp pain that propels a guttural sound from my throat.

Jay puts a gentle hand on my wrist. "You need to relax. You've been through a lot. Please, try not to move."

I draw a few shallow breaths, and the pain eases. "Why did you leave my mom?" I ask again.

When he finally answers, his voice is ragged, almost broken. "I didn't want to go. I didn't. And I was so angry at Martin, I can't even begin to tell you. I actually ripped up his check and threw it in his face."

That makes me smile, but it quickly fades when I remember that he'd still walked away, from my mother and, by extension, me.

"I'd planned to tell Abby what he did, how he thought bribing me could separate us," he explains.

"Why didn't you? Why didn't you tell her?"

Jay's thoughtful; then, with new conviction, he says, "Because I knew how much Abby loved her father and how important family was to her. I thought if I just went off to college and never told her what he'd done, she could still salvage her relationship with her dad." Softly, he adds, "I just wanted her to be happy. She deserved that."

"But she wasn't happy," I remind him. He'd read the journals. He knows as well as I do that was the end of my mom's relationship with her father. She'd lost both Jay and Martin all at once. All because of lies and secrets.

"I didn't think Martin would be bold enough to admit to Abby that he offered me the money." He shakes his head, a muscle thrumming along his jaw. "And I never thought him vindictive enough to lie and tell her I took it. If I'd known that—I would have made sure she knew the truth." He closes his eyes for longer than a blink. "And when I got that letter and I realized that she thought I knew about you all those years ago and still walked away—that nearly killed me."

I study him carefully, and in the lines around his eyes, I see the sorrow over everything that went so terribly wrong all those years ago. He lost seventeen years with a child he never knew he had. I grew up without a father. And to top it off, my mother believed that she had been deceived by the boy who'd been her first love when, in truth, she'd been lied to by her own father. It's a story that reads like a tragic novel where no one lives happily ever after.

"Dad," I say hesitantly. The oddity of the word is so foreign on my lips that I'm a little startled by the sound.

Jay's eyes swing to mine, awe filling his strained face. "You've never called me that before."

"I know. And to be honest, it feels kind of weird," I say. "But—I think I could get used to it—if you don't mind."

Jay nods and his smile widens until it consumes his face and his eyes glisten. "Yeah." He reaches out and touches my hand, giving it a gentle squeeze. This feels good, and for the first time in a long time, I want him to stay with me. But then I remember there is something I need to do.

"Where's Connie? I have to apologize to her. I said some awful things, to both of you, and I'm so very sorry. I didn't know—I didn't understand."

"It's okay, Paige."

"No, it's not." I swallow hard, recalling the hurtful accusations I'd thrown at them. "I spent so much time pushing you away, both of you, I didn't bother to see what I had. I just felt—"

"Abandoned," Jay supplies. I lower my lashes. "Paige, I know this has been difficult for you. And you think I only invited you here because I felt obligated."

I stare down at the blankets.

"That's not true," he says firmly. "What I said before— it was only because I was angry. I wanted you here with us the moment I found out about you." His heavy sigh is filled with unspoken words, and he rubs his index finger across his lower lip in thought. "I don't know why your mother would trust me to raise you after all these years, and believe me, there is not a day that goes by that I don't think about that. But all that matters is that she did trust me, and I will do everything I can to prove to you that she didn't make a mistake when she made that decision."

I glance up and meet gentle eyes. "Look, Paige, I knew it wasn't going to be easy for you to come here, and I was scared. I admit that. But please believe me when I say that I wanted you here. Maybe I didn't show you that in the ways I should have, but this is all new territory for me."

"Me too," I admit.

"You and I are more alike than I realized. We're both strong-willed and maybe a little stubborn at times." I raise an eyebrow. "Connie's words," he says quickly, and I have to agree that's a pretty fair assessment. I haven't given Connie the credit she deserves. "But she's also the one who told me that we need each other. And I think she's right about that, too." He eyes me hopefully.

On the verge of tears once more, I nod. "Could you go get Connie? I really need to talk to her and apologize."

Jay reaches over and gently cups my cheek. I lean into his warm palm. "Sure." He turns to go, but then stops. "You should also talk to Cade when you get a chance. I think he'd like to see you, too."

My heart immediately does a grand jeté inside my chest. "Is Cade here?"

Jay's smile softens. "He stayed until he knew you were going to be all right. Then he left."

The light wave of hope that swelled in my chest sinks. Cade left. He didn't want to see me. I hurt him too deeply to be forgiven.

"You were right," Jay says. "I didn't give him a fair shake. He's a decent kid. If it wasn't for him, I don't know how we would have found you."

"What are you talking about?" I ask.

"When you didn't come home, we didn't know where to begin looking for you," Jay says. "I went to Cade's house on the off chance you were there. He and Shawn offered to help look for you. They found your car parked at the trailhead." Jay shakes his head. "Thank God Shawn was with him. He knew just what to do. The doctors say if you'd spent just a couple more hours out there alone— things could have ended much differently." Jay shudders at the thought of what he and I both know would have happened. "I don't think I've ever seen a kid so scared."

A new warmth fills my insides.

"I'd like the chance to get to know him better. So, if you want to invite him over to the house, you have my blessing."

It might be too late for that gesture, but I don't tell Jay that.

"Oh, one more thing." He motions to the journals in my lap. "Did you read both of these?" I look down at them, stroking the leather with my fingers, and shake my head. "You should. Especially that one." I hold up the brown journal with my mother's initials etched in gold on the front cover. "I think you need to read Abby's last entry." With that, he smiles and touches my hand before heading for the door.

Cade doesn't come back to the hospital that night, but Connie comes to see me, just as I'd asked. She sits rigidly in the chair across from me. I don't blame her; our last conversation was pretty awful.

Connie's face breaks. "I'm so sorry, Paige."

"Stop, please," I tell her, shaking my head, ashamed that she would try to take the blame for my embarrassing behavior. "I'm the one who's sorry. I shouldn't have said those terrible things to you."

"It's all right—"

"It's not actually, and there's something I need to say to you." She clasps her hands in her lap and nods. "I had no right to take out my anger on you. I was upset. You were there. I felt like I'd made a mess of everything, and when I saw you with my pointe shoes—"

"I shouldn't have snooped, I just—"

"Please, let me finish," I say. "This isn't about what you did. You just happened to be the third person that day who was trying to get me to face something I wasn't ready to face. I couldn't handle that. But you were right. I don't talk about my mom because if I did, I would have to deal with a lot of painful stuff," I confess. "I'd have to admit that I'm so angry and hurt and lost right now—and I just couldn't do that. But I had no right to say such terrible things to you. You have gone out of your way to be more than nice to me since I got here. You didn't deserve to be treated like that, and I'm really, really sorry." My voice is barely a whisper by the time I expel my final words.

"Paige, I never wanted to take your mother's place," Connie says, casting her red, swollen eyes downward as if they harbor something she doesn't want me to see.

With every bit of strength remaining in my upper body, I coax the fingers of my left hand to slowly maneuver the small space between us to where Connie's hands are clasped together on the edge of the bed. I give them a gentle squeeze. Connie's head lifts, and she stares at me in wonder and confusion.

"I understand now why you tried so hard to reach me.

Jay—Dad—told me about Nathan."

Connie draws in a sharp breath. When she manages to swallow it down, her shoulders relax, and she nods.

"You couldn't save him, and I'm so sorry about that, but you saved me. Even though I didn't know I needed saving. You convinced Jay to take me in, and I haven't been the most grateful or easy houseguest."

"Let me be very clear about one thing, Paige. You are not a houseguest," she says firmly. "You are a member of this family."

"See? How can you be so nice after the way I treated you?"

"Because that's what you do for family," Connie answers matter-of-factly, tucking a strand of her thick, blond hair behind her ear. "I knew what you were going through and it wasn't my place to tell you to get over it. We all heal in our own time. I had faith that you'd eventually come around."

"I've come around," I manage, embarrassment heating my cheeks. "And I'm truly sorry for everything." The tears come easily to the corners of my eyes and slide down my face. "Thank you for not giving up on me."

Connie pats my hand. "I'll never give up on you, sweetie." She leans forward, brushing away the tears, and kisses my cheek.

"Maybe someday you could tell me about my brother Nathan—and I could tell you about my mom."

Connie smiles, wiping at her moist eyes. "I would like that very much."

# CHAPTER THIRTY-NINE
## Paige

"You are a badass, my friend," Quinn declares, sitting cross-legged on the foot of my hospital bed. The last time the nurse came into the room, she'd reminded Quinn in a firm, motherly voice that the bed was only for patients, and she directed her to the chair, where "visitors are encouraged to sit." Quinn had smiled politely and apologized in her sweet, syrupy voice that she reserves for adults in authority, but as soon as the nurse was gone, she'd hopped right back up on the bed.

"I think you're confused about what badassery really means," I say, gesturing with my hand to the hospital equipment surrounding me and gritting my teeth at the twinge of pain in my shoulder. "No badassery here. This is clearly the result of good, old-fashioned idiocy."

"Still," Quinn says. "Think about it. You could have died. But you were rescued in the nick of time."

"It wasn't like Prince Charming rode up on his mighty steed," I say, amused by the glimmer in her eye. "I was rescued by a Coast Guard helicopter crew."

Quinn snorts. "Yeeees—but they wouldn't have even known you were there if it wasn't for the hot guitar player who risked his life to save yours. Don't look at me like that; I overheard Jay talking to Cade's family."

"You're right. Cade saved me, and I'm thankful," I say. My fingers fiddle with the frayed edge of the blanket in my lap. "But he hasn't bothered to come see me since I woke up. That can't be a good sign."

"Relax," Quinn says. "I'm sure he's just waiting for everyone else to have a chance to see you first. That waiting room is a pretty happenin' place. Everyone is here to make sure you're okay."

I appreciate all the friendly faces who have stopped by to check in on me in the last forty-eight hours, from Aunt Faye and Tyler to Zoey and Sam and a bunch of girls from the dance team who I barely know. Even Mrs. Hopkins sent a teddy bear and a balloon with a "Get Well Soon" card. But still, the fact that Cade hasn't been one of the people to step foot in my room—that worries me. Regardless that he'd risked his own life to save mine, it doesn't erase the fact that we'd said some hurtful things to each other on the beach two days ago. And despite Quinn's reassurances, there is still a good possibility that just because Cade saved me didn't mean he ever wanted to see me again.

"When are you getting out of here?" Quinn asks. "Hospitals creep me out."

"Hopefully, later today, if everything checks out. Jay's

trying to track down the doctor for a status report."

"Is your doctor cute at least?" Quinn asks, and I laugh. I've binged enough medical shows with her on Netflix to know precisely what she's thinking.

"He's a grandfather," I say.

Quinn wrinkles her nose. "Bummer."

There's a light tapping on my closed door. "I hope for your sake that's not the nurse again." Quinn rolls her eyes as I call, "Come in."

My heart stutters when the door opens, and Cade walks into the room.

# CHAPTER FORTY
## Cade

Paige stares at me like I'm a mirage standing in her doorway. I step into the room and take in the full sight of her, her arm in a sling and the bruises and scrapes across her face.

"You up for another visitor?" I ask. She doesn't respond.

"All righty, then." Quinn sighs, sliding off the bed. She snags her jacket from the chair and wriggles into it. "I think I'm gonna go check out the cafeteria. I hear the chocolate pudding rocks." She gives Paige a hug and heads for the door. As she passes me, she flicks my arm and says, "It's about time you showed up, punk."

I suppress my smile and move to the foot of the bed, where Paige's weary eyes assess me. "Hey."

"Hey," she repeats, her guarded gaze filled with questions.

"Looks like we're going to have matching scars." I gesture to the bandage on her forehead. Paige lowers her lashes. "Sorry I'm late." Tentatively, I lean in to kiss her uninjured cheek, and I'm relieved that she lets me. Forcing myself to break our connection, I take a seat in the chair. "So, a funny thing happened the other day. A girl on the beach told me I needed to get my shit together and—how did she put it exactly?—Oh, yeah, 'Stop throwing a selfish tantrum.'"

Paige flinches. "Just so you know, that girl was a whack job. She didn't know what she was talking about."

I reach for her hand. "You had every right to say what you did."

"No, I didn't," she says. "I was horrible to you. I think I just wanted someone else to hurt as much as I did. What's going on between you and your dad is none of my business, Cade. I shouldn't have said what I did. I'm really sorry."

"No one's ever spoken to me like that before," I say.

"And no one should," she insists.

"Actually, someone probably should have said it a long time ago. I might have decked 'em if they had, but I needed to hear it." I release her hand and sit back. Paige's face falls at the distance between us. "Everything you said to me was true. I never gave my dad a chance to explain why he did what he did. So—I went to see him."

Wide eyes stare back at me. "You did?"

I nod. "Yesterday. That's why I wasn't here. Because I couldn't face you until I talked to him."

"Wow, Cade, that's big," she whispers.

I stand and circle around to the foot of her bed, my thumbs hooked in my pockets. "I sat in the parking lot at the correctional facility with Macy for half an hour trying to get up the nerve to go inside. I thought about what you said, about how I was hurting her and—" I shrug. "I finally went in."

"How was it?"

I blow out a long breath. "It was weird. I mean, I haven't seen my father in nearly four years. He looks older. He looks—different."

"How so?" Paige doesn't know what my father looks like. She's never even seen a photo of him because I made Macy pack them all away years ago. I couldn't stand the sight of him.

"I'm not quite sure how to explain it. He was definitely surprised to see me, that's for sure," I say, closing my eyes and telling Paige the whole story.

*"It's good to see you, son," my father had said as he took a seat across from me at the large metal table. I bristled at the word "son." When Mac called me that, I felt a connection, but coming from my father's mouth, that one small word was more like a fork scraping across a plate than a term of endearment.*

*"I'm glad you're here," he said when I didn't respond. "Look at you; you're so grown up. How tall are you now?"*

*"Just stop," I said, holding up my hand. "This isn't a family reunion. I need some answers."*

*He nodded, staring down at his clasped hands on the tabletop. "I know you do. I'm just so happy to see you, Cade. I've missed you."*

*"I said enough!" I barked and shot out of my chair. The guard in the corner shifted his footing. I took a deep breath and sat back down. "You can't destroy a family and then expect to*

pick up the pieces like it's no big deal. It doesn't work like that."

My father closed his eyes and sighed. "You're right. You have every reason in the world to hate me for what I did."

"You destroyed me, you selfish asshole!" I spit. "Do you not get that?"

"Cade, please calm down."

"Don't you dare tell me to calm down," I said through gritted teeth. Our gazes locked, my father's wavering and uncomfortable, mine steely and focused. I wouldn't let him play the victim. "Are you even sorry for what you did?"

He rubbed his forehead. "I'm sorry I hurt you, Cade."

I shook my head, my jaw clenched to prevent me from erupting again. "You have a funny way of showing it."

"I've written you dozens of letters. You'd know I was sorry if you'd opened them. But your sister says you haven't. Son, it's hard to ask for forgiveness when you won't give me a chance."

"Are you serious?" I seethed, astonishment colliding with cold anger. "You have no idea what you did when you decided to crap where you ate."

"Where in the world did you hear that expression?"

I leaned into the table, anger pulsing in my chest. "I'll tell you exactly where I heard it. From Mr. Sloane. Right after you were arrested and right before he kicked me out!" My father's face paled, and his shoulders collapsed, as if I'd just leveled him with a punch to the gut. "I ended up on the streets because I was no longer welcome in his home. Because of you!"

My father ran a hand over his bowed, shaved head and a strangled squeak escaped from his lips as his shoulders shook. When he lifted his eyes, they were filled with tears. "I'm so sorry." His immediate remorse affected me in a way that I wasn't prepared for. I didn't want to see him broken. I wanted to see that all of this was just an act, like I'd convinced myself it was. It's easier to hate a liar than a man breaking apart from years of regret.

"When your mother died, I—" He shook his head at the memory, and my chest grew tight. "I was lost, Cade. I don't expect you to understand that, but I didn't have a clue how to go on without her. She was everything to me, the reason I got out of bed in the morning. When I lost her—I was so wrapped up in my grief, it consumed me. So much so that I didn't see that you were grieving, too." Tears stung my eyes, but I blinked them back and stared at the ceiling, refusing to engage him.

"For that, I am sorrier than you will ever know. It doesn't erase what I've done. I have to answer for that, and I am, I am doing that, and I will be for a long time. I don't expect you to forgive me, Cade. I don't deserve it, and I won't ask you for it." He paused, and silence filled the space between us, so heavy that I finally gave in and met his gaze. Pain swirled in his gray eyes. "I know that I failed you on so many levels, and if I could take it all back, I would. All of it. But you and I both know that's not possible." He closed his eyes, taking a moment to expel a deep breath. "But what I can do is make sure that I grab every opportunity I can to tell you that, no matter what, I love you. I always have and I always will."

I look up when Paige shifts in her bed. Clearing my throat, I wipe at my eyes.

"How are you feeling now?" she asks.

"I'm fine."

"Fine is not a feeling," she says, then a smile turns up the corners of her mouth. "That's something Aunt Faye always says to me."

"I'm all right."

"Really?"

I nod. "Yeah. One visit doesn't fix everything, but I feel like maybe I left some of my anger behind in that room. Not all of it, because I've been angry at my dad for a long time."

"Are you going to see him again?"

I shake my head. "I don't know. Maybe. I think I just need to let this first visit sink in, you know? We have a lot more we need to talk about, but this was a start." She raises her hand and motions for me to come closer, patting the mattress beside her. I lower myself onto the edge of her bed.

"Visiting your dad couldn't have been easy, but it's huge that you did it. Things will get better from here." I lean down and press my lips to hers in a kiss that's clearly too short for her liking. Paige frowns.

"I need to tell you something that I should have said to you a long time ago," I say, swallowing hard and gathering my courage. "I lied to you."

Worry creases her forehead. "Lied to me about what?"

"I do believe that things happen for a reason," I say. "Not everything. Not losing your mom—*that* was a horrible accident. It shouldn't have happened. But I think everything after that did happen for a reason."

"What do you mean?"

"I mean you and me. Meeting in the airport that day, as ridiculous as that was." I laugh softly at the memory of the girl who'd so adamantly accused me of being a suitcase thief. My expression draws serious once more. "My life hasn't been the same since the moment I met you, Paige. You're not like anyone I've ever known. You accepted me for exactly who I was, flaws and all, and you forced me to be honest with myself for the first time in a long time. None of that was a coincidence."

Paige tilts her face to the ceiling. Tears leak from the corners of her eyes and I swipe gently at the wetness with my thumbs. "Why are you crying?"

"I've been so lost since my mom died," she whispers. My heart aches at her pain, and I want to make things better for her. But sometimes things just hurt and there's nothing you can do about it.

"I was angry at her for sending me here. For not warning me. For not even telling me about my dad in the first place," Paige says. "But most of all, I think I was angry because she never gave me a chance to have a say in any of this."

I tighten my hold on her hand, and she meets my eyes. "The truth is, if I'd had a say in it, I never would have come here," she admits. "I would have stayed in San Diego with Aunt Faye, and I would have missed out on so much. I would have missed my chance to get to know my dad and Connie and the kids. And you and I would never have met." She stares at my lips. "Honestly, I can't even imagine that.

For so long, you were the only thing in this town that made any sense to me."

"You called him your dad," I say, and she smiles and nods.

"Yeah. We're okay now. It's a long story, and I'll tell you about it later." Paige rubs at the spot on her wrist where her watch used to be, it's absence now marked by tan lines.

"Your watch," I say.

She glances down at her wrist, her sigh heavy with sadness. "I lost it. I don't know where, but it's gone."

"No," I say. "Paige, it's not gone. I completely forgot to tell you, I took it."

"What?" Her brows lift, then drop as her eyes cloud with confusion. "Why? Where is it?" She sits up immediately, wincing at the discomfort that follows.

"When I was holding you on the ledge, waiting for the rescuers, I saw that the glass was cracked. Before they got to us, I took your watch. I gave it to Macy to have it repaired. She's working on it."

"Oh my gosh, Cade! Are you serious?" she squeals, flinging her uninjured arm around my neck and wrenching me into a hug.

"Take it easy, you have a hurt shoulder," I remind her.

She squeezes me harder and cries into my neck, mumbling, "I don't care. This is the best news! Thank you, thank you so much!" When she pulls back, she's laughing through her tears, and even after everything Paige's been through, she's as beautiful as ever. I stroke her cheek.

"I know how much that watch means to you."

She shakes her head. "I'm not just talking about the watch. You saved me."

"I think the Coast Guard gets the nod for that one. And Shawn was the one who called for help."

Paige smiles and squeezes my hand. "I'm grateful for all of that. But that's not what I'm talking about either. Cade, you saved me long before you ever rescued me from that cliff. And I will never forget that."

# CHAPTER FORTY-ONE
## *Paige*

The doctor released me from the hospital with strict instructions to rest and take it easy. I think I'm going to have a nasty scar. Tanner says I should tell everyone I got in a bar fight with a biker gang and that I won. That kid cracks me up.

Quinn, Zoey and Sam have come to visit me so much, Jay felt the need to enforce strict visiting hours. At first, he allowed them only one hour each evening until I was back on my feet. Fortunately for them—and for me—that only lasted a week. Now, I'm back in class, but still moving slowly while all my bruises heal. Jay has been much more lenient with Cade, and he's stopped by the house every day to check on me.

Aunt Faye extended her stay to keep an eye on me. She took a couple of days to visit Tyler at the university, but then she returned to oversee my recovery.

"Maybe you should have been a nurse," I say as she tucks me into bed after dinner. "I think you missed your calling."

"I don't know," she says, fluffing the pillows behind my back. "I only have patience for certain people. You happen to be one of them." She picks up a few stray articles of clothing from the floor and tosses them into my hamper.

"You don't need to clean my room. Can you just sit with me?" She does as I ask, and I make room for her on the bed.

"How's your shoulder?" she asks.

"Much better." I no longer have to wear my sling, and the soreness is lessening with each passing day. "I'm hoping I'll be back to normal pretty soon."

"Don't rush it," Faye says. "What's your hurry anyway? Looks like you're getting out of a lot of chores in your condition."

I try to suppress it, but a hint of a smile appears. "Yeah, that part's not so bad."

"Uh-huh, that's what I thought," she says.

"The truth is, I want to get better because I have some things I need to do."

"Like what?"

I take a deep breath. "I want to start dancing again. There are some advanced classes starting at Lily's dance studio, and I want to enroll."

Aunt Faye is quiet, but her eyes instantly sparkle with tears. "I think that's an amazing plan."

"You were right," I say. "I miss dancing. And I can't give it up."

"And there she is." Aunt Faye reaches out and pats my hand. "I knew she'd be back." She hands me a cup of tea from the nightstand.

"What are you talking about?" I ask.

"That little spitfire I've known all my life. She got derailed for a little while, but I knew she was still in there," Aunt Faye says. "You're just like your mother." That's one of the greatest compliments she's ever paid me.

Faye kicks off her shoes and hoists her legs up to sit cross-legged in front of me on the bed. Just like Mom used to do. "So, what changed your mind?"

I want to tell her that she did. And Cade did. And remembering my mother and how much she loved me changed my mind. But instead, I say, "I guess I just realized I don't want to be in a world where I can't dance. That doesn't work for me."

"Abby would be so proud of you right now. Do you know that? All she ever wanted was for you to be happy. I can't count how many times she wrote that in her journal."

I stare down into the mug.

"Paige?" Aunt Faye asks. "Did you read her journals?"

"I read the first one, the one she wrote in high school," I say. "That was really hard for me, and she wrote it so long ago. But the other one—that's the end, you know?" I say. Faye nods with understanding. "Does that make me a coward?"

"Not at all," she says.

"But you've read it, and Dad's read it, and you both say I should."

Faye touches my leg. "How about we read it together? Would that make it easier?" Hope, anticipation and unease swirl together into a tight ball that settles in the pit of my stomach as I nod. "Okay," she says softly. "Where is it?"

I motion to the nightstand drawer, where she'd first put the journals nearly two months ago. She retrieves the leather-bound book, and I carefully ease myself over just enough to make room for her on the bed beside me. Faye stretches out, and I lean into her, resting my head on her shoulder as she opens the journal. She flips through the pages to my mother's last entry, which is dated September 14. I close my eyes and try to ignore my racing pulse. Aunt Faye begins to read.

*Today was another long day at the studio. I'm so proud of Paige for how hard she's working. I know I've been intense with her these past few weeks, and I'm pushing her really hard, but it's because I know what she's capable of. I don't want to jinx us, but I think she's going to nail her audition. Any company would be lucky to have her. But even if they don't choose her for whatever reason, it won't matter. She's such a gifted dancer, she will find her place and opportunities to amaze people with her talent. I am so impressed by her drive and tenacity. I wish I could say she gets them from me, but I don't think I ever possessed those traits as strongly as she does.*

Faye hesitates, her voice cracking. I lift my lashes, seeing fully for the first time the pages she holds in her hand. My mother's words swirl before me as Faye swallows and continues.

*It's hard for me to believe Paige is seventeen already. When did that happen? My spunky little girl is now a strong, kind,* talented young woman with an incredible head on her shoulders. Sometimes I think, "Way to go, Abby, you must have done everything right." But I know it wasn't me at all. Paige is an extraordinary person to her core. I am truly blessed to be her mother. I can't wait to see what she will do next, and all the lives she will touch in big and small ways.

Tears slip from my eyes as Faye places two fingers to her lips and then presses them to the page. She closes the journal, and we sit in silence, holding hands as we each think about my mother in our own ways. I miss Mom so much, and I will always feel as if a piece of me is missing. The pain ebbs and flows, and sometimes, like now, the wound is as fresh as it was all those months ago. My world has been permanently altered, and I feel cheated by that. Compounding my heartbreak is the new realization of how much my mother lost when her life was snatched away from her.

Mom wasn't a perfect human being—none of us are—but in my eyes, she came pretty close. She was selfless, always trying to do the best she could for me, even when I didn't appreciate it or even notice. She impacted my life in a million little ways by merely being a part of it. When I think of it like that—I finally get it. I finally understand the one thing I didn't before. I thought my grief was a punishment for all I had done wrong, for not being able to save Mom. But the truth is—my grief is proof that I loved her, and that she loved me in return. And that, by any measure, isn't a punishment. It's a gift.

# EPILOGUE

## *Paige*

I glance at my watch again and grow more anxious as each minute passes. The dance studio is deserted except for the receptionist, who sits behind the desk out front, playing solitaire on her phone. The last class ended at seven, but I begged her to keep the doors open. When I confessed to her the reason for my request, she was more than happy to oblige.

It's now almost seven thirty. I stand squarely in front of the big mirrored wall and tap my pink-toed foot nervously on the hardwood floor. When I hear muffled voices out front, I turn with anticipation. It's not long before Cade appears in the doorway, shaking the rain from his hair. His smile is wide when he spots me.

As I nearly skip across the room, my heartbeat quickens. I'm used to the sensation by now. Since the day we met, it's how my body reacts each time he looks my way. Cade studies me carefully, his eyes taking in my black leotard. "You look great." I reach up on my tiptoes and give him a kiss. "Are you ready to go? I brought Macy's car so you wouldn't get drenched on the motorcycle."

"Actually," I confess, "I don't need a ride home. I have my car."

Confusion clouds Cade's eyes. "No? Then—?"

I take hold of his wrists and draw him farther into the room. "I asked you to come here because I want to show you something." Cade raises an eyebrow. When he looks at me like that, I nearly melt like an ice cream cone in the summer sun. "I want to show you what I've been working on."

"Really?" His smile is bright, almost radiating a warmth that floods the space between us. I nod. Cade's never seen me dance. For months, I couldn't bring myself to do it. Now that I am back in the studio and trying to make up for all the time I've squandered after losing my mom, I'm finally ready to share this piece of myself with him.

I draw a full breath, filling my lungs with courage, and turn to the stereo. "Keep in mind, I'm still a little rusty," I call over my shoulder.

I cue up the music and press Play. As the song bleeds through the speakers and out across the large room, I stroll to the center of the space, facing the determined girl in the mirror and trying to forget about the deep, copper eyes watching my every move. I begin to dance, letting the music guide me, my arms and legs executing the movements just as they've been trained to do for so many years. It feels incredible to be here in this space, doing what I love more than anything else in the world. My injuries have completely healed, and I've spent the last several weeks getting back into shape and trying to recover the flexibility that once came so naturally. I'm getting there, although it hasn't happened as quickly as my impatient self would like. It's true that muscles have memories, and mine, even though I'd abandoned them for months, seem to have snapped right back into form when I started training again.

I glide across the floor, my powerful legs propelling me effortlessly into the air as I leap, my arms brushing the air gracefully in a grand jeté before I land once more. For a moment, I close my eyes, losing myself in the rhythm, dissolving into the joy exuding from every limb. I whip my leg powerfully in a double fouetté en tournant followed by three more as pure bliss pulses through me. As I move, I envision all I've endured—the pain, the emptiness and the longing for a world I'd lost without warning—and I imagine it dissolving into the floor beneath me. In its place springs hope and love and endless possibilities. There's room now for all that. There's room for the happy, confident girl who'd been exiled the day her world crumbled beyond her control.

*"You, my sweet Paige, have a gift,"* my mother's words whisper in my mind. *"Hold on to it and never let it go."* I smile, acknowledging her words with a silent promise. As the music fades, my body folds into the final movement of the dance, spent from the intensity of the last several minutes, but genuinely exhilarated at the sensation that,

after everything that's happened, I am finally where I belong. I wish I'd known all those months ago that it could feel like this. I wish I'd understood that when bad things cloud your world, it's easy to forget that there was ever good in the first place. I'd convinced myself that the bad was all there was, all there ever would be. I was wrong. I was so very wrong.

I relax out of my stillness and stand. Exertion mingles with pride, and I give the tiniest nod to the girl staring back at me in the mirror. I turn to find Cade. "What do you think?"

"Wow," he says, coming toward me, his face awestruck. "That was amazing."

"Thanks," I say, wiping my damp forehead with the back of my hand. "But I didn't dance for you because I was fishing for compliments."

Cade wraps an arm around my waist and draws me close. He dips his head and says, "What exactly do you want, then? Because I gotta tell ya—that was hot." He brushes his lips against my jaw as I laugh, then I playfully push him away. "Stop! That wasn't why I danced for you either." He feigns disappointment.

I lead Cade over to the bench by the doors and motion for him to sit down. When I stand in front of him, he puts his hands on my hips and jerks me playfully toward him. I run my hands through his soft hair as he eyes me curiously.

"I asked you to come here tonight because I want you to know that I heard what you said to me. And you were right—and so were Tyler and Aunt Faye. Dancing is part of my life—a huge part, actually—and I should never have abandoned it." Cade lowers his forehead and rests it against my stomach. "I love it; I always have," I continue, fingering the soft strands at the base of his neck. "Dancing is my dream, and it was my mom's dream." I look around the room as Cade lifts his head. "When I'm out on the floor, moving to the music and feeling that fire inside me—I think she's here with me."

"That's great. I'm so glad. You're really talented, Paige."

I take a seat next to him on the bench, an easy smile turning up the corners of my mouth. "I've applied to the University of Oregon. They have a dance program and I think I want to stay in Oregon. I'll be closer to Jay and Connie. And of course, Tyler will be there." I smile. "And you're here."

"What about the ballet company and the audition?"

I shrug. "I kind of blew that last fall. I suppose there's always a possibility I can try again, but I really feel like Oregon is where I should be. Quinn just got her acceptance letter, and if I get in, we're going to room together in the dorms. I'm really excited about it."

"Sounds like you've finally got things figured out."

"Thanks to you."

"I don't think I had anything to do with it," he says. "But if you say so, who am I to argue?" Cade kisses my temple, then presses his gentle lips to mine. I cup his cheek in my palm, drawing him closer and kissing him back in a way that lets him know that right here, at this moment, despite everything that's happening or will happen, he is the most important thing in the world to me.

More than a few seconds pass before I'm willing to let him pull back. When he finally does, I say, "Macy told me you went to see your dad again. How was that?"

"Let's just say it's a work in progress. I'm not sure if I can forgive him—not yet anyway. But we're talking, and that's a good place to start."

"I know this isn't easy, but I'm proud of you," I say, leaning my head on his shoulder. I breathe in the familiar scent of him, the worn leather from his jacket mixed with rain and the sea air.

"Yeah, I'm proud of me, too," he says.

"So, what are your plans?" I ask, turning up my face and staring at his jawline. "I mean, after your band gets scouted by some big-time record label, of course."

"Where? At Java Joe's?" He nudges my leg with his own. "I'm sure that's gonna happen."

I ignore him because while we may be joking around, he is exceptionally talented, and someone somewhere is bound to notice sooner or later. "I'm just trying to plan ahead for when I'll have to pay hundreds of dollars to some scalper for a backstage pass just so I can get close to you." I waggle my eyebrows, and Cade laughs.

"Let's hope so. That sounds great." I elbow him teasingly, and he laughs again. "No, seriously. I'm actually thinking I may want to do something else with my life."

"What could possibly make you want to give up music?"

"I don't know, I was thinking maybe I'd look into becoming a paramedic."

I sit up. "Really?"

"Yeah. I've been hanging out with Shawn at the fire station, and I'm learning a lot."

"That's great," I say. "That's really great, Cade."

"I never thought much about what he does for a living, you know? Not until the night we found you." He stares down at our entwined hands. "Shawn was amazing. He was so calm, and he knew just what to do. You were in bad shape." He shakes his head at the memories. "It was impressive to watch him."

Goose bumps prickle on my arms and at the back of my neck as I think about that night. "I can never thank him enough for what he did for me," I say softly. "And you, too."

"It got me thinking about what a great job he has," Cade says. "He can *save* people. I think I want to do that, too."

"You'd be great at it," I tell him.

He exhales a long, satisfied breath. "We'll see."

"Do you think you'll end up getting a place with Jared?" I'd heard the two of them talking about renting an apartment as soon as Cade graduates in June.

"I think for right now I'm gonna stay with Macy and Shawn. I like it there, and they're probably going to need the extra set of hands soon."

"What are you talking about?"

Cade breaks into a wide grin. "I'm gonna be an uncle."

I throw my arms around him. "Oh my gosh, that's incredible! When?"

"Labor Day." Cade laughs, shaking his head. "What are the odds?"

I'm so happy for Macy and Shawn. They will be amazing parents, and there is no doubt in my mind Cade will be an awesome uncle. He's so great with Tanner, and Lily adores him. She even talked him into playing Barbies with her once. He'd agreed, as long as she promised to let him drive the sports car. Cade rests his arm around my shoulders and stares out across the studio, grinning like life couldn't be better than it is right now.

"Just promise me one thing," I say.

He peers down at me. "What's that?"

"Promise me you won't stop playing your guitar."

"Of course I won't." He raises an eyebrow. "Why is that so important?"

I reach up and hook a hand around the back of his neck, drawing him closer until our foreheads touch. "Because girls love guys who play in bands," I whisper. Cade laughs as his lips find mine again. I melt against him, kissing him with an intensity reserved just for him. And it's in that instant that everything becomes clear, free from the cloud of self-doubt and the pity that has been a stronghold in my life for too long. At that moment, with this amazing guy in my arms, with so many possibilities before us and so much goodness filling our once emotionally tattered worlds, I feel it.

No matter what lays ahead for me, no matter where this crazy life takes me and no matter what obstacles try to slow me down—I can handle it. All of it. And this time, I'm not going to give up on my happy ending. Because I deserve it.

# About the Author

Kelli Warner has loved books ever since she could hold them in her hands. Driven by a ferocious imagination as a child, her love for writing began by creating simple short stories and soap opera scenes while her mom watched General Hospital. Kelli went on to become an award-winning and Emmy-nominated TV newscaster and reporter while continuing to write young adult and contemporary romance novels. She's passionate for good coffee (even a bad cup on a desperate day), her amazing and hilarious family, and she's a big fan of lazy Saturday mornings spent watching the Food Network. Kelli and her husband live in Oregon with their two kids and an outstanding border collie named Lucy.

Facebook: fb.me/KelliWarnerAuthor
Twitter: @KelliWarner_
Instagram: kelliwarner_author
KelliWarner.com